D1590788

DEATH
IS POTENTIAL

Charleston, SC
www.PalmettoPublishing.com

DEATH IS POTENTIAL
Copyright © 2023 by Bob Burnett

All rights reserved

No portion of this book may be reproduced, stored in a retrieval system, or transmitted in any form by any means—electronic, mechanical, photocopy, recording, or other—except for brief quotations in printed reviews, without prior permission of the author.

This is a work of fiction. Names, characters, business, events and incidents are the products of the author's imagination. Any resemblance to actual persons, living or dead, or actual events is purely coincidental.

Paperback ISBN: 979-8-8229-1685-2
eBook ISBN: 979-8-8229-1686-9

DEATH
IS POTENTIAL

A Kate Swift Mystery

BOB BURNETT

TABLE OF CONTENTS

SUNDAY

(9am): Laura

"You're driving too fast." Detective Sergeant Daniel O'Malley muttered, as he looked up from reading his phone messages.

Dan sounds like my father, Detective Laura Sanchez thought. *He's old enough to be my father*. "I'm going sixty in a fifty-five zone. We're driving in a new Dodge Charger Pursuit. I'm a graduate of the Bondurant driving school at Laguna Seca. Just close your eyes and relax, Sarge. Leave the driving to the professional."

"You know, Sanchez, you have potential. But your attitude could give you problems."

"No one has ever told me that before." She laughed. They were headed south on Highway One, headed for Satori Institute below Big Sur. Their black sedan cleared Carmel Highlands and entered Garrapata State Park, more than two-thousand acres serving as the mountainous entrance to the southern Monterey County coastal wild.

I

"Have you ever been to Big Sur?"

"My dad and I have been fishing at Molera State Park," Sanchez said. "But I've never been any further south than the gas station in the campground. What about you?"

"Patty and I have been camping in Big Sur," Dan said. "And I was on the grounds of Satori a long time ago."

"What was it like?"

"Rich hippies running around in the nude, taking drugs."

"Sounds like my kind of place," Sanchez laughed. "Except for the 'rich' and 'hippie' part. Why were you there?"

"Something similar to this call: a body washed up on the beach."

"What was the story?"

"What you'd expect: a rich hippie got stoned and fell off the cliff."

"Ouch. And it was ruled an accident?"

"Yes. But the guy's family sued Satori for negligence."

"What happened?"

"I heard through the grapevine that there was an out-of-court settlement. Satori didn't acknowledge any responsibility, but agreed to taking additional security precautions, such as putting up fences."

"Sounds like the Sheriff's Department doesn't get called to Satori very often."

"Our records show nothing in the last couple of years. That's probably because Satori is so isolated; it's only 30 miles from Monterey but it takes more than an hour to drive down Highway One. When the Institute has problems, they take care of them themselves."

"Except for when there's a dead body." The two deputies drove over Bixby Creek Bridge, a graceful, 700-foot-long, single-span concrete arch. "I love this bridge. We should get out and take a selfie."

Dan studied his twenty-seven-year-old partner and then smiled. "You almost had me."

"I would have texted it back to Homicide: 'having wonderful time, wish you were here.'" They both laughed. "Since the last dead body was obviously an accident, why is homicide involved now?"

"Because this dead guy is a big shot. One of the Satori founders."

"Okay. I get it." They drove through the historic Brazil Ranch and passed the Hurricane Point turnout with its view of miles of Big Sur coastline, the Santa Lucia mountains rising dramatically from the Pacific Ocean. "Another great place for a selfie."

Dan continued to study his phone messages.

"Explain to me what happens at Satori, besides nudity and drugs."

"I'm not sure I can explain it very well. It's a conference center at a hot-springs resort. They advertise 'increasing your human potential.' People come from all over and take classes."

"What kinds of classes?"

"They offer different kinds of therapy. Like couples' therapy."

"That's what Gary and I need."

"Because?"

"Because he wants us to be a couple and then spends all of his time in San Francisco." Sanchez sipped her cold coffee. "Maybe I can get therapy while I'm there, to work on my issues."

"What issues?"

"Where do I start? I have a boyfriend who is afraid of commitment. I have a mother who won't stop badgering me about producing a grandchild. I have co-workers who won't take me seriously because I'm a woman. I have citizens who don't believe I'm a cop, who call me 'Chica' behind my back." Sanchez waved her right hand in the air and then regripped the steering wheel.

"At least you weren't the first Hispanic woman in the department. You should be grateful that Dr. Hidalgo became coroner."

Sanchez rolled her eyes. "It's like following in the footsteps of Marie Curie."

"Who is Marie Curie?"

Sanchez bit her cheek. "A famous restaurant owner." She waited 30 seconds. "What other kinds of classes do they have as Satori?"

"Massage. Painting." Dan scratched his head. "Music Therapy; Patty's friend Julie took some classes at Satori."

"Who was the dead guy?"

"Malcolm Eastwick." Dan read his notes. "He and Richard Staybrook founded Satori thirty years ago. They're both therapists. They wanted a place, on the coast, to give workshops and bought the Satori property because of the location and the fact that it has natural hot springs," Dan mumbled. "Staybrook is also deceased. Happened at Satori but doesn't say how, just 'accidental.'"

"Interesting coincidence."

"Yes. When I get cell reception, I'll ask for more details.

"What do we know about Eastwick's death?"

"Not much. Someone saw the body on the beach at the bottom of a cliff. It took a while to get down to it. When they got there, they realized the victim was Eastwick; they couldn't leave him where they found him, because of the incoming tide, so they carried him up to the office. And then they called us."

"Why were we assigned?"

"Because of your attitude, Sanchez. Sheriff John wanted to reward you for your attitude." Dan smiled. "Actually, Malcolm Eastwick was a major contributor to the Sheriff's reelection campaign; so, he has taken a personal interest in this case."

"And he wanted his best investigators on it. Good judgment by Sheriff John."

CHAPTER 2
(3PM): Tom

I arrived at Satori in the afternoon, intending to hit the baths but the bed in my private room looked so inviting, I ended up napping until dinner was served.

As I walked to the dining hall, I passed a black Monterrey County Sheriff's Department sedan parked next to the office and wondered if they were investigating drug sales, a perennial Satori problem. I stepped into the small, redwood-paneled bar for a glass of wine and immediately ran into a couple of staff members that Fiona had worked with the last time we'd been at Satori.

"Nice to see you, Tom," Marcia Ball, the Satori outreach coordinator, said. "Are you here for a workshop? Where's Fiona?" Marcia was a well maintained, middle-aged white woman with an extravagant French braid.

"Fiona passed away eighteen months ago," I rasped as my throat constricted. "Her breast cancer returned."

Marcia choked up. "I'm so sorry to hear that." Marcia was joined by her assistant, Grace, a slight twenty-something

Hawaiian woman. "We always enjoyed working with her, working with your company."

"Fiona loved it here. When I saw that David Sanders was giving his 'Transitions workshop.' I thought I would take the course and contemplate my life after Fiona."

"You must miss her a lot," Grace said. "How long were the two of you together?"

"Almost twenty years. We met right after I finished business school at Stanford."

"Do you remember Carl?" Marcia asked as a tall young Black man joined us. "Carl works in public relations. Carl, this is Tom Scott."

I didn't remember Carl, but we shook hands warmly. He stood out in his white-shirt and navy-blue blazer, a stark contrast to the other men who were dressed like surfers.

"Did you hear the big news?" Carl asked.

"I haven't heard anything," I said. "I just got here."

"They found a body on the beach this morning."

"Someone said that it's Malcolm," Marcia added in a shaky voice.

"Wow," I said. "I noticed a Sheriff's Department vehicle parked by the office. Wow. They found Malcolm's body? What happened?"

"I don't think they know what happened," Carl said.

"Did you know him?" Marcia asked.

"I met him during one of the events we helped you stage. Fiona had several conversations with Malcolm."

"What did Fiona think of him?" Grace asked, arching one eyebrow.

She thought Malcolm was a predator, I thought but didn't say. *He tried to hit on her even though he knew she was married.* "Smart. Lots of ideas. Tried to interfere with our plans at the last minute."

"Sounds like Malcolm." Marcia chuckled. "When he was around, he had a tendency to micro-manage."

I started to say something but was interrupted by David Sanders. "Tom, so good to see you. I'm sorry to hear about Fiona's passing. How are you doing?"

David and I had known each other for twenty years. He was about ten years older than me. We were the same height, but David was twenty pounds heavier and had a lot more hair. His was turning grey. *In another five years, David will look like Santa Claus.*

"I'm in and out," I said. "On the one hand, I'm glad she doesn't have to suffer anymore – the last year of her life was very painful. On the other hand, I miss her companionship; I miss her buoyant personality."

"You're an upbeat guy," David said. "And resilient."

"I hope so. I expect to live forty more years and I don't want to mope around with a black cloud hovering over my head."

"Like the cartoon character, Joe Btfsplk?" David chuckled. "You're not remotely like him." He clutched my hand. "I'm glad you're going to be in the workshop. Most of the participants are newbies."

"I heard they found Malcolm's body on the beach," I said.

"That's what I just learned," David answered. "I'm not sure if Cheryl knows yet; I've been trying to find her." Cheryl Taylor was a senior therapist on the Satori board; she had been married to Richard Staybrook, the other Satori founder, who died. "Excuse me but I need to find her."

David strode off.

"Are you coming to our fundraiser, on Wednesday night?" Marcia asked.

"I was planning on it. Do you think they'll still hold it, given Malcolm's death?"

Marcia furrowed her brow. "I think so. We've got the whole board coming in." She glanced at Grace who sighed but said nothing. "I'll let you know if it's cancelled."

"Okay."

"Would you like to join us for dinner?"

"Thanks." I followed Marcia, Grace, and Carl to the food line.

CHAPTER 3
(5PM): Laura

"It could have been worse," Detective Sanchez said. "The body could have been in the water for several days. I hate it when they're partially decomposed."

The detectives stood on the deck of the old conference center, a rambling two-story, wood-frame structure that had been the original Satori facility. Stretched out before them on a sun-bleached picnic table was the partially clothed body of Malcolm Eastwick. They knew it was Eastwick because they'd studied the picture on the driver's license, found in the leather wallet in his back pocket.

"Looks pretty clear that he died from a head injury," Dan O'Malley said. The right half of Eastwick's face had been compressed by the impact of landing on rocks at the bottom of a nearby cliff. "That's about all we know. We don't know what happened or where it happened."

"When Bruno Oliver gets here, perhaps he can tell us when it happened."

O'Malley used a gloved hand to lift Eastwick's head off the table. "The skin's pliant enough that it probably happened within the last twenty-four hours."

"Which means last night, because no one saw anything until this morning when they looked off this deck and saw the body on the beach below."

O'Malley lowered the head to the table and used one gloved finger to close Eastwick's open eye. "There's no telling when your friend Bruno is going to get here." O'Malley turned to Laura. "Bruno is very sharp, but strange. He won't look me in the eye."

"That's because he doesn't know you. He's on the spectrum."

"What's the spectrum?"

"Technically it's called the Autism-Spectrum-Disorder."

"But he can do his job."

"Of course, Bruno is very intelligent. He just has difficulty in social situations. The better he knows you, the more typical his behavior is."

"You seem to know a lot about Bruno, Sanchez."

"I've known him all my life. I went to school with his sister, Eunice."

O'Malley looked out at the choppy Pacific Ocean. "Do me a favor, Laura, and go down to the beach and see if you can find anything. Chances are there's nothing, but you might get lucky and find where he hit the rocks."

"Sure thing, Sarge." Sanchez was happy to get away from the smell of Eastwick's body, a combination of the odor of mothballs and rotten eggs. She walked off the deck, circled the front of the old conference center, and headed down the well-kept path to the beach. For the last ten yards she had to scramble down the remains of the staircase which had been compromised by wave action. Reaching the small, sandy beach she tried, without success, to determine where the body had come ashore.

The beach ended after twenty yards and Detective Sanchez began to clamber north, over wet rocks, some packed with barnacles and others smooth. After fifteen minutes she'd moved to a spot directly under the westernmost overhang of the conference center deck. Sanchez defined a search perimeter and methodically examined it. There were several dark marks that might have been blood, but nothing that looked like flesh or brain particles. *Gulls probably got them*, she thought.

The Detective was about to abandon the search when she spotted a white cloth trapped between two rocks, three feet below the perimeter floor. She lay flat on the uneven wet surface, extended her gloved right hand into the crevice, and snared the item with two fingers.

Sanchez held up a silk handkerchief bearing the monogram, "ME."

CHAPTER 4
(7:45PM): Tom

I showed up ten minutes early for David Sanders' "Transitions" workshop. It was scheduled to start at 8PM in the "Carl Rogers" workshop room located roughly seventy-five yards up the hill from the Satori dining room. "Carl Rogers" was circular with vertical redwood panels to the east and floor to ceiling windows to the west. In the classic Satori tradition there were no chairs; workshop participants either sat on the floor or lounged on the over-sized pillows that were piled against the north wall.

When I entered, David was sitting yoga-style on a pillow with his back against the wood wall. No one else was in the room. I grabbed two pillows, one for my back and another to sit on, and plopped down next to him. David nodded and kept reading his notes.

Over the next ten minutes, the workshop participants drifted in. An equal mix of men and women. Some apprehensive, others overly casual. *The usual white privileged group*, I thought. *A* frizzy-haired guy stumbled across the room and fell on a pillow. *Stoned?*

By 8:11 all the space was filled except for an opening to the right of me. An attractive woman burst into the room, mumbled "Sorry I'm late" and searched for a place to sit down.

It's Kate Swift, I realized.

She gasped and mouthed, *Tom?*

I pointed to the opening next to me. Kate hesitated, then moved toward me. I stood up and gave her the pillow I had been leaning against. Kate sat down and muttered, "I can sit somewhere else."

I blushed. "This is fine."

Since we last met, three months before, Kate had restyled her brown-blond hair into a bob. Her new look emphasized her athletic bearing and determined personality. She was dressed in a white linen jumpsuit accented by dangling turquoise earrings.

David got to his feet. "Welcome to the semiannual Satori transitions workshop. For those of you who have not been to the Institute before, there will be an orientation in the front office at 8:30 tomorrow morning." He looked around the room, as though trying to ascertain how many workshops members were newbies. "The workshop rules are elemental: Show up on time -- the schedule is in the workshop packet and will be repeated verbally each day. Pay attention. Tell the truth. And keep your commitments." David looked around to see if anyone had questions. "To repeat, it's essential that each of you tell the truth about why you are here, why you are in the middle of a transition. This may be difficult or embarrassing, but the more you tell the truth the more you will benefit from this work." Again, David paused. "You have a commitment to each other to keep what is said here confidential." David walked to the center of the circle and turned, looking each participant in the eye. "You may hear things that disturb or shock you – things that jolt you out of your comfort zone. That's okay. This is a safe space. For the next six days, our objective is to create a sanctuary where you can ask for and receive support. Do any of you have questions?"

A woman across the room raised her hand. "So, can we take notes?"

David shook his head. "Unlike most Satori workshops, I prefer you don't. When we are in this room, I want you to give the other participants your total attention." He slowly turned. "Any other questions?"

No one spoke.

David retreated to his starting position and sat down on a pillow. "There are two facilitators: me and Cheryl Taylor." He acknowledged the petite woman, sitting on his left. She wore wire-rimmed glasses and had black hair with one gray streak. "We've both been on the Satori staff a long time. We've both been in lots of workshops. We've both seen lots of shit: some good and some bad. Our objective is to create a safe space. If you don't think you will feel safe you may want to leave now." David looked around the circle.

No one left.

"We'll begin by hearing each of your stories. Take as long as you need to tell us why you came here and what help you need. When you tell your story, you will not be interrupted." David paused. "That's a very important rule. By the way, that means that it's not okay for you to leave the room to use the bathroom while a participant is speaking. If you need to pee, go during the breaks. Do you understand?" He looked around the room. "If Cheryl or I feel that you, the speaker, is stuck, we may say something, but no one else is permitted to talk until you are finished. When we believe that you are finished, we will say something like, 'Are you finished?' If you signal that you are, we will ask, 'Are you ready to take questions from your group?' If you signal that you are, we will take questions until there are none. At that point, we will either take a break or move on to the next participant." David paused. "We'll start tonight and proceed until everyone has had their turn. However long this takes. Typically, about two days." David looked at each participant. "During this process, we ask that you not be absent. Please do not schedule a massage during this time. We are building trust and that requires that each of you gives this process your one-hundred percent commitment." David paused. "Do you understand?"

There were some murmurs and more nods.

"I can't hear you. Say 'I understand.'"

The group echoed: "I understand."

"Good. Now we'll get started. We'll proceed around the circle counterclockwise, starting with my friend Tom here." David put his hand on my shoulder. "Tom will speak for as long as he needs. At the end, I will talk to him, and then if he wants, he'll answer your questions."

I got to my feet, stared at the group, and cleared my throat. "It's easier for me to do this when I am standing. No matter how many times I do this, it's always scary to address a Satori group." I took a deep breath and exhaled. "I'm Tom Scott. Just turned forty. Recently widowed; my wife died eleven months ago." I sighed. "I'm a classic privileged California WASP. I grew up near Los Angeles, attended Stanford, and now live in San Francisco. My wife and I own a successful event management company. I was trained as a computer scientist and, in my spare time, play around with event-scheduling software." I took a swig of water from my thermos.

"I'm here because I'm single after being in a close relationship for fifteen years.

"After I graduated from Stanford Business school, I started an event management firm with a couple of friends. We put on all kinds of events and then specialized in 'difficult' events; that is, events with special security or logistical challenges – for example, a celebrity wedding. About the time I was in the process of buying out my partners, I met Fiona. She and her sister, Stella, were running an event company servicing the 'human potential' community. By the way, Fiona spent a lot of time at the Institute; she knew David and Cheryl. I was impressed with Fiona both personally and professionally. We fell in love. We began living together in San Francisco. We joined forces and started our company 'Carpe Diem.'

"We always planned to start a family but never made the time." My throat tightened and I struggled to speak. "Seven years ago, Fiona was diagnosed with breast cancer. It wasn't a total surprise; her mother was a breast-cancer survivor and her aunt died of it. Fiona was in good shape, had a positive attitude, and excellent medical care. She underwent a course of chemotherapy and, after three years, was judged to be cancer free."

I took another swig of water. "We went on with our lives, and tried to start a family but were unsuccessful." Again, my throat constricted. "Fiona's Ob-Gyn said that Fiona was impacted by the chemotherapy, that it was likely temporary, and we shouldn't be discouraged.

"Three years ago, a lump in her left breast appeared. Fiona had the lump removed but not the breast as she had always dreamed of breastfeeding our children."

Tears filled my eyes and rolled down my cheeks. David slid a box of tissues to where I stood, and I used one to wipe my face. "Fiona started another course of chemotherapy. It was not successful. She was given the choice of extensive surgery or more experimental drugs. Fiona chose the drugs. They didn't work.

"More than a year ago, Fiona realized that she was going to die. We had a long talk about what that would mean. Fiona wanted to die at home and not in a hospital or a hospice. We got her a special bed and arranged for nursing support.

"My mother was a nurse and, while I was attending Stanford as an undergraduate, I worked as an orderly at the VA hospital. Which is to say that I have the temperament to deal with sick folks." I looked around the room. "Fiona spent her last days in our home. I was able to sleep next to her every night." My eyes stung with fresh tears "I was there when she suffered."

When I looked around the room, most of the workshop participants were crying. "Fiona began to use the morphine drip and that helped with the pain, helped with the suffering, but it dulled her humanity." I sighed. "I could feel her drifting away from me. Even though we had a nurse to help us, I stopped going to work and spent all my time with Fiona. I helped the nurses clean and feed her. Her death was imminent, and I didn't want to miss that moment."

David Sanders touched my shoulder. As I turned, he placed a large beige pillow at my feet, and backed away. I knelt and began to talk to the pillow as if it was Fiona in bed. "At the end, you declined morphine; you wanted to be able to talk to me. I sent the nurse back to her quarters and you and I talked for hours. I wish I had had the presence of mind to record what you said, but I didn't. The main thing that I remember was that you told me not to be bitter. You believed that the rules of the universe are unfathomable, and we just need to roll with them. You told me to go on and live my life. You knew that I would remember you and treasure our relationship, but you encouraged me to go out and meet new people; you said, 'It's okay to love again. You have a big heart, Tom; there's room for me and someone New'.

"Fiona and I cried and laughed. And then she was gone." The workshop participants were still crying. I placed my hands over the pillow and slowly lifted them towards the ceiling. "A light left Fiona's body and drifted upward until it passed through the ceiling.

"It seemed important to personally care for her body. I washed her and tied her hair back in the same style of pony tail she was wearing when we met. Then I wrapped her in a clean sheet. I called our doctor and he arranged for paramedics to move Fiona to the mortuary." I stood up. "After the death certificate was issued, I had Fiona cremated, as she requested. Then I began scattering her ashes in the locations she'd suggested.

I even brought some with me to scatter here at Satori, below the baths."

I looked around the group. "Fiona and I weren't particularly religious, so we didn't have a memorial service, per se. A month after she passed, I hosted a 'Celebrating Fiona' party at one of our favorite San Francisco clubs. There were no speeches, just music and dancing. Fiona would have enjoyed it."

I turned back to David. "I think I'm finished for now."

David got to his feet. "Are you ready for feedback from the other workshop members?"

"I think so."

David looked around at the group. "If you have feedback for Tom, please raise your hand."

A woman across the room raised her hand and got to her feet. "I lost a sister to breast cancer, so I deeply related to your story." She dabbed her eyes with tissue. "I just want to say how privileged Fiona was to have you with her in the last days." Several folks murmured agreement. She sat down.

"I was privileged to be with her," I said. "It was an awe-inspiring experience."

"What did you learn, Tom?" David asked.

"I learned how precious love is. I learned that when you have love, you should treasure it each moment." My heart pounded and tears rolled down my cheeks.

"I'm going to stop here," David said. "I know some of you may have feedback for Tom, but you can convey that privately. We're going to take a ten-minute break and then move on."

As the workshop members got up, I returned to my pillow and sat down. Kate took my hand and whispered, "You are so brave."

I started to respond but was interrupted by five workshop participants who wanted to talk to me about their somewhat similar experience with the death of a loved one.

       ᴄᴇᴏ

The workshop reconvened fifteen minutes later. David stood and turned to Kate. "You're next."

She bounced to her feet. "Wow. Tom's a tough act to follow. My name is Kate Swift. I'm 36 and single. I've never been married and that's one of the things I want to talk about." She glanced at me and then looked away. "I'm a professional manager. I live and work in the City." Kate reached down and took a sip of water from her thermos.

"I'm here because I feel I'm in a dead-end job and I need to make a career change." She sighed. "But I'm primarily here because I am terrible at relationships, and I need to do something about that. I'm a successful professional. In many ways I have a fortunate, privileged life. I have wonderful friends. But I'm unable to have a sustained intimate relationship with a man."

Kate looked around the room. "How many of you have been in a relationship where your partner told you they loved you, and you let your guard down, and said to yourself, 'At long last I have met my soulmate. Now I can relax and get the love I deserve.' And then they cheated on you? Raise your hand."

Almost all the participants raised their hands.

Kate nodded. "You understand my problem. I have good judgement about many things but terrible judgement about men. I keep hooking up with losers." She sighed. "I decided to come here after I found out that my boyfriend, Earle, was cheating on me." Kate moved into the center of the room. "Even though Earle had a checkered reputation, I believed him when he said, 'I love you, Kate. I know I've catted around in the past, but those days are over. I'm a new man. I'm ready to commit to one woman; to commit to you.'"

She punched one fist into the other. "What the fuck is wrong with me? I believed Earle. My gut told me better, but my poor needy heart wanted to believe him. So, I ignored what my friends said and moved in with Earle. Only to find that he had lied. Only to find that he was fucking Marci, one of the women in our office." Kate began to cry.

David pushed a box of tissues across the floor to Kate. She used a tissue to wipe her eyes.

"I feel so stupid." Her voice choked. "I knew better, but I trusted Earle." The tears poured out.

David Sanders walked next to Kate. "This is your moment, Kate. You can use it as you like, but I suspect that you're carrying anger as well as grief. Perhaps it would help if you expressed your anger."

Kate took two deep breaths.

David moved closer to her. "It's your choice, Kate. This would be a good place to let your anger."

"You're right, David," Kate said. She looked down at the floor and muttered, "Fuck you, Earle." She jumped up and down on the floor. "Fuck you, Earle."

Several of the women in the group joined the chant, "Fuck you, Earle."

Kate continued to jump up and down. "Fuck you, Earle."

I'd been in another of David's workshops where he had encouraged a woman to get her anger out by punching a pillow. I got up, wadded up my pillow, and approached Kate. David encouraged her to punch the pillow.

Boff. "Fuck you, Earle."

The first time she punched the pillow, I remembered that Kate's a martial-arts practitioner.

Boff. "Fuck you, Earle."

Now all the participants were chanting, "Fuck you, Earle."

Kate kicked the pillow with her left foot. "Fuck you, Earle."

The tempo increased and the chanting got louder. "Fuck you, Earle."

Kate alternated hitting the pillow with her right hand and left foot. She screamed, "Fuck you, Earle." I backed up.

Kate feinted with her left foot, swung it in an arc, and hit the pillow with the back of her right foot. "Fuck you, Earle."

The pillow split open, and feathers flew over both of us.

There was a moment of shocked silence and then Kate and I started laughing. Kate tilted her head to one side and mouthed, "I'm sorry."

I put up both my hands. "No harm, no foul."

David got up. "Clearly, it's time for us to take another break." He turned to the participants along the wood wall. "Would one of you please open the closet. I think there's a vacuum cleaner in there."

I wanted to talk to Kate, but she was immediately surrounded by female participants who wanted to talk to her about dealing with their errant boyfriends. I went to the men's room and cleaned off the feathers.

⌒℮⌒

Fifteen minutes later the workshop reconvened. The feathers had been cleaned up. Kate broke away from her fan club and plopped down next to me on a new pillow. "Are you okay?" she asked.

"I'll be fine as long as I don't mention my middle name is Earle." I smiled.

Kate tilted her head to one side and mouthed, "No." then she punched me softly in the right shoulder. "Let's talk after the group is over."

David stood up and laughed. "I can tell that this is going to be a good group." He turned to Kate. "Do you have more to say?"

"I'm fine," Kate said and addressed the group. "Thanks for being so supportive."

Most of the participants applauded.

"Okay it's your turn," David said to the young man next to Kate.

He remained seated but scooted forward. "My name is Earle."

Everyone laughed.

"Not really, my name is Rory." He sighed and looked down at the carpet. "I'm afraid I'm like Kate's ex. I'm a womanizer. A sex addict."

Rory was a twenty something wearing faded jeans and a black sleeveless t-shirt that revealed a large dragon tattoo on his right shoulder. Judging from his manner, I thought *Rory is someone who has been at Satori for a while. Probably an intern.*

"I'm Rory Goodrich. I'm originally from Glendale. After I graduated from USC I was at loose ends, so I ended up here." He kept moving. "I've always been very social. Always had a lot of girlfriends." He sighed. "Recently, one of them told me, 'Rory, you're great at sex and terrible at intimacy.' That's me. I'm terminally shallow." He turned towards Kate and nodded.

Kate moved close and whispered to me, "Keep me from throttling him."

"I joined this workshop to work on my addiction. Now that I'm here, I don't know what to do." Rory turned to David.

"Why don't you start by telling us more about yourself." For the next hour David worked with Rory, getting him to describe his unorthodox upbringing that featured a lot of material comfort but little real affection. Halfway through this process I tuned out and started thinking about Kate.

Six months before, she and I had met in San Francisco at a Democratic fundraiser, "Women Who Make a Difference." The Speaker of the House, who lived in San Francisco, hosted a gathering that featured prominent women. One of them was a Federal Judge that Kate, a US Marshall, was assigned to protect.

My firm was responsible for event management and general security. The Secret Service provided for the Speaker's protection. At a planning session, Kate and I realized that we both regarded the head of the Secret Service detail as a bloviating incompetent. Kate and I bonded in our distaste for this individual. This led to a couple of coffee dates, which I thought we both enjoyed, and telephone conversations. We scheduled a dinner date and then Kate broke it off saying, "I like you Tom, but I don't have time, right now, for a real relationship. I'll call you."

I waited for her call, but it never came. I told myself a story that perhaps, after Fiona, I would never have another major relationship. I immersed myself in work. Decided to come to David's workshop. And Kate reappeared. I struggled not to make too much of this.

Meanwhile, Rory's struggles to differentiate sex and intimacy found a receptive audience. Everyone in the group got engaged. Everyone but me.

"Okay," David said, glancing at his watch. "Why doesn't you all sit down, and we'll wrap up." The cluster around Rory went back to their pillows.

"It's after 10," David said. "We're going to break for now and resume at 9am tomorrow morning. Our Monday schedule will be 9 to noon, 2 to 5, and 8 to 10. When you return, I want you to take the same positions that you were in today." He looked around the circle. "Tom, Kate, and Rory, if something came up that you need to process, you can talk to me or to Cheryl after the group adjourns." He looked at Cheryl. "Anything else?"

"Don't forget the baths," she said. "If you're feeling emotional, it may help to soak it off in the Satori hot baths."

"Good advice," said David. "Good work, everyone, see you tomorrow."

∝◦∋

"What's the deal with the baths?" Kate asked.

"There are maybe a dozen tubs, some communal, some smaller. They are located directly below here, overlong the ocean. It's very nice."

"Clothing optional?"

"Yes. Everyone tends to go nude."

"I don't think I can do that."

"That's okay. No pressure."

"Do you go in the baths?"

"Yes,' I said. "I like to go in early in the morning when no one's around. Often the whole area is covered with fog. It's a good time to meditate."

"Maybe I could do that," Kate said. She looked around. Rory was talking to Cheryl but everyone else had gone. "Can I buy you a drink, Tom? I owe it to you." She tilted her head to the side and smiled.

"You don't owe me a drink, but I would like to understand why you never called me."

"Let's walk down to the dining room," Kate said. "I'll tell you what happened."

We got up, put on our shoes and coats, and started walking down the gravel path to the dining room. The path was well lit, but several times, when we came to steps, I put my hand on Kate's arm to help.

"You're a gentleman, aren't you?"

"Old school, I'm afraid."

"I bet Fiona liked that."

"She did. It was one of the things she mentioned on our first date."

"Does it hurt to talk about her?"

"Not right now. My process felt cathartic."

"It was awesome." We turned a corner. "You know David Sanders?" Kate asked.

"Yeah. As a therapist, not as a social friend. Over the years I've done a couple of workshops with him."

"You and Fiona?"

"No. Once I did a men's workshop with him while Fiona was here working. Another time I did a sort of 'wilderness experience' workshop with David where we rode horses back into the mountains."

"Sounds interesting. Do you like to ride?"

"Yes. But I don't do it very much. What about you?"

"My family has a ranch in the hills above Fresno. I've been riding since I was a little girl." We stopped to look at the view and then Kate asked, "What do you think about Cheryl Taylor?"

"She's been at Satori a long time. I've never done a workshop with her, but Fiona did. Cheryl and Fiona became friends."

"How's that for you?"

"It doesn't bother me."

"I didn't get a read on Cheryl," Kate said.

"I think she and David will work well together. David has this very 'avuncular' style; he's warm and fuzzy. Cheryl is more conventionally clinical, more spiritual." I ran my hand across my forehead. "David's training is eclectic. Cheryl studied at the Jung Institute in Switzerland. David is an outdoorsman. Cheryl is a meditator; a Zen Buddhist, I think."

"Thanks. That's helpful."

We came to another set of stone steps. I put my hand on Kate's arm and she reached across and covered my hand with hers.

"I still like you," Kate said.

I flinched. "As a friend."

"More than that." We'd reached the dining room. "Let's get that drink."

Unfortunately, the bar was closed. "What about tea?" I asked.

Kate made some spicy tea for herself, and I got chamomile. We walked out onto the deck and sat in Adirondack chairs facing the fire pit. In the distance we could see the dark ocean.

"I owe you an apology," Kate said. "What happened was all my fault. After talking to my therapist, I realized that I was afraid of having a relationship with you and I took the coward's way out."

I had been holding my breath, but now I let it out. "Thanks, but it wasn't all on you. I hadn't let go of Fiona. It was stupid for me to wear my wedding ring to our coffee date."

"I notice you're not wearing it now."

"No. I talked to my therapist about what happened between the two of us and he pointed out that I was still wearing my ring." I sipped my lukewarm tea. "I thought about it and realized it was time to move on. The next day I went to my jeweler, and he helped me get the ring off."

Kate drank tea and looked at the fire. "My therapist helped me understand that I sabotaged our relationship. I was afraid that I would get involved with you, it wouldn't work, and I would be devastated. So, I chose a 'reclamation project.' I chose Earle because it was a familiar, fucked-up pattern."

I started to ask Kate a question but stopped myself.

"I have an insidious self-esteem issue: I don't think I'm worthy. Therapy has helped me understand it stems from my relationship with my father, who was a star in the Fresno PD. I never thought I could come up to his standards." Kate took a deep breath and turned to look at me. "My therapist helped me understand that I thought that I wasn't good enough to be in relationship with you. I believed I wasn't a star, like Fiona."

I started to respond but Kate stopped me with her hand.

"It may be too late, but I would still like to explore our being together."

"It's not too late. I'm not seeing anyone. Before I came here, I had half reconciled to being single the rest of my life." *I've done nothing but work.*

"There was a picture in *the San Francisco Chronicle* of you and an attractive woman."

"That wasn't my date; that was Stella, my sister-in-law and business partner."

"Oh." Kate smiled and looked into my eyes.

My heart was racing and my next words came out in a whisper. "This would be an opportunity to explore being together."

Kate's eyes misted.

We sat in silence for a few minutes and then Kate said, "I'm exhausted. I need to go back to my room and go to sleep." She got up from her chair and extended her hand. "Walk me back, Tom. There's something important I need to tell you."

We went into the dining room, deposited our cups in the "dirty dishes" tub, and exited the side door. As we crossed the lawn, Kate started talking. "I'm here as part of my psychological leave. I'm thinking of leaving the Marshall's office."

"I thought you liked your job? I thought you just got a big promotion?"

"True. I'm the first female supervisor in the San Francisco office. But something terrible happened."

I stopped and looked at Kate, but she kept walking.

"U.S. Marshalls do three things. We protect US government officials, particularly judges – that's what I was doing when we met. We arrest people that are subject to Federal warrants. And we administer the witness protection program."

"You are on psychological leave because of something that happened in that program?"

"Yes." Kate stopped in front of her room and turned to me. "One of my families was murdered by the Mexican mafia. The wife tried to contact me, but I got her message too late. I rushed to their residence, in the Mission district, and found the bodies of my assignee, his wife..." Her voice broke. Kate paused, composed herself, and finished, "and their three little children."

"Ugh." I stopped and clasped her hand.

"Tom, in my line of work, I've seen some heavy shit. I've seen really bad traffic accidents. I've seen the aftermath of gang fights. I've seen mafia guys blown away with sawed-off shot guns. But this was the worst." Tears flowed down her cheeks.

I wrapped my arms around her.

"It was so fucked up." She sobbed into my chest.

I had to bend down, to kiss her hair, her cheek, and taste her tears. Then I got an erection.

After a few moments, Kate's tears turned into chuckles. "I'm glad you like me."

I pulled back. "I'm not good at keeping secrets."

"Apparently not." She chortled.

"I'm embarrassed." I kissed her hair.

"Don't be. It's sweet." She nuzzled into my chest.

Kate's roommate, Norma, walked up and offered, "If you want to have the room to yourselves, I can sleep somewhere else."

"That's a kind offer," Kate said. "But Tom and I are saying goodnight. Go ahead into the room. I'll be right in."

Norma walked around us, unlocked the door, and went inside their cabin.

"I don't want to let go of you, but I'm going to," Kate said.

My heart hammered in my chest.

Kate let go of me and took a step back. "Did you mean what you said, that we can use this time to explore being together?"

My throat tightened. "Yes," I rasped.

"Good." Kate kissed me on the cheek, turned around, and went into her cabin.

MONDAY

CHAPTER 5
(6:30 AM): Tom

I woke up at my usual time, made myself a cup of coffee, shaved, and headed for the baths. The air temperature was in the sixties, but a thick mantle of fog hung over Satori.

The baths were located at the southern end of the campus, perched on a cliff overlooking a rocky cove. I walked for ten minutes and got to the bath house as the maintenance crew was finishing their work. I stripped, showered, grabbed a towel, and headed for the most remote tub, where I would be alone. As I submerged my body in the 104-degree water and the heat loosened my muscles. I drifted across the tub and came to the edge that overlooked the ocean. *Twenty-one years ago, I met Fiona in this tub. Fiona loved Satori; it was her safe space.*

Thinking of Fiona didn't hurt anymore; it warmed my heart. *Kate is different from Fiona but smart, independent, funny. They would like each other.*

As I contemplated this, a gaunt man from the workshop entered the adjacent tub. He knelt at the edge of his tub and bowed his head in prayer. I looked away.

In a few minutes my meditation was interrupted by the splash of another two people entering my tub. Although they were at the other end, I could hear their conversation.

"No matter what the police say, I don't believe it was an accident," the man muttered. "Malcolm had too many enemies. Think of all the women he wounded. He hurt you."

"I hurt myself," the woman said. "I knew what kind of person Malcolm was and still I let myself be lured into his web." She laughed. "I wanted his validation that I was worthy."

"What was his appeal?" the man asked. "I never got it."

"Obviously, he was handsome. And when he focused on you, he made you feel that you were the only woman in the world. Everyone else was a pebble and you had been elevated to be a diamond."

"For one night."

"For one night."

"And then?"

"And then I woke up and knew I had been used."

"And you felt how?"

"All the feelings you expect: shame and sorrow and anger."

"Angry enough to kill him?"

"Not that angry. Angry enough to cut his balls off." The woman laughed.

CHAPTER 6
(7:30AM): Laura

"At least the coffee is decent," Detective Sanchez said. She and detective Sergeant O'Malley were sitting in the Satori lobby waiting for the staff to arrive for the meeting scheduled at 7:30. "Maybe we should go get breakfast and then come back.'

"They're all on Satori time," O'Malley said. "They always show up late. If we leave now. They'll stagger in, assume the meeting was called off, and disappear."

"How about if I get us some pastries?" Sanchez asked.

Just then a lanky, spectacled man approached, carrying a briefcase and key ring. "Are you Detectives Sanchez and O'Malley?" he asked. They nodded. "I'm Bruce James, the executive director. Come on into my office. We'll start talking and the others will join us over the next few minutes." James unlocked the door behind the receptionist desk, and they entered an office corridor. The detectives followed him to the end and James unlocked a heavy redwood door. He entered the office, threw his briefcase and keys on the desk, and then drew open the drapes. The office overlooked the main Satori lawn to the ocean.

The fog was beginning to lift, and they could see the outlines of pine trees at the edge of the bluff.

"Go ahead and take a seat," James said, as he flicked on the lights. "When Sequoyah gets here, I'll have her fetch more coffee and some pastries."

"Did your maintenance crew tell you what we found out?" O'Malley asked. "We talked to.." he referenced his notes, "Juan Romero."

"Juan called me at home and said that you had identified Malcolm. He fell off the deck at the old conference center." James ran his hand over his face. "That's bizarre."

"We don't know if he fell or was pushed," Sanchez said. "The coroner's team will be here today. Maybe they will be able to tell. For the time being, we're treating it as a suspicious death."

"We want to talk to your staff to identify Malcolm's movements just before his death," O'Malley said.

A buxom blonde wearing overalls entered the office. "Sorry to be late, Bruce. We had a crisis in the garden." She turned to us. "I'm Sequoyah, Bruce's personal assistant. Can I get you some more coffee or pastries?"

"That would be grand," O'Malley said.

Sequoyah sauntered out.

O'Malley referenced his notes. "Malcolm Eastwick had a residence in San Francisco, how often was he here?"

"Not as often as he used to be," James said. "At the beginning he was very involved, but recently he's left the day-to-day management to me and my crew."

"How many people are in your crew?" Sanchez asked.

A dignified, middle-aged woman with an extravagant French braid bustled in. "Sorry to be late."

"This is Marcia Ball, my outreach coordinator," James said.

Marcia shook hands with the detectives and then sat down.

O'Malley turned back to Bruce James. "When did Malcolm Eastwick return to Satori?"

"I'm not sure," James said. "We knew he would be here for Tuesday's board meeting and the fundraiser on Wednesday evening."

"You didn't see him when he arrived?"

"No, but that's not unusual. Malcolm has a house on the northern end of the property. These days we don't see him in the office unless there is a board meeting or a special event."

"Can you give us access to his house?" Sanchez asked.

"Yes," Marcia replied.

"Who might know when Malcolm arrived?" O'Malley asked. "Who might be aware of his movements on Saturday night?"

"I don't know," James said. "Perhaps Cheryl Taylor, she's a member of the board who has a house nearby. She's known Malcom since the beginning; she was married to the other co-founder, the one that died."

"Where could we find Cheryl Taylor?" Sanchez asked.

"She'll be here today," James said. "She's co-leading a workshop. We can get word to her, and she could talk to you during a break."

"The first thing we will do is to examine Malcolm's residence," O'Malley said. "Then we will begin interviewing folks who might have contacted Malcolm on Saturday."

"You can interview here," James said. "I have a vacant office."

CHAPTER 7
(8:45AM): Tom

I looked for Kate at breakfast but didn't see her, so I headed to the "Karl Rogers" room, arriving minutes before 9AM. As before, David Sanders was sitting yoga-style on a pillow with his back against the wood wall. A few participants had already arrived.

Over the next few minutes, the workshop filled up. At 9:04, Kate ran in and plopped down next to me, wearing dark-blue leggings and a "Fresno State' sweatshirt. Her face was flushed and her hair wet. "I took a longer run than I planned," she whispered.

Cheryl walked in and closed the door.

David sat up. "Before we begin, I want to tell you sad news. Malcolm Eastwick, one of the Satori founders, is dead. There was an accident on Saturday night; Malcolm fell off the deck at the old conference room and landed on the beach rocks. The Monterey County Sheriff's Department is here investigating the incident." David sighed. "The detectives will probably want to talk to anyone who knew Malcolm, particularly anyone who saw him on Saturday." David looked around the room. "They'll talk to me and Cheryl. Who here knew Malcolm?"

I raised my hand, as did another man I didn't know.

"How well did you know him?" Kate whispered.

"Not well. He was one of Fiona's clients. I'll tell you later."

"We'll going to continue to go around the circle," Cheryl said and checked the roster. She nodded at a middle-aged, brown-skinned woman sitting next to Rory. "Norma, it's your turn."

Norma wore black pants and a grey tunic. Her long gray hair was tied behind her back. *She looks worn down*, I thought. Kate's roommate scooted forward on her cushion. "My name is Norma Jefferson. I'm a cancer survivor. I had pancreatic cancer and underwent chemotherapy and surgery and survived. For the last four years I have been cancer free."

There was a round of applause.

"I'm from Portland," Norma said. "I was married for thirty years to Eugene Jefferson; we divorced several years ago. Our daughter, Sherry, lives in Boston, where she's going to graduate school." Norma sighed and clasped and unclasped her thin hands. "It's hard to talk about."

"Just breathe and take your time," Cheryl said.

"Eugene and I were in love when we got married. At least I was," Norma said. "And we were happy for a while. I worked as a nurse and Eugene as an accountant. We bought a house. Joined a church. Had friends. Parented Sherry." Norma reached behind her for her thermos, unscrewed the top, and took a sip of water. "Eugene and I drifted apart. We stopped being intimate. Stopped having sex." Norma blushed and looked at the rug. "I told myself this was normal; told myself I shouldn't expect more."

"Then I got sick." Norma sighed. "By this time, Sherry was at BU. I could drive myself to my doctor's appointments, but not to chemotherapy; it was too debilitating." She looked down at the carpet. "At first, Eugene took time off from work and drove me. Then, when I was coming home from a chemotherapy session, I threw up in the car. That night, Eugene asked me to find someone else to drive me. We had a big argument; he said it was too upsetting for him." Norma began to cry.

Cheryl pushed a box of tissues across the floor to her.

Norma wiped her eyes. "I tried to find other rides with friends. A couple of times I used Uber. Sherry found out about this. Just before I went into the hospital for my surgery, she took a leave of absence from graduate school and moved home to take care of me." She sighed. "I'm not exactly sure what was said, but while I was in the hospital, Sherry and Eugene had words; when I got home, he was gone.

"Eugene moved into an apartment. Each month he sent me a check. Sherry insisted that I talk to an attorney and, when I was well enough, I did. He negotiated a reasonable divorce settlement." Norma cried. "Eugene didn't care much about the money; he just didn't want to be around me."

"What an asshole," Kate muttered.

"Put him on your 'Earle' list," I whispered.

Kate gave me her signature look, her head tilted to one side and grinned. "I smell a business opportunity."

I stifled a laugh and turned back to Norma.

"Sherry stayed with me until I recovered and then she returned to BU. I sold the house and used my portion of the proceeds to buy a nice condo, downtown. I went back to work at Portland General."

"One day I realized how angry I was. I had a dream where I had run over Eugene in our car – the car he drives now." Norma shook her head. "I realized how I had been holding everything inside. It frightened me. I began therapy."

Norma leaned back, grabbed her water bottle, and took a drink. "I go to individual therapy with Rachel Deavers and group therapy led by her associate, Myrna. The group encouraged me to come here." She stopped and looked at Cheryl.

Cheryl scooted forward until she was sitting in front of Norma. "You are very brave to tell us your story, Norma. I hear your anger. What other feelings are there?"

"I feel very sad." Norma teared up. "When I really needed Eugene, he left me."

"I hear that, Norma." Cheryl waited to see if Norma had anything more to say. "What are you hoping to get from this group?"

Norma glanced at me. "When Tom talked about Fiona's death, he said he realized how precious love is." Tears rolled down her cheeks. "I survived my cancer because I wanted to live. I want more love in my life."

"You want more love in your life," Cheryl echoed.

"Yes. Sherry loves me. My girlfriends love me, but I want more."

"You deserve more." Cheryl moved closer and clasped both of Norma's hands. They sat in silence for several minutes.

"You are very brave, Norma. Would you like feedback from the group?"

"Yes."

For the next period, participants applauded Norma and shared their experiences in failed relationships. *Betrayal is a common theme*, I thought.

Kate whispered, "I hope you know how lucky Fiona was to have you stick with her at the end."

My heart throbbed.

"Loyalty is a rare commodity," Kate said.

I thought of Malcolm Eastwick and wondered, *Who did Malcolm betray?*

The group conversation subsided. Cheryl looked around the group. "Any more feedback for Norma?" No hands went up. "Thanks, Norma. You did great."

Cheryl and Norma scooted back to their places. Cheryl turned to the man next to Norma. "Your turn, Otto."

The man stood. He was around sixty with a stiff, military bearing, and neatly trimmed gray hair. "My name is Otto Weber," he said, speaking with a slight accent. "I was born in Germany, near Bremen. I went to University at Heidelberg. My wife, Inga, is also German. I moved here in 1982 to work for Siemens and I have been here ever since. Now, I am retiring." He reached down and took a drink of water. "Inga wants to return to Germany and live the life of a retired person. I want to remain here and start a second career as a therapist." He looked around the group. "That's why I came here; to decide what to do."

David got up and walked in front of Otto. "I hear that you are being pulled in several directions: stay here or return to Germany; retire or pursue a second career. How do you feel about this?"

"I feel sad." Otto closed his eyes. "I feel that Inga and I have drifted apart. We want different things; we see the world differently."

"That's what I'm hearing," David said. "Do you have children?"

"Yes, two grown children. Tim and Mia. Both in university."

"What do they think?"

"They want to stay here. They were born here."

"What reason does Inga give for wanting to return to Germany?"

"Inga thinks Germany is safer." Otto clasped his hands tightly together. "She never integrated into American society as much as I did. Inga stayed at home and took care of Tim and Mia. And after they were grown, she joined the German-Lutheran church in Sunnyvale."

"So, this difference in perspective is not a new development?" David asked. "It sounds like this has been brewing over several years?"

"Yes. Five years ago, we came to a Satori Institute couple's workshop," Otto said. "I enjoyed it. Inga did not. I talked to a lot of people. Inga did not. I went into the baths. Inga did not." Otto kneaded his hands. "We had very different experiences."

Cheryl got up and walked to where David and Otto were standing. "How was that for you?" she asked.

"It was very upsetting. I tried to talk to Inga about it, but she couldn't. She does this thing where she, what is the expression 'turns to stone.'"

"That's always hard when one couple member wants to talk about a problem and the other doesn't," Cheryl said. "Did you and Inga try therapy back in Sunnyvale?"

"Yes and no," Otto said. "Yes, I tried to get her to go to conventional therapy, the sort of therapy you teach here. No, she wouldn't attend but suggested that we do 'therapy' with the assistant pastor of her church, spiritual counseling."

"Did you talk to the assistant pastor of her church?"

"We did," Otto answered. "It was very unsatisfactory for me. He said that we had been 'joined' by the church and that was that. He advised us to read the bible together."

"How did you feel about what he said?"

"I felt that it was not good advice. I was very upset."

"What did you do about these feelings?" Chery asked.

"I found a therapist in Sunnyvale, Byron Jordan. He's the one that suggested I come to this workshop." Otto kneaded his hands. "In fact, it was my experience working with Byron that got me interested in becoming a therapist."

"So, you worked with him for quite a while?"

"Yes. For several years."

"And what did you learn?"

Otto's voice choked and he spoke so softly I could barely hear him. "I learnt that Inga and I want different things from life. I learnt that she is set in her ways. Inga wants to return to Germany and live in a Lutheran retirement community. That's not what I want." Otto looked up at the top of the room and then peered intently at Cheryl. "It is very hard for me to say this because Inga is a good person, the mother of my children. Once I loved her as a lover; now I love her as a friend. Once I wanted us to be together always; now I do not mind if we live apart."

Cheryl moved closer to Otto and placed her hand on her heart. "How do you feel, Otto? Is it a bad thing for you to separate from Inga?"

Otto mirrored Cheryl and placed his right hand on his heart. "No." One tear rolled down his cheek. "Life is precious. What I've learned here is that I need to take responsibility for my own life, for my own happiness." He wiped one eye with his shirt sleeve. "I believe Inga stopped growing. I do not want to stop growing."

Cheryl went back to her pillow and sat down. "What do you need from this group?" David asked.

"I think I got what I wanted," Otto said. "Thank you."

"Do you want feedback from the group?"

"Yes. I am interested in what they have to say."

Again, participants applauded Otto and shared their relationship stories. *Relationships are hard work*, I thought and remembered that Kate and I had to do individual therapy before we felt ready to pursue a relationship. *If either one of us hadn't gone to therapy, we wouldn't be here now.*

"Let's take a ten-minute break," David said.

"Wow. That was intense," Kate said.

"Yes. Good people trying to get the most out of life."

"Like you and me," she said.

∞

"We'll take two more and then break for lunch," Cheryl said. She addressed an attractive young woman sitting next to Otto. "It's your turn Julie."

The woman scooted forward. "My name is Julie Peters." She glanced at Kate. "I'm afraid this is another Earle story. I'm twenty-five; my mother and I own a horse ranch, outside Whitefish, Montana. We bought it from my father, who decided that he wanted to move to L.A. and become a screenwriter." She flashed a wry smile. "I graduated from UM as a pre-med in veterinary medicine. I started in the Vet program at Washington State but had to drop out when my mom broke her leg." Julie paused for a sip of water. "Like the songs say, it's lonely out there on the prairie. A couple of years ago, I was at a horse show in Missoula, and I met a horse dealer from Bozeman, Glen Sanders. He was ten years older, married, with a kid. We hung out and he told me how his wife didn't love him anymore, she wanted to move back to Jackson Hole." Julie teared up. "We didn't sleep together then, but a couple of months later there was a show in Great Falls, and I saw him there." Tears rolled down her cheeks. "I won't bullshit you guys; I've been hit on all my life. I thought I had a pretty sophisticated B.S. detector but somehow Glen got past that."

Cheryl got up and slid a box of tissues to Julie.

"I thought he loved me; I thought he was going to leave his wife and daughter and come live with me." She wiped her eyes with a tissue. "Then, three months ago, Glen called to say that we had to break it off. His wife was pregnant, and he couldn't leave her. So, I realized that I had been had." She sobbed.

Cheryl slid across the room, close to Julie. "Take your time. Focus on breathing."

"I feel so stupid. I know you can't trust men, but I did anyway."

"I feel there is sorrow and anger," Cheryl said. "Are you ready to express your anger?"

"I don't think so. I feel like going into a cave and closing the entrance." Julie put her hands over her face.

"It sounds like there is a part of you that is angry at Glen and a part of you that is angry at yourself."

"Uh huh," Julie's voice was barely audible.

Cheryl leaned closer. "Are you willing to try something?"

"Uh huh." Julie moved her hands away from her face.

"If the part that is angry at yourself could talk, what would it say?"

"How could you be so stupid? How could you let Glen fool you?"

"Good." Cheryl handed Julie a tissue and she wiped her face. "Suppose that a friend told you this story. Suppose that a friend said, 'How could I be so stupid?' What would you say to your friend?"

Julie thought as she wiped her face. "I would say, 'It's Glen that's stupid. You are a good person, friend. It's Glen's problem that this didn't work. Glen is a fucking idiot.'"

Several women clapped.

"You're brave, Julie," Cheryl said. "How can this group help you?"

"I'm not sure. It feels good to be here." Julie wiped her face with a tissue. "I've been depressed. My mom was worried about me. She's the one that suggested that I come to this workshop."

"Smart mom."

"Yes. Smart and tough. She's had to make her way in a man's world, and she's held her own." Julie looked at Kate. "You remind me of her. Except that you are more dangerous."

Cheryl said, "If that part of you that admires Kate's dangerousness, her lethality, could speak, what would it say?"

Julie smiled, "It would say, 'Would you mind coming to Montana and taking out Glen?'"

The group laughed.

Cheryl glanced at Kate and then refocused on Julie. "It sounds like you would like some Taekwando training."

"That would be good," Julie laughed. "I'd like that."

"That could be arranged," Kate said.

"Good," Julie laughed.

"Is there anything else you need from us?" Cheryl asked.

"I don't think so."

Cheryl looked around the group. "Do any of you have Feedback for Julie?"

Several women applauded Julie and shared their "Earle" stories. I thought about Malcolm Eastwick. *Malcolm was an "Earle." Did one of his conquests take him out?*

The conversation stopped. Cheryl hugged Julie and they both stepped back to their places in the circle.

"Okay, Theo," David said. He turned to the man sitting next to Julie. "Your turn."

Theo stood up. I would have thought him to be in his twenties if I hadn't noticed the flecks of grey in his black hair. "My name is Theo Wang. I'm Chinese American; born in San Mateo. My father grew up in San Francisco's Chinatown. My mother came here from Taiwan in 1950. I went to San Mateo schools and then to Stanford. I'm married with two children. We live in Portola Valley."

Theo scanned the group. "This is difficult. I feel more nervous than I usually do."

David leaned in. "Take your time. Focus on breathing."

Theo took two deep breaths. "I'm a physician, an oncologist. I have a practice in Palo Alto." He sighed. "I have a wonderful family and a successful life, but-" he hesitated and his voice trembled, "-I've hit the wall." Theo looked down at the rug and then fixed on David. "I've been very depressed; somedays I can barely find the energy to go to my office. I talked to my wife about this, as well as my therapist. He's been working with me and suggested I come here." Theo closed his eyes.

David walked across the room until he was close to Theo. "Oncology is a tough field."

"Yes. Too many of my patients die." Theo lowered his voice. "I have to talk to my clients and their families about death all the time."

David leaned closer. "That must be hard."

"It is hard." Theo paused. "It wears me down. I don't know if I can do it anymore."

"I'm imagining that you have internal dialog about your situation," David said.

Theo nodded.

"So, what are these parts saying?"

For the next thirty minutes, David worked with Theo on his conflicts regarding his situation. A part of Theo wanted to leave oncology and another part, his internalized father, felt he should tough it out. I considered that I was lucky because I didn't have a father part telling me what I should do; my father left my mother when I was five years old and ceased to be a factor in my life. I remembered, years before, seeing Malcolm Eastwick lead a workshop; he'd been a commanding presence. *Malcolm was charismatic. He was probably a father figure to some women.*

The more I thought about Malcolm's death, the more convinced I was that it was a revenge killing: Malcolm, the father, was seen to have betrayed his conquest. *He screwed over the wrong woman. And she killed him.*

David's work with Theo ended. Several participants gave him feedback.

"Theo," David said. "Thank you for your hard work." He looked at Norma, Otto, and Julie. "Thank you all for your hard work. You've set a high bar for those who follow."

"We're going to break now," Cheryl said. "We'll meet again at 2PM. Please be on time."

The workshop participants slowly rose, as if waking from a trance state. "Let's have lunch," Kate said and reached for my hand.

CHAPTER 8
(11am): Laura

Marcia Ball let Sanchez and her partner, O'Malley, into Malcolm Eastwick's bungalow. It was a spacious one-bedroom dwelling with a luxurious bathroom and book-strewn sitting room.

"If it wasn't for the suitcase on the bed," Detective Sanchez said, "I'd think Eastwick hadn't been here for weeks."

"It looks like Eastwick unlocked the front door, threw his suitcase on the bed, and left," O'Malley said. "Probably walked to the old conference room to meet someone."

Sanchez and O'Malley put gloves on before conducting the search. "Eastwick threw his keys on this counter," Sanchez said. "One of them probably works with the Tesla parked outside. Let's look around and see if we can find his phone." O'Malley scanned the bedroom while Sanchez moved to the sitting room.

After a few minutes, O'Malley called out. "I found his laptop in his briefcase but no phone."

"There's something in the sitting room I want you to take a look at," Sanchez said.

O'Malley moved to the doorway.

"Notice how all the pictures have the same wooden frame?" Sanchez said. "Except for this one." She moved to a picture over the couch and grabbed hold of it. "It has a thicker frame and different orientation to the wall." The detective grabbed hold of the frame and tugged it. "Voila." The frame swung out revealing an inset safe.

"Now all we have to do is find the combination."

⁓

"Did you find anything, Bruno?" Sanchez asked the coroner's assistant, who was sitting at a table inside the old conference room, writing notes.

"It's difficult terrain," Bruno Oliver said. "The tide washed in and out several times after the body fell. There's nothing on the beach or on the rocks where you found the handkerchief."

"Can you tell if Eastwick was struck before the fall?" O'Malley asked.

"No. We can't determine that," Bruno said. "The only thing we can do is provide the toxicology report. That might determine if he was drugged before the fall."

"There's one more thing," Sanchez said. "We found a laptop in Eastwick's cabin. It's password protected. If you could open it, we can look at his schedule to determine if he planned on meeting anyone here on Saturday night. Or if there are recent emails about a meeting."

"Tell him about the safe," O'Malley said.

"Thanks for reminding me." Sanchez turned to Bruno. "We found a wall safe in Eastwick's residence but, of course, no combination. When you examine the laptop, see if you can find the safe combination."

"When do you expect to have lab results?" O'Malley asked.

"Possibly Wednesday. It depends on how busy we get."

"Bruno, do me a favor."

"Sure, Laura."

"When you talk to me you look at me, but when you talk to O'Malley you look away. Try to look at him; he's actually a nice guy."

"That's good to know." Bruno slowly moved his eyes to O'Malley's face.

⁕

"I can't believe no one was around Saturday night," Sanchez said to O'Malley. They had just finished the last of eight staff interviews.

"Well, we did learn that Eastwick was a womanizer," O'Malley said.

"And that no one on the Institute staff liked him because he was difficult and bossy," Sanchez said, before lowering her voice to add, "Unlike managers at the Sheriff's Department."

O'Malley looked at her and raised his eyebrows. "Attitude, Sanchez. Attitude." He looked at his list. We've got a couple of people to interview that are in the 'Transitions' workshop; they'll be around at lunch time."

"Here's an interesting item," Sanchez said. "There's a US Marshal in the workshop; a woman."

"What's she doing here?"

"I have no idea, but it's possible she may know something. Her name is Kate Swift."

CHAPTER 9

(noon): Tom

Kate and I went through the lunch line and sat at a long red-wood table with Norma, Otto, Theo, and Julie.

"Will you really teach me Taekwando?" Julie asked Kate.

"Of course, Julie. You're athletic, you shouldn't have any trouble picking it up." Julie had informed us that she was going to live a couple of months in San Francisco before she started veterinary school at UC Davis.

While the ladies talked, Otto asked, "Are you and Kate friends?"

I glanced at Kate, who didn't appear to have heard the question. "Yes. We met in San Francisco, lost contact, and reconnected here."

"She likes you," Otto said. "I notice she keeps touching you."

My heart pounded giddily, like I was a teenager.

Two Sheriff's deputies approached our table. "Do you mind if we interrupt?" the woman said. Her name tag read Detective Laura Sanchez.

"Not a bit," Kate said. "How's it going?"

"It's going," the other detective said. His name tag read Detective Sergeant Dan O'Malley. He leaned across the table. "Are you US Marshal Swift?"

Kate frowned and muttered, "How can I help you?"

"Do you mind if we talk to you for a few minutes?"

"Not at all." Kate got up and whispered to me. "So much for traveling incognito." She followed the deputies out of the dining room.

CHAPTER 10

(12:15PM): Laura

Marshall Swift followed the deputies back to their temporary office in the administrative suite.

"We're here investigating the death of Malcolm Eastwick and realized that you were among the workshop participants," Laura said. "We thought that we should make contact with you."

"I'd like to help you, but I never met Eastwick. From what I gather, he had an unsavory reputation."

"What have you heard?"

"Nothing specific, but some women regarded him as a predator."

Detective Sanchez nodded. "We're having trouble tracking his movements. We know he arrived here sometime Saturday, but we haven't talked to anyone who saw him before his body was found Sunday morning."

"He was a therapist. Maybe he was seeing clients."

"Any idea where we could find his client schedule, if there was one?"

"The obvious," Kate said. "His phone or pocket planner."

"Which we didn't find."

"The office might know."

"They claim to know nothing."

"What about the cloud? Did Eastwick have a website?"

Sanchez turned to O'Malley. "That's another thing that Bruno can help us with."

"Eastwick probably used scheduling software to keep track of his appointments. If you find his laptop, you can access his schedule and his contacts."

"We found his laptop," Sanchez said. "The coroner's investigators are trying to get into it."

CHAPTER 11
(12:30): Tom

I stayed in the dining room, waiting for Kate to return. I could tell our friends were curious about the interaction with the Sheriff's deputies.

"I didn't know Kate is a Marshall," Norma said.

"She's trying to travel incognito."

"You knew her before the workshop?" Julie asked.

"We met in San Francisco, lost contact, and reconnected here."

"Why did you lose contact?"

I thought before answering Julie. "The best explanation is that when we met, we liked each other but we weren't prepared to have a romantic relationship."

"And now you are?"

"Yes. I think we are."

"I hope so," Julie said. "You guys seem like a good fit."

ↄↄↄ

Kate returned and told us the Sheriff's deputies were investigating the death of Malcom Eastwick.

"It sounds like they think that Malcolm's death wasn't an accident," I said.

"That's the impression I got but they didn't say that. What do you think?"

"I think that Malcolm made a lot of enemies."

"How did he get along with you and Fiona?"

I shook my head. "Malcolm was like several of our rich entitled male customers, always trying to hit on Fiona."

"How did she handle it?"

"She laughed at him. Called him *Puer Aeternus*."

"What's that mean?"

"I think it literally means 'eternal boy.' She took a course in the Enneagram and told me that Malcolm fit the category of men who never grow up."

"She wasn't pissed off at him?"

"No. He might have been pissed off at her, for laughing at him, but he still gave us business."

∽

The six of us walked together to the afternoon session. Kate and Norma arm in arm with Julie.

When we entered the conference room, David asked Kate, "Did the police talk to you?"

"They found me at lunch, but I didn't have anything to tell them about Malcolm," Kate said.

"I hate to malign the dead," David said. "But the Institute will probably run better now that Malcolm's out of the picture. The last few years, he's been a pain in the ass."

Kate looked at me and raised her eyebrows.

We sat down and waited for the room to fill.

"We're going to continue around the circle," Cheryl said. "Aoife, it's your turn." She nodded at a distinguished, red-headed woman sitting next to Theo.

She scooted forward. "My name is Aoife. A-O-I-F-E. You pronounce my name EE-fa; somewhat like e-VA."

The entire group said, "EE-fa."

"I'm a tenured mathematics professor at Cal, with a specialty in numerical analysis. I live near the campus with my husband, who's a doctor, and our two daughters. I was forced to leave my campus duties because I was stalked." Aoife's eyes teared.

Cheryl moved forward and slid a box of tissues near Aoife.

"Last year, I was assigned to the dissertation committee of a mathematics student I will call Ray. I didn't know him; he'd never been in any of my classes. Shortly after Ray submitted a dissertation proposal, the chair of the committee, Nance, became ill, and I took over. I received Ray's proposal and found it incoherent. It wasn't just poorly written; it made no sense. I attempted to contact Nance to discuss this proposal, but his illness had become more severe – he died a couple of months later. I invited Ray to drop by my office and discuss his proposal." Aoife stopped and took a sip of water.

"Ray came in and I was shocked by his manner and appearance. You may understand that at the University of California at

Berkeley we are accustomed to students affecting a wide range of lifestyles. We also have a large number of students for whom English is a second language and, therefore, I am accustomed to students who have difficulty expressing themselves. Even given this background, I was shocked by Ray's appearance and conduct. He dressed in tattered clothes, smelled like he hadn't bathed in a week, and talked gibberish."

Aoife told us she had tried to work with Ray but was unsuccessful. Finally, she recommended that he be dropped from the PhD program. After that occurred, Ray stalked her. When he began delivering threats and ominous messages to her home, Aoife took a leave of absence.

"That sounds very hard, Aoife." Cheryl moved closer. "How can we help you?"

"I'm not sure. It feels good to be in such a supportive group, with so many strong women." Aoife looked at Kate.

The female participants offered support to Aoife. Kate suggested they talk during the break.

"You're next, Paul," Cheryl said to the middle-aged man sitting next to Aoife. He was the same guy I had seen praying in the baths, that morning.

Paul was thin, and dressed in a worn gray tracksuit. His hair and beard were neatly trimmed and flecked with gray, and his shoulder were slumped. *He would be good looking*, I thought, *but he appears to have given up*. His shoulders were slumped.

"I congratulate you all for your bravery," the man said. "I can relate to all your stories. Particularly that of Theo. Theo is burnt out as an oncologist. I am burnt out as a priest."

"Tell us your full name," David said.

"Good idea," the man laughed. "My name is Paul Rossi. I am fifty-two years old, born in San Francisco. I have been a Catholic priest for the last twenty-five years." He reached down for his thermos and gulped water. "I studied with the Jesuits at Santa Clara. Because I am a fluent Spanish speaker, I worked as missionary in Central America for fifteen years. The last ten years I have been working in the East Bay."

"There's a lot about being a priest I like. I like the isolation. Until recently, I found comfort in our daily routine: mass, simple living, prayer, and so forth." Paul paused and looked around the room. "Until recently I enjoyed pastoral care; I enjoyed hearing confessions; I enjoyed talking to lay people. Then something changed; I felt that I had used up my allocation of empathy. I felt that my heart had dried up." Paul looked down at the floor. "I prayed on this, and I talked to my confessor, Brother Ray. A couple of months ago, I decided to leave the church. Brother Ray convinced me to come here and take this workshop to help clarify my thinking."

David got up and walked close to Paul. "How are you feeling?"

"I feel defeated. I feel that my heart has been damaged and, therefore, I have nothing further to offer the church."

David closed his eyes and then opened them. "You believe in the soul?"

"Yes."

"In your belief system, are the soul and the heart synonymous?"

Paul placed his hand on his chest. "They are close but different parts."

"Okay. I want to try something," David said. "Have your soul talk to your heart. Have your soul ask your heart what's happening and what it needs."

"Out loud?"

"Whatever feels comfortable," David said. "If you'd rather have an internal dialog, do that and then report back."

Paul closed his eyes and pressed his hand to his chest. His lips moved but his words were inaudible. After a couple of minutes, Paul spoke. "My heart needs to be replenished. I want to be guided by spirit, but I need to care for myself."

"What does 'care for myself' mean?"

Paul laughed. "It means to have some fun. It means that I need to receive love as well as give it."

"Do you want feedback?"

"Of course."

No one raised their hand. I thought when *Fiona died, my heart needed to be replenished. That's why, at first, I wasn't ready for a relationship with Kate.*

"Thanks again," David said. "We're going to take a ten-minute break."

"I'm going to talk to Aoife," Kate said. "I have an idea how I can help her." Kate squeezed my hand and got up.

❧

After ten minutes the group started up. "It's your turn, Tammy," Cheryl said to the woman sitting next to Paul.

Tammy was in her forties and attractive in a "country-club" fashion. Overdressed for Satori, wearing clothing more suitable for a golf event than a psychological workshop. Too much make-up and hair gel. She slid forward on her pillow. "Hi everyone. I'm Tammy. I live in Fresno." She made a face. "I'm a member of the Earle club."

The women laughed.

"I've been married to my husband, Ernie, for twenty-five years. We have two kids, both in college." She wrapped her arms around her chest and sighed. "We met at UT, the University of Texas. We were married in Plano, moved to Dallas, and then ten years ago came to Fresno, when Ernie got a promotion."

Tammy scanned the room, looking at the women in the group. "Ernie is a good old boy. If he was here, today, you'd probably all like him. But he's a player. Since I've been with him, he's played around, always had a woman on the side. And I've gotten sick and tired of it."

"You might ask, 'Why do you put up with shit, Tammy? You seem like a smart gal.'" Tammy began to cry.

Cheryl slid tissues to Tammy.

Tammy picked up a tissue and wiped her eyes. "You might ask that and the reason I usually give is that Ernie is a good guy. When he's around and focused, he's lots of fun. He's been a good provider and good in bed – at least he used to be." Tammy looked at the floor and mumbled, "We haven't had sex in six months."

Tammy dabbed her eyes. "You might ask why I put up with Ernie?" She sighed. "The real reason is that I never learned how to set limits. Year after fucking year, I've let Ernie roll over me because I can't seem to say 'enough.'" The tears fell faster. "I'm just like my mother, as much as I hate to admit that."

"A year ago, Carol, one of my tennis partners, told me that she had gotten a handgun to protect herself from Antifa. At the time, there were rumors that Antifa was going to attack Fresno and we were all scared, even though we live in a gated community. Carol said she felt safer with her little gun, and she enjoyed firing it at the shooting range. I went with her, and I liked shooting it, too. So, I started thinking about getting a gun."

"Then, last month, Ernie and I were going to go to the Eastern Star's gala. At the last minute, Ernie cancelled, saying he had to be away on business, even though he knew how much it meant to me. I knew that he was going somewhere to fuck Trini, his current girlfriend. I was very angry, and it occurred to me that if I owned a gun, I could use it on Ernie – maybe not shoot him dead but do something like shoot him in the balls. I talked to my therapist, Myrna, about it, and she suggested that before I bought a gun I should come here."

"Good idea," Cheryl said. "What do you need from us?"

"I'm not sure," Tammy said. "I needed to come here and tell everyone how angry I am."

"And get laid," Kate whispered to me. I bit my tongue.

Cheryl peered at Tammy. "Does Ernie know how angry you are?"

"He sure as shit ought to. I've yelled at him enough."

"Have you tried going to couples counseling?"

"My therapist suggested that, but Ernie wouldn't do it. We did have a meeting with our pastor, John. He suggested that we pray and read the bible together. Ha." Tammy laughed a hollow laugh. "My church doesn't believe in divorce." Tears rolled down her cheeks.

Cheryl handed her a tissue. "It sounds to me like you are stuck."

Tammy stared at her hands. "I guess that's right.

"Imagine that you had a friend who came to you with a relationship story similar to that of you and Ernie. What would you tell your friend?"

Tammy cried and Cheryl waited.

"I'd tell her to get out," Tammy said in a faint voice.

"I don't think everyone in the group heard you."

"I'd tell her to get out of the relationship while she still has her self respect."

Cheryl waited.

"You think I should get out of the relationship?"

"It doesn't matter what I think. You just told us that if a friend came to you with a relationship story like that of you and Ernie, you would advise her to leave the relationship."

"Uh huh."

Cheryl waited.

"I'm taking everyone's time," Tammy said after a few minutes.

"Fortunately, you're at the Satori transitions workshop and you can take as much time as you need." Cheryl waited.

Tammy dried her eyes. She had a sip of water. "I should divorce Ernie," she whispered.

Cheryl remained silent.

"My church won't like it, but I should divorce Ernie."

Cheryl waited a few more minutes. "You've done some good work here, Tammy. Would you like some feedback?"

"I guess."

Several people put up their hands. Cheryl selected Norma.

"You might ask yourself: which option would my church prefer? That I divorce Ernie or that I shoot him?"

Everyone in the group laughed.

Norma continued. "Given my experience, you would be better off if you lived by yourself."

Several participants signaled their agreement.

"But I haven't lived by myself for twenty-five years," Tammy whispered.

"You're actually living by yourself now," Norma said. "You aren't willing to acknowledge it. Ernie has left your marriage."

"That's harsh," Tammy said.

"It may be harsh," Norma continued. "But it's the truth. You came here because you knew your marriage was over and you didn't know what to do next."

Tammy stared at Norma for a minute and then nodded yes.

"That's a good place to wrap up," Cheryl said. "You've done good work, Tammy."

Tammy spontaneously hugged Cheryl and then the two of them scooted back to their positions in the group.

David spoke to the man sitting next to Tammy. "It's your turn, Lucky."

The man got to his feet. He was short, well built, clean-shaven with short curly black hair. The guy I thought was stoned last night.

"My name is Lucky Moretti. I'm from New York City, I live in SoHo." He paced while he talked. "I'm gay and I've been a gay activist for many years." He made a fist and tapped it into his open left hand. "I was active in 'Act Up' and other militant gay groups. I'm HIV positive but avoided AIDS; my partner, Jose, was not as fortunate and died eight years ago. I'm a script writer working primarily with TV series, so I have plenty of money." Lucky sighed. "I'm an alcoholic and a coke addict."

He retrieved his thermos and sipped water. "Eight months ago, I was stopped for speeding on the Jericho turnpike; the cops searched my Jaguar and found my pipe and some crack cocaine. I got a good lawyer and fought the charges. There were issues with the search and so we finally bargained the charges down to a fine and probation. To fulfill my probation orders, I started going to therapy. One thing led to another, and my therapist suggested I come here."

"What did you expect?"

"I thought I'd get out of New York City, come to Northern California and chill." Lucky flashed a wry smile. "When the workshop started, I thought I didn't belong, but now, because you all have been so honest, I feel like I do belong. I feel like I have a problem that I need to work on in a supportive environment."

"Good," David said. "How can we help you?"

For a moment, Lucky seemed at a loss for words. He coughed. "My therapist helped me see that deep down I suffer from lack of self-esteem. Between rejection by my family, getting hassled by the community, and losing Jose, I wanted to kill myself. So, I chose to do this through alcohol and cocaine binges."

"What do you think?"

"I think her analysis makes sense." Lucky's eyes teared up. "Jose was good for me; he made me feel loved and accepted. His death was a big deal."

David handed Lucky the box of tissues and Lucky dabbed his eyes. "What do you need from this group?"

"Straight talk." Lucky looked around the room. "How many of you have had problems with drugs or alcohol."

Six people raised their hands including Rory, Theo, and Tammy.

"I need for you to call me on my bullshit," Lucky said.

As Lucky interacted with the group, I reflected on the similarities and differences in our stories. Both of us had suffered from the death of our beloved partner. Lucky had turned to alcohol and cocaine. I had chosen to work night and day. I thought, *I didn't turn to addiction because of Fiona; she was in recovery, because of her I had stopped using drugs and alcohol.* Then I remembered that, as part of her recovery, Fiona had come to Satori and had intensive therapy. I recalled that Fiona had known Malcolm then. She'd said something about Malcolm and drugs, but I couldn't put my finger on it. *Could drugs have something to do with Malcolm's death?*

"Good work everyone," David said. "Let's take a break."

CHAPTER 12
(3:30PM): Laura

"If you don't want to talk to us here, you can talk to us in Monterey," Sergeant Dan O'Malley said. He and Detective Sanchez were attempting to interview Bryn Moore, the Satori bookkeeper.

"Bruce James is in his office," said Laura Sanchez. "Do you want me to get him to talk to you?"

"I was hired by Malcolm Eastwick," Moore said. "I reported more to him than to Bruce James."

"Malcolm Eastwick is deceased," O'Malley said.

Moore blanched. Sighed. "So, it's true?"

"We're here because his body was found on the beach."

"Who signs your paycheck?" Sanchez asked.

"Bruce James."

"Mr. James authorized you to talk to us, so talk."

"I don't want to get anyone in trouble," Moore said.

"I hear that," Sanchez said. "But we'll be the judge of whether something you say gets anyone in trouble. Did you see Eastwick on Saturday?"

"No. But I knew he would be here for the board meeting, and I expected that he would talk to me about my report."

"What's in your report?" O'Malley asked.

"The usual accounting information: Satori revenue and operating expenses; actual versus budgeted expenses."

"Sounds boring," O'Malley said.

"It is," Moore said. "It should be."

"But there is a problem, isn't there?" Sanchez asked.

"Yes."

"What is it?"

"it's technical," Moore said. "You may not understand it."

"Try us," Sanchez said. "We're smarter than we look."

Moore sighed. He extended his arms, linked his hands together and cracked his knuckles. "Satori Institute is a non-profit, a 501(c)3. It typically runs at a loss; that is, the revenue from workshops does not cover the operating expenses. We make up the deficit from contributions and 'special' income."

"What's special income?" Sanchez asked.

"In this case it's income derived from licensing the Satori brand. Malcolm had a good idea, years ago when the institute began. He copyrighted 'Satori,' and no one can use it for any purpose without paying a fee. In the same sense that you can't sell 'Disney' peanut butter without compensating the Disney company."

"I get it," Sanchez said. "What's the problem with the licensing income?"

"Mr. Eastwick was administering it and there has been no income reported so far this year."

"Why not?"

"Mr. Eastwick said there were 'irregularities in the payment stream.'"

"What's that mean?" Sanchez asked.

"It means that we are short about $1 million."

"Does the board know this?" O'Malley asked.

"Bruce James does. You'll have to ask him about the board."

꿈

"We've just finished interviewing Bryn Moore," O'Malley said when he and Sanchez entered the office of Bruce James. He relayed what Bryn Moore had told them about the million-dollar shortfall.

"Yes. I just heard about this." James put his hands over his face.

"What are you going to do?"

"I don't know." His voice quivered. James removed his hands from his face.

"Who else might know about this problem?" Sanchez asked.

"I don't know." James sighed. "No one else on staff but possibly some board members, if Malcolm told them."

"You don't know if Malcolm told anyone?" Sanchez asked.

"No. I suspect not. Malcolm was very tight lipped about financial matters."

"The Satori Board meeting is on Wednesday?"

"Yes. The board members show up tomorrow and we have a board dinner tomorrow night."

73

"We'll need to interview the board members when they arrive," O'Malley said.

"You're going to tell them about the problem?" James asked.

"Malcolm Eastwick is dead and $1 million is missing," Sanchez said. "Someone needs to inform your board as soon as possible."

CHAPTER 13
(6:30PM): Laura

When Detectives Sanchez and O'Malley joined the supper line in the Satori dining room, they found themselves next to Kate Swift and her friend Tom Scott. "How's it going?" Kate asked.

"It's going," Laura answered.

"That bad, huh?" Kate laughed. "You look like you need a drink. Let me buy you one."

"Good idea," Laura said and turned to O'Malley. "Sarge, save me a place wherever you sit. I'm going to have a glass of wine with Marshal Kate."

"Tom," Kate said, "when you go through the line would you get extra food for Detective Sanchez and me?"

"Your servant, Marshal." Tom smiled and made a bowing motion.

Kate and Laura walked off, bought wine at the bar, and settled in the Adirondacks on the deck. There was no wind, and the temperature was in the low seventies. The ocean glistened in the evening light.

"My face gave me away?" Laura asked.

"I'm good at reading people," Kate said. "It helped me as a detective on the Fresno P.D."

"That's where you were before you joined the US Marshal's office?"

"Yes. Following in the very large footsteps of my dad, who retired as Deputy Chief."

"Was that good or bad?"

"Mostly good. It was my dad who encouraged me to become a Taekwondo Dan."

"What's a Dan?"

"I hold a blackbelt plus ten years of experience."

"Impressive." Laura sipped her drink. "What was bad about following in your dad's footsteps?"

"Just the fact that it's hard being Superman's daughter. Everyone's always watching you." Kate studied her wine glass. "I think that was one of the issues when I first met Tom. He had recently lost his wife, Fiona, and I felt like I was following in the footsteps of Superwoman."

"So, you and Tom met before this workshop?"

"Yes. We met at a political event and hit it off. We went out for coffee, and everything seemed to work, but I cut it off."

"Why?"

Kate looked out at the ocean and then back at Laura. "Because I felt this was going to be a capital 'R' relationship and neither one of us was quite ready. Tom because he hadn't finished grieving for Fiona. Me because I needed to get enough therapy to convince myself I was worthy of someone like Tom."

"He seems like a good guy."

"Tom is." Kate sipped her wine. "I woke up this morning and told myself how lucky I am that Tom likes me. He's a lot of good things but above all, he's not a player."

"What do you mean, exactly?"

"He doesn't play games."

"How can you be sure?"

"I trust my instincts but, to be safe, I asked one our workshop leaders, Cheryl, about him."

"Cheryl Taylor?"

"Yes. Cheryl Taylor has been at Satori since the beginning and has known Tom almost that long. She was Fiona's friend when Fiona met Tom. Cheryl said that in her experience there were two categories of men -- the good men which includes a select few and the other men which are the vast majority. She said that her late husband, Richard, and David, our workshop leader, and Tom were good men."

"Interesting," Laura said. "I wonder where she placed Malcolm Eastwick."

"I didn't ask her. You interviewed her. What did she say about Malcolm?"

"She had a lot to say but nothing very helpful. She characterized Malcolm as 'Puer Aeternus,' the eternal boy."

"From what everyone says about him, he was a player."

"I'd agree," Laura said, before falling silent.

"You think he was killed."

"Yes. But I don't have any proof."

"But your gut tells you that." Kate studied her new friend. "Why?"

"There's $1 million missing from the Satori accounts."

"No shit? That's a lot of money." Kate got up from her chair. "I think that calls for more wine. I'll buy you a refill." She walked inside to the bar.

Kate came back, handed Laura a glass of wine, and sat down. "How can I help you?"

"I'm not sure. We're going to stay over tonight, interview the Satori board, and then head back tomorrow." Laura drank half her glass. "If I find anything new, I'll let you know."

"Good." A fog bank had formed to the west, creating a gloomy vibe.

"Changing the subject, you feel hopeful about your relationship with Tom?"

"Yes. I feel like we're both ready." Kate grinned. "I'm excited. It reminds me of when I was ten years old, and my parents bought me a new pony to ride."

Laura laughed. "Perhaps not a metaphor you want to share in mixed company."

Kate blushed. "Perhaps not."

CHAPTER 14
(6:30PM): Tom

Kate went off with Detective Sanchez and left me to handle the food. Detective Sergeant O'Malley helped me fill two extra trays and then joined me when I sat down with Otto, Norma, Julie, Aoife, Theo, and Lucky. I bought wine for the table. At first, O'Malley demurred; then he reconsidered and seemed to relax. "What kind of workshop are you in?" O'Malley asked.

"Sex, drugs, and rock 'n roll," Lucky said with a straight face.

O'Malley blanched while the rest of the group laughed. "That's just in Lucky's room," I said. "Seriously, we're part of a *Transitions* workshop that, hopefully, will help us to manage the transition we're going through."

O'Malley frowned and Otto tried to explain. "For example, I'm going through the transition of retirement, trying to decide what I'm going to do next."

"I'm about to retire," O'Malley said. "I know I don't want to be home all the time, but I'm not sure what I want to do other than be a cop."

Fortunately for O'Malley, our group had lots of suggestions about what he might do. By the time Kate and Laura came back, O'Malley seemed to think he should come to Satori for the next *Transitions* workshop.

At 7:30, the detectives left to conduct more interviews. Because Kate was involved in a lengthy discussion about Aoife's safety, I didn't get a chance to ask her about what Laura Sanchez had said when they were outside.

⌒⌒

"Welcome back," David said. "You're doing an excellent job. Tonight, we'll hear from our last three participants and then we'll talk about the Tuesday schedule."

Cheryl pointed to a young woman with red hair and freckles. She was wearing overhauls and a *Cranberries* t-shirt. "Lucy it's your turn."

"I'm Lucy Collins. I'm here as part of the Satori work-study program. Cheryl is my therapist; she suggested that I attend this workshop."

"Since the '*sine qua non*' of this workshop is brutal honesty, I will start with this admission: I have an eating disorder. Rather, I have had a series of eating disorders: I have been bulimic and anorexic now I am obese because I have trouble regulating my eating. I'm working on it."

She stood up straight. "A lot of people tell me that I would be attractive if I gained weight or lost weight or did this or that. This does not register on me because I almost never see myself

80

as attractive. I have a lot of difficulty looking in the mirror and seeing someone who is worthy of respect."

Lucy retrieved her thermos and drank water. "Can you come over here, Cheryl. I'm nervous." Cheryl walked across the room and sat down in front of her client.

"Like many women and girls who have eating disorders, I have been abused. In my case by my stepfather, Don. The abuse started when I was twelve and ended when I was seventeen and left for college. The abuse was complicated by the fact that my stepfather was also the pastor of our church."

Kate growled. I squeezed her hand.

Lucy stopped and looked around the room. "In case you are wondering, Don died in a traffic accident, two years ago. He was driving drunk with a teenage girl from our church. Fortunately, she lived."

Lucy teared up but kept talking. "I'm here to try to be a normal workshop member. I have trouble with boundaries; I overshare or numb out without noticing my own experience."

She looked at Cheryl. "How am I doing?"

"You're doing great, Lucy. Take a deep breath and take your time. Check in with yourself: How are you doing?"

Lucy gulped and briefly closed her eyes. "I'm okay. Maybe a little scared that I broke my silence."

"You should adopt her," I whispered to Kate.

"My thought, exactly," she said.

"Lucy, what do you want from the group?" Cheryl asked.

"I want to be accepted."

"What does that mean to you?"

Lucy's lips moved but no words were audible.

"You'll have to speak up," Cheryl said.

"I want to be respected."

"Lucy, we've done the self-respect process before," Cheryl said. "Can we do it in front of the entire group?"

"Sure," Lucy said in a voice that slightly quivered.

"Okay. Imagine that a close friend was telling you positive things about yourself. What would they say?"

"They would say: Lucy you are a good friend. You show up when I need you. You keep your commitments. You tell the truth. You love me no matter what." Lucy teared up.

"Good. What else would your friend say?'

"They would say: Lucy you are smart. You can figure things out. You can take care of yourself."

"Good. What else would your friend say?"

Lucy's lips moved.

"No one can hear you."

"My friend would say: Lucy, you are beautiful. I know that you have trouble seeing this, but you are beautiful." Lucy blushed beet red and looked at the floor.

"Good," Cheryl said. "Is it okay if I repeat what you said to the entire group? Is it okay if I reintroduce you to the group?"

"Sure."

Cheryl slowly scanned the group as she spoke. "This is my friend Lucy. She is a good friend. Smart. Resourceful. And beautiful."

Lucy continued to blush.

"How does it feel to hear that, Lucy?"

"Good." Her voice lowered. "But embarrassing."

"Maybe we should stop here, and you can get feedback from the group."

"Okay."

Several hands went up.

Cheryl selected Lucky. "How old are you, Lucy?"

"I'm 22."

"You are very brave. You have the beauty of the brave."

Several people applauded.

Lucy blushed.

Cheryl recognized Aoife. "Lucy, where was your mother when all this happened?"

"She was drunk. We're not in contact anymore."

Aoife sighed. "Can I give you a hug?"

Lucy smiled. "I'd like that."

Aoife hugged Lucy. And then was joined by Kate, Norma, and Julie. They hugged for a long minute.

"Thank you," Lucy said. "I feel safe here."

"That's probably enough," Cheryl said. "Thank you, Lucy." The women both scooted back to their positions in the group.

"Let's move on to Greg," David said.

The last man in the group stood up. He was Asian, probably the same age as me, and in good shape. The man was wearing a black acrylic full-length t-shirt and white chinos. "My name is Greg Tanaka. I live in Danville and I'm a CPA." He opened his thermos and drank water.

"The problem with being a CPA is that you get exposed to people who have way too much money. Some of my clients try to write off things like their mistress's apartment or their new Lamborghini. My neighborhood is awash in new money, and it warped my judgment." Greg smiled a weak smile. "I took a chance to make a lot of money and it didn't work. I got caught."

"One of my clients got involved in money laundering. He needed help setting up a phony company and I assisted him. A lot of money washed through this company, and I saw a chance to siphon off a little bit for myself. There was so much money that I thought no one would notice." Greg shook his head. "I was wrong. The FBI did notice." He looked around the group. "Did you know the FBI employs accountants? I didn't." he chuckled. "Maybe if I did, I would have made other career choices." He shuffled his feet. "I made a mistake. I was arrested. I agreed to cooperate with the FBI. I was found guilty of securities fraud and sentenced to two years in prison." He sighed. "After the workshop is over, I report to the Federal prison at Lompoc."

David got up and walked in front of Greg. "Thanks for your story, Greg. I want to remind you that participants in this group must come here voluntarily. Is your participation part of your plea bargain?"

"No," Greg said, shuffling his feet. "I've lost everything and need to rethink my life. I thought I would come here to begin a new start. I'm not going to get any career counseling in prison." Greg's voice broke. "It's hard to admit that I've been such a fool."

"Shame is the hardest emotion to express," David said. "It takes a lot of guts to admit that you've been a fool."

Greg studied the floor. "Thanks."

"Would you like to get some feedback?"

"I think so." Greg's voice was barely audible.

David looked around the room.

Tammy held up her hand. "Greg, I want you to know that I think you are very brave to tell your story."

Otto raised his hand. "Greg, since you cooperated with the FBI, are you worried for your safety when you go to prison?"

"My attorney says the FBI will protect me."

I looked at Kate.

She made the "maybe, maybe not" hand gesture.

There was no other feedback. David thanked Greg and they both moved back to their positions in the group.

Cheryl spoke, "Now we move on to our last participant, Lois. After she tells her story we're through with phase one."

A striking middle-aged woman stood up. She had long black hair with streaks of grey, pulled back into a loose braid. She wore a beige jumpsuit and an elaborate woolen shawl that had beads woven into the fabric. I figured her for an artist.

"My name is Lois Waters. Thank you for all your amazing stories. You are all very brave." She clasped her hands tightly in front of her. "We began with Tom's tale of death and end with my tale of death. The death of love."

Lois stepped into the circle and slowly scanned the room. "I just turned 50. I'm a lesbian and I live alone; just down the road in Carmel." She stopped in front of Lucky. "I didn't always know I was a lesbian. For many years, I was in denial of my sexuality; I even lived with a man for a while. Then, thirty years ago, at another Satori workshop I had an affair with a woman and realized my true nature."

Lois walked across the circle and stopped in front of Kate and me. "I was satisfied, sexually, but I had difficulty establishing a lasting relationship. My therapist told me that this was because I had trouble trusting. She said I was not secure enough in my identity as a lesbian to be able to love completely."

Kate gripped my right hand.

"Ten years ago, I was at a gallery opening in Carmel when I met a young artist who had just arrived in town, Moira. We spent the night together and it was very good. Moira wanted us to continue and so we became an item. She moved into my spare bedroom."

Lois walked back across the room and got a sip of water. "I was 40 and Moira was 25. I felt loved and satisfied in the relationship, but I was aware of the age difference. I talked about this with Moira, suggested she find someone her own age, but Moira insisted that she loved me, and the fifteen years made no difference. We were happy for five years and then Moira met Kim, someone her own age." Lois teared up.

Kate handed her tissues.

"I was at the party when they met, and I knew right away there was chemistry between them. When we got home, Moira denied it. Then she started sneaking off to see Kim. I confronted her with it, and she got angry, wouldn't meet my eyes. Then one day I came home and found that Moira had moved out." Tears rolled down her cheeks. "She didn't even leave a note."

"How did that feel?" Cheryl asked.

"Terrible. Moira had lied to me, and I had been a fool to believe that our age difference wouldn't matter." Lois dabbed her eyes. "For the last several years I have been alone. Moira and Kim live in Carmel Valley; they seem to be happy. I am growing old by myself." She walked back to her place in the circle. "I came here because I realized that I have been stuck; I don't have enough love in my life and I'm afraid to love."

Cheryl got up and walked close to Lois. "Would you like to work on being stuck?"

"Sure."

"Okay. Close your eyes and go inside and see if you can find the part that wants to be loved."

Lois sat silently for a minute. "I found it. It's like a big soft heart."

"Good," said Cheryl. "Now ask that part why it finds it difficult to accept love."

Lois considered this. Her lips moved but no sounds were audible.

"What did you learn?"

"My heart says it wants love but is afraid of being hurt."

"Okay," Cheryl said. "I'm going to ask you to do one more thing, if you can. When you go inside and see your heart, look around and see if there is another part that is acting as a 'defender.'"

"A what?"

"It's a part that is protecting your heart. Perhaps in the same way that you might keep a bulldog in your front yard to keep visitors from knocking on your front door. The bulldog might keep away unwanted visitors, but it might also keep a lover from your door."

Lois smiled. "I get it." She closed her eyes for a brief time. "I found a couple of defender parts."

"Pick one and tell me about it."

"It's the part that's too busy to date. I tell myself that I am too busy with my art and my social projects and, therefore, I do not have time to pursue a new relationship."

"Very good," Cheryl said. "Do you think we can examine another defender part."

"Yes." Lois closed her eyes. "I found a good one." She teared up. "This is the part that is fearful that if I open up to love, I will be severely hurt." Tears rolled down her cheeks. "It tells me that if I open to love, I will die."

"I think I have a part like that," Kate whispered.

"Very good," Cheryl said to Lois. "I want you to try to talk to that part."

"Okay."

"Tell that defender part that it has been doing a good job. Thank it. And then tell it that you are stronger now and you do not need it to completely block your heart. Tell it that you will call it out when you need to."

"I can do that." Lois sat quietly for several minutes. As her lips moved silently, she wiped tears from her eyes. "Thank you," Lois said to Cheryl.

"We can stop here," Cheryl said. She leaned closer to Lois. "You did terrific work. You were very brave."

"Thank you. It was hard work."

"Are you ready for feedback?"

"Yes."

Several hands went up. Julie said, "I think I have a part like Lois, a part that's afraid to open up."

"Me, too." Kate and Norma said.

Cheryl looked around at the women. "Tomorrow we're going to meet as a woman's group. Perhaps I can teach you all about dialoguing with your defender parts."

The women nodded.

Lois hugged Cheryl and they scooted back to their positions in the group.

After a few minutes, David spoke. "Wow. What a group!" he looked slowly around the circle. "Having a successful transitions workshop requires that the participants take risks. You are a bunch of risk takers. Good for you." He turned to Cheryl.

"Thank you all for your work. We'll see you all tomorrow morning at 9AM."

The men got up and began leaving the room. The women stayed in a cluster around Cheryl and Lois. Lucky, Otto, and Theo walked over to me, "What are you going to do now?"

"I'm not sure. If Kate stays here, I'm going to the baths. Otherwise, I am going to hang out with her."

"We're going to the baths," Lucky said. "Maybe we will see you there."

I waited by myself for a few minutes. Finally, Kate broke away from the group and approached me. "I know I told you that we would be together. but it looks like the women are going to do more work with Cheryl. Can we wait until tomorrow night?"

"Okay. I think I understand but there's a part of me, like a small child, that wants to hold onto you."

Kate smiled. "I have that part, too." She held out her hand. "Now I'm going to shake your hand because if I hug you, I may not be able to let go."

෴

I walked to the baths and got into a large tub with Lucky, Otto, and Theo. "Have you noticed that the women's group is more cohesive than the men?" Lucky asked.

"That's because they don't have any outliers," Otto said.

"What do you mean?" Theo asked.

"The four of us are involved in the group process," Otto said. "But Rory isn't because he is too wounded. And Paul isn't because he's too depressed."

"What about Greg?" I asked.

"I don't know about Greg," Otto said. "I don't understand him."

"He's not engaged," Lucky said. "Maybe he's preoccupied with the thought of going to prison."

"That would make sense," Theo said.

"Have any of you talked to him?" I asked. "He's not around much at mealtime."

"He's a weird guy," Lucky said. "I tried to talk to him last night and he was very strange."

"Maybe it was homophobia," Otto said.

"No, it wasn't that," Lucky said. "Believe me I know how to recognize homophobes. It was like Greg was on *ludes* or a similar downer."

"That would make sense if he were very afraid of going to prison," Theo said.

We talked for another thirty minutes and then Lucky and Theo left. When it was clear that we were alone, Otto said, "I'm thinking about asking Norma out. What's your opinion?"

"I like Norma; she is a terrific person. Why do you need my opinion?"

"Because I haven't dated in thirty years. I'm rusty."

"I take it that you and your wife have separated."

"Inga has gone back to Germany. I don't expect her to return."

"From what you said, it sounded like you and she had irreconcilable differences."

"Yes. Plus, she began to regard sex as evil."

I blew out a breath. "That must have been hard."

"Yes. So, I haven't been on a romantic date in a very long time."

"Norma is a perfect person for you, Otto. She may not be your soul mate, but she is a very kind person."

"That's what I think. Thank you, I will ask her out." After a few minutes, Otto got out of the tub.

I sat in the tub and pondered, *Is Kate my soul mate?* I realized that I didn't need to decide that now.

I was about to get out of the tub when a woman got in. At first, because of the poor lighting, I thought she was one of the women from the *Transitions* group. Then I realized it was detective Sanchez. "Did you solve the case?" I asked.

"Hardly," she laughed. "I'm celebrating the end of a particularly frustrating day."

"Where's your partner?'

"Probably in bed. Don't tell him I'm here. He doesn't approve of the tubs." She looked around. "Where's Kate?"

"She and the other women in our workshop are doing a special process."

"From what she told me, I should be in the workshop, working on my relationship."

"David gives this workshop a couple of times a year. You can come the next time."

Sanchez mulled this over. "Kate said that you guys met a couple of months ago and that it didn't work out."

"Yes." When she didn't continue, I asked, "What else did she say?"

"Kate thought you were both ready to have a relationship."

I let out my breath. "Yes."

"How do you feel about that?"

"I'm amazed. I'd come to believe that with the death of my wife, I had used up my karmic relationship quota and that I probably would never have another big relationship."

"And now you don't believe that?"

"Now I believe that Kate and I will work it out."

"That's very romantic. It gives me hope."

I waited for Laura Sanchez to say more but she didn't. She turned around and looked over the edge of the tub at the seascape below. "You didn't like Malcolm Eastwick," she said, slightly turning her head,

"He was a client, so I tolerated him. He was full of himself. My deceased wife, Fiona, made fun of him, but I couldn't do that."

"You weren't around on Saturday?"

"No, I drove down on Sunday."

"It turns out that not many people were here on Saturday."

"That's strange," I said. "There should have been workshops."

Laura turned around so her back was against the side of the tub. "It turns out that there was a gap in the Satori schedule last weekend. Normally, weeklong workshops end on Friday morning and weekend workshops begin Friday night. But in this case, there was no weekend workshop because the workshop offered in the Satori catalog – something about Shamanism – didn't sell."

"And there wasn't a backup workshop?"

"No. The only thing scheduled was a team-building exercise with the work-study students that was led by David Sanders and Cheryl Taylor."

"You're telling me that no new guests showed up on Friday night."

"Yes," Sanchez said. "No new guests showed up and the old conference center wasn't in use because the workshop that was to occupy that space didn't occur."

I scratched my head. "So, on Saturday night, everyone was on the south end of the Satori campus."

"Exactly. Malcolm Eastwick showed up at his residence on the north end of campus and no one was around."

"Can I ask a question?" I waited for Laura to respond. When she didn't, I kept talking. "Access to the grounds is closed, at least on the south end. Do you have a record of who came in and out on Saturday?"

"There's someone assigned to the south gate 24/7. They write down names and license plates on a form and, later, that data gets input to a computer. We've gone over the list for Saturday, and everything checks out."

"They write down who enters the campus, but not who leaves."

"Exactly."

"What about the north campus? Is there is a gate up there?"

"There's a gate regulated by a keypad. It doesn't show who entered, merely when. However, there is a camera there and we checked the entry times against the video record. Malcolm Eastwick showed up Saturday at 2:10PM in his Tesla. Only two folks showed up after that: One was the maintenance guy, Juan Romero, and the other was a staff member named Carl something."

"I met him. He works in HR."

I waited a couple of minutes before asking, "How long are you going to be here?"

"Another day. We plan to interview the Institute board. Tomorrow afternoon, we'll drive back to Monterey." Sanchez got up. "Tell Kate I'll talk to her before we leave." She swam across the tub and got out.

I thought about what I had learned. *Sanchez thinks Malcom was murdered. She suspects one of the staff members did it.*

TUESDAY

CHAPTER 15
(6:30AM): Tom

I woke at my usual time, made myself a cup of coffee, shaved, and headed for the hot tubs. The temperature was in the low sixties and the ground wet from early fog.

When I got to the tub area, the maintenance crew had finished their work, and the tubs were empty. I stripped, showered, grabbed a towel, and headed for the most remote tub. There, I drifted across the hot water and came to the stone-and-concrete edge that overlooked the ocean. Alone in the universe except for the sound of crashing waves and an occasional gull cry.

My mind cleared and I felt buoyed by positive emotion, happy with the workshop and excited about my burgeoning relationship with Kate. Malcolm Eastwick's death was intriguing but did not seem to have anything to do with me.

As I floated, I remembered a dream I'd had the previous night. I was swimming in a lagoon in a tropical setting with Fiona and

Kate. When we reached the shore and stood up on the sandy bottom, Fiona lifted her hand and handed something to Kate. A beating heart.

My meditation was interrupted when I heard someone enter the tub. The intruder moved close to me; I felt their movement in the water and smelled perfume.

"I hoped I would find you here," Tammy said.

I opened my eyes. "I was meditating."

Tammy ignored my response and drew close. She was nude and made sure that I had a good look at her attributes. "I think we would be good together," she said.

Wow, I thought, *Tammy is really desperate*. "I'm starting a relationship with Kate."

"You barely know her. You should give me a try."

"Thanks, but I'm monogamous."

"No one would know," Tammy said with a quiver in her voice.

"I would." I was scrambling for the right words to get her to back off without hurting her. "There's something you should understand; something nobody else knows. Kate and I didn't meet here by chance; we arrived at this workshop after having participated in an elite dating service. We were matched psychologically and biologically."

"Really? I never heard of such a thing."

"It's a new San Francisco startup, 'Super Tryst.' Kate and I were matched on the Myers-Briggs test and the Stanford Pheromone profile." I piled it on. "It cost me $10,000."

"Really? Where did Kate get that kind of money?"

"They don't charge single women as much; I think Kate paid $4000."

Tammy took a step back.

"Maybe I could use their services." She sat down with her back against the tub wall. "I need to find someone other than Ernie."

"Remind me at the workshop and I'll give you their URL. And if Kate and I don't work out, I'll be sure to let you know."

Tammy reached out with her right hand, and I squeezed it. "That would be nice, Tom. I think we would be good together," she said in a defeated tone of voice.

<hr/>

When I got to the dining room, Kate was sitting by herself. I sat down next to her and had the momentary sensation of an energy surge throughout my chest.

"Did you enjoy working with the other women?" I asked.

"I did. Cheryl is very talented. She worked with us for another hour, then she left, and we all stayed and talked until after midnight. What about you?"

"I had two interesting conversations in the tubs." I told her about my late-night conversation with Laura Sanchez. "I think she's worried that someone on the Institute campus killed Malcolm Eastwick."

"Laura told me she thinks Eastwick was murdered but she left out the part about the killer still being around."

"She didn't say that. I inferred it from her questions."

"You're probably right. Who else did you talk to?"

I told Kate about my encounter with Tammy.

Kate growled. "Talk about brazen. What did you do?"

"I didn't want to hurt her feelings, so I made up a story about how we'd been matched by a new high-tech dating service."

Kate tilted her head to one side and chortled. "That's priceless. And she bought it?"

"Totally. She even asked me to give her info on the dating service."

"Poor Tammy, she's not very bright." Kate took my hand. "You know Tom, the average guy here would have accepted Tammy's offer and fucked her in one of the massage rooms."

"I guess I'm not the average guy."

She leaned close. "That's why I like you."

CHAPTER 16
(8:30AM): Laura

Sanchez and O'Malley held their first interview in the Satori Institute board room, a large room in the administration suite; the redwood walls were lined with photos of Satori boards past and present, while the west-end overlooked the south campus. Jean Little, the acting president of the board was an energetic middle-aged woman who ran a San-Francisco-based venture capital firm. *Overdressed for Satori*, Laura thought, as she appraised Little's expensive pantsuit.

"I'm sorry I can't help you," Little said. "Malcolm and our accountant, Bryn Moore, always handled the Institute financial details."

"I find it unusual that you've been on the board for five years, yet you don't understand the outsized role that license fees play in the Institute's finances," O'Malley said.

"You may find it strange," Little said, "But the reality is that non-profit board members have specialties. Mine is fundraising in Silicon Valley. Until Malcolm's unfortunate demise, there was no need for me to understand the details of Satori finances."

"Who else might understand the finances?" Sanchez asked.

"I'm not sure." Little frowned. "You talked to Bruce James?"

"Yes, and he said only Bryn Moore dealt with the books. And we already talked to Bryn, and he doesn't understand the license revenue."

"Have you talked to anyone at Malcolm's San Francisco office?" Little asked. "Penny might know about this."

"We didn't even know there was a San Francisco office," Sanchez said. "Where is it and who is Penny?"

"The office is on Russian Hill," Little said. "Penny is my oldest daughter. She runs the office for Malcolm. She knows everything." Little's scratched her head. "By the way, did you know the FBI visited Malcolm last week?"

Sanchez shook her head, while O'Malley's mouth fell open.

CHAPTER 17
(9:00AM): Tom

Kate and I walked into the second full day of the Transitions workshop and took the same positions in the circle. At 9:06 David Sanders spoke: "Welcome to Tuesday." He looked at each person in the circle. "You're doing a fabulous job; this is an extraordinary group. Cheryl and I are impressed by your candor and energy. We're particularly impressed by the way the female participants have bonded. Good work, ladies."

Chery scooted forward: "We've found that it helps participants go deeper if we briefly divide into a women's group and a men's group. That's what we will do today." She looked around the room. "The women will stay here, and the men will go with David to the Freud room. We'll reconvene after dinner."

I kissed Kate on the cheek and began to get up. "See you later, badass. Don't miss me too much."

She reached out with her left hand and pinched me on the butt. "I'll see you tonight."

⁙

The Freud room was a smaller version of the Carl Roger's conference room. We formed a men's circle.

"Before we start," David said, "Has anyone seen Greg Tanaka?"

"Not since last night," I said. "He didn't go to the baths with us."

"He wasn't in the dining room this morning," Otto said.

"Maybe he scheduled a massage," Lucky said.

David frowned. "You were told not to have a massage during the workshop intervals. If he doesn't show up by our break, I'll check with the office."

"We'll go around again," David said. "Starting with Tom. Speak for as long as you want with, I hope, particular emphasis on what help you need."

I pulled forward on my pillow. "I'm Tom. I've already made progress on the relationship front – with Kate Swift here at the workshop."

"Today I'm going to talk about my plans outside relationships." For the next few minutes, I talked about my plans for the new scheduling software I was writing. Then I fielded questions.

I was getting ready to sit down when David said, "Tom it sounds like things are moving well for you. Do you want to talk about your new relationship?"

"I don't want to take too much time."

"We have plenty of time," David said. "Why don't you go inside and see if there is anything you want to share."

I immediately thought of my dream. "Last night, I had a dream where I was swimming in a lagoon and Fiona and Kate were swimming with me."

"Uh huh."

"We swam close to a sandy beach. We stood on the bottom and Fiona handed Kate something. I walked closer and found it was a beating heart."

David scooted closer to me. "What do you make of this dream?"

"When Fiona died, I felt like a piece of my heart had been ripped out. Maybe Fiona is handing Kate that part to reinsert."

"How does that feel?" David asked.

"It feels right. Late yesterday, I was thinking that Fiona and Kate would have liked it each other. What do you think? You knew them both."

"What I think is not important," David said. "You believe that Fiona and Kate would have liked each other. What does it mean to you that Fiona handed the heart to Kate?"

"Symbolically, it means that Fiona approves of Kate taking her place in my heart." As I said this, my voice choked, and tears came to my eyes.

"A direct message."

"Yes." I could barely get the words out.

"Take a few breaths, Tom. Relax and take this in."

We sat in silence for a few minutes.

I exhaled loudly. "Thanks, David. It seems very clear, but it still shakes me. Thanks for being here." I put out my hand and David clasped it. Then I moved back.

David looked at the other men. "What just happened with Tom illustrates that it is okay to share your dreams and intuitions with this group." He turned to Rory.

"What do you have to share?" David asked Rory.

"I'm having a bad day," Rory said. "I've been spending time with Jenny, in the work-study program. Last night she broke up with me and ripped me a new one."

"Do you want to talk about it?"

"I guess. Although at the moment I don't feel very optimistic. I guess I'm doomed to be a shallow asshole."

"Do you want to tell us what happened?" David asked.

"The usual. We hooked up. We had some good times and then Jenny dumped me because I'm shallow."

David moved closer to Rory. "What's that mean?"

"Like I said, I'm good at sex but not good at relationships.'

"Stop me if I'm wrong, but I think you mean that you don't know how to be intimate."

"Yeah, I guess."

David got closer to Rory. "Why do you think that is?"

"Perhaps because no one in my family was intimate with me."

David didn't say anything.

"I can't be intimate with someone I like because I don't know how."

David waited.

"I don't know what to do."

David nodded.

Rory looked at David. "What do you want me to say?"

"Are you happy right now?"

"No."

David held Rory's gaze.

"I'm stuck."

"Uh huh."

"I'm unhappy and I'm stuck."

David waited.

"I don't know what to do to get out of the hole I'm in.

David nodded.

Rory began to cry. "I don't know what to do. I've been here three months and I'm stuck. I haven't figured out what to do."

"But you have had a lot of sex," David said.

"Uh huh." Rory kept crying.

"You've made a lot of young women unhappy."

"Uh huh."

"You're a smart guy, Rory. Imagine that we traded places and you were the therapist, and I was your client. Imagine that I came to you and said, 'I'm stuck. I'm great at sex and terrible at relationships. I don't know how to be intimate.' What would you tell me to do?"

"I don't know."

"Take a guess."

Rory looked out into space and then said, "Be honest."

"Very good," David said. "Let's try a little role play. Okay"

"Sure."

David turned to me, "Tom you're secure in your masculinity. Imagine that you're a new female arrival at the Institute. You meet Rory in the dining room, and you have a glass of wine together. Say something."

I said, "Hi Rory. I'm Tomasina. I'd like to get to know you better but I'm a little gun shy because I'm recovering from a bad experience with my boyfriend, Earle."

Lucky snorted.

"Perfect," David said before he turned to Rory. "What do you say?"

"Well, I would usually say, 'Why don't we go to the baths together, that's a good place to relax.' But I should try something else. How about, 'I would like to get to know you better, but I should warn you. I'm here at Satori because I have some hang ups around intimacy.'"

I clapped my hands.

"Perfect," David said. "Then what?"

"We talk."

"Do you go to the baths? Do you have sex?"

Rory looked at me.

I thought, *How did I get to be Rory's big brother*. "No. You keep talking and then you say something like, 'I like you Tomasina but I am training myself to go slow.' And then you shake hands." *Like Kate and I did.*

"And that's it?" Rory said.

"And then you go back to your room and take a cold shower."

Everyone laughed.

"How does that sound, Rory?" David asked.

"Okay."

"You don't sound convinced."

"I can try it."

"That's all I'm asking." David looked at me. "I have a suggestion, the next time you meet someone you like, ask the advice of your big brother, Tom." David looked at me and back to Rory. "How's that feel?"

"Okay, I guess. Is that okay with you, Tom?"

I'm adopting strays just like Kate, I thought. "Sure," I turned to Rory. "We have a deal."

"How's that feel, Rory?" David asked.

"Good."

"Anything else?"

"No. I'm good for now." Rory scooted back and whispered, "Thank you," to me.

"Okay," David said, turning to Otto. "It's your turn and then we will break for lunch."

Otto scooted forward. "I have decided to stay in California and become a therapist." He sighed. "Life is precious. What I've learned here is that I need to take responsibility for my own life, for my own happiness." He wiped one eye with his shirt sleeve. "I believe Inga stopped growing. I do not want to stop growing. I have decided to divorce Inga, even though we were together for a long time, and she is the mother of our children. I have decided that I must take responsibility for my own happiness."

"How do you feel those decisions?" David asked.

"I feel good about them. I feel like a load of bricks has been lifted off my back."

"Uh huh. What more do you need from this group?"

Otto looked around the group. "I'm not sure. Maybe, like Tom, I'll talk about my dream."

"Go ahead," David said.

"I had a dream where Inga and I go to the airport. When we get there, I realize that we are on different flights. I can't find Inga, but I realize that she's left me with all the luggage. There's so much to handle that I am fearful I will miss my flight. Then I wake up."

"What do make of this dream, Otto?"

"The obvious part is that Inga and I are going in different directions; we get to the airport and get on different flights." Otto laughed. "Not subtle."

"What about the part about the luggage?"

"That's not subtle either." Otto chuckled. "She left me to handle all the baggage of our marriage."

"How do you feel about that?"

Otto's jaw dropped. "I feel angry."

"Uh, huh," David said.

"I am not used to feeling angry."

"Take a few breaths, Otto." They sat for several minutes.

"I am angry, and I am glad Inga is gone. But I see that she left me with the short end of the stick." Otto looked at David. "Is that the right way to say it?"

"It is. What does that mean to you?"

"It means that Inga is running away. She is abandoning me and our children, leaving me to clean up everything – take care of the baggage."

"That's what it sounds like."

"I do not like it," Otto said. "I am angry at Inga. But I can handle this."

"I'm sure you can," David said. He looked around the group. "Are you ready for feedback?"

"Okay."

After I put up my hand, David selected me. "Good work, Otto. I'm sure you can handle it." Other men agreed.

"On that note, we will break for lunch," David said. "I'll see you back here at two."

⁓

We got to the dining room before they started serving. I grabbed a cup of coffee and looked for a place to sit. I spotted Detectives Sanchez and O'Malley eating peanut-butter sandwiches. "Mind if I join you?"

"Be our guest," Sanchez said. "We're about to head back to Monterey. Where's Marshal Swift?"

"She and the other women in the group are doing some special process."

"Think it's too late for me to join their group?" Sanchez asked. O'Malley grimaced.

"Probably. When are you coming back?"

"We don't know. The case got complicated." She handed me her card, after writing what I assume was her personal cell phone number on the back. "Have Kate call me if anything comes up."

O'Malley got up from the table and Sanchez followed. "If we need the Marshal's assistance, we'll leave a message at the office." They left the dining room.

⁓

Kate and the women weren't back by the time service started. Lucky, Otto, Theo, and I filled our plates and grabbed a big table by the window. I looked around the dining room but did not see Greg Tanaka.

After a few minutes, Rory joined us and sat across from me. "Were you serious about being my big brother?" He asked.

"Yes. Why?"

"A cute girl just joined the work-study program, and I was thinking about talking to her."

"As your big brother, I have two pieces of advice for you. The first is to slow down. You don't have to talk to her tonight or anytime soon. Stay cool."

"Okay. What's the second piece of advice?"

"Find Jenny, the girl who just broke up with you, and apologize."

"What should I say?"

"Tell her you realize you made a mistake with her. Tell her that you understand that you did not treat her right and you are sorry."

"Okay."

"Think you can do that?"

"Can you come with me?" Rory asked.

"Only if you pay me."

All the men laughed.

"Okay, I think I can do that," Rory said. "Explain why you think I should."

"Two reasons. First, it's the right thing to do; you hurt Jenny's feelings and you should begin to make amends."

"Okay, I understand that" Rory said. "What's the second reason."

"You've probably gotten a bad reputation with the women in the work-study program, as a guy who just wants to have sex, who doesn't care about intimacy; you need to begin to repair your reputation."

Rory ran his hand over his forehead. "Yeah. That makes sense."

Kate came to the table and sat down beside me. "We're having so much fun. All the women are great."

"I can't say that the men are 'having fun,' but we're definitely making progress."

"Tom adopted me," Rory said.

"David suggested that I become Rory's 'big brother' while I was here."

"That sounds like a good idea," Kate said to Rory. "Just don't hit on Julie or Lucy or you'll have to deal with me."

Rory's face turned white. "I promise I won't."

"What else is new?" Kate asked me.

I told her that detectives O'Malley and Sanchez had left and handed her Laura Sanchez's card. "She'd like you to stay in touch."

"They're doing an autopsy on Eastwick today," Kate said. "I'm curious about the findings."

"Changing the subject," I said. "I was wondering if you want to go on a date with me, tomorrow evening."

"Sure. But won't we be having the workshop?"

"No. On Wednesday evenings there isn't a scheduled workshop. I was invited to a Satori Institute fundraiser at the old conference center: drinks and hors d'oeuvres. I thought it would be fun for us to go together."

"A real date," Kate laughed. "What a concept." She tilted her head to one side. "But I'm not sure I brought anything to wear to a cocktail party."

"I imagine that the cute white-linen outfit, you wore Sunday night, would work. Or you might borrow something from Cheryl. She's been to a lot of these."

"Okay." Kate clasped my hand. "Our first date."

"So, what does the women's group plan for the rest of the day?"

"We haven't finished telling our stories. After we conclude, I'm going to give the ladies an introduction to Taekwondo. Next, Aoife will teach us Irish songs. Then, Lois will lead us in drumming. And then, the grand finale..." Kate patted her hands on the table.

"Yes."

"After dark we're all going to get into the big hot tub together."

"No kidding."

"Really. Turns out that in our group, only Cheryl, Lois, and Lucy have been in the tubs. So, we agreed that after dark we would all go in together."

"Women only?"

Kate tilted her head to one side and smiled. "Perhaps we would let in a few worthy men."

CHAPTER 18

(noon): Laura

"You're driving too fast." Detective Sergeant Dan O'Malley muttered as he looked up from reading his text messages. The two detectives were heading north on Highway One and had just passed the lighthouse and naval facility at Point Sur.

Detective Sanchez sighed. "This is getting old, Sarge. I'm going fifty in a forty-five zone. Take a deep breath."

O'Malley's phone rang. "It's Bruno Oliver," he said.

Sanchez listened to the brief conversation.

"Slight change of plan," O'Malley said after he ended the phone call. "Instead of going back to Monterey, we're heading to Salinas. Bruno and his crew finished the autopsy. He says the medical examiner wants to talk to us at headquarters." The coroner's department was in the same building as Sheriff's Department.

"Why is Doctor Hidalgo involved?" Elena Hidalgo was the Medical Examiner for Monterey County.

"Bruno didn't say, but she wouldn't be involved unless they found something disturbing."

"Something that would indicate that Eastwick's death wasn't an accident?"

"That would be my guess," O'Malley said.

"I guess I better step on the gas," Sanchez laughed.

An hour later, Sanchez and O'Malley parked in front of the Sheriff's Monterey County headquarters, a modern two-story office building with a solid concrete façade. They took the elevator to the second floor and headed to Bruno Oliver's office in the east wing.

The door was open. As they entered, Bruno got up and said, "Don't bother to sit down. Dr. Hidalgo wants to see us immediately."

Sanchez and O'Malley followed Bruno down the hall to the Medical Examiner's office. Bruno spoke to her secretary, "Please tell Dr. Hidalgo that the detectives are here." A few minutes later, they were ushered inside the large office that had two broad tables covered with paperwork. Dr. Elena Hidalgo was a fifty-year-old Hispanic woman with a reputation as someone who worked hard and didn't like long meetings. She wore a grey pin-striped suite with a white blouse; her black hair with grey streaks hair was cut in a bob. Her wire-rimmed glasses reinforced her sober style. Dr. Hidalgo shook hands with Sanchez and O'Malley and had them sit down.

"Bruno and his guys completed the autopsy on Malcolm Eastwick. As you are aware, he's a celebrity and we need to be careful how we handle this." Sanchez and O'Malley nodded. "Our investigation indicates that, at the time of his death, Eastwick was narcotized. It seems likely the assailant drugged Eastwick, interrogated him, and then, after obtaining what he or she wanted, they threw him off the cliff, figuring the waves would carry his body out to sea. Fortunately, Eastwick's body washed in on the beach, so we were able to recover it and ascertain the circumstances of his death." Hidalgo looked up from the typed report on her desk.

Sanchez looked at Bruno. "Could you walk us through what you think happened?" Bruno looked to Dr. Hidalgo for permission and, when she nodded, began to speak: "We believe that Eastwick willingly let the assailant into his Satori cabin. They sat in his front room and drank wine. Eastwick's wine was laced with Rohypnol."

"A 'roofie?'" Sanchez asked.

Bruno nodded yes. "The Rohypnol rendered the victim unconscious. "While he was out, the assailant restrained him. Then they woke him up and commenced interrogation."

"How do you know that?"

"Because they injected him with Scopolamine, a class of drug used by 'spooks' for interrogation."

Sanchez leaned forward. "They injected Eastwick with 'truth serum'?"

"That's what we think. They injected him with Scopolamine, he gave them the information they wanted – probably the combination to the wall safe, and then he died." Bruno looked at Dr. Hidalgo. "Probably due to the interaction between drugs and alcohol. The autopsy indicated that he hadn't had much to eat that Saturday. He may have had a couple of drinks before the assailant showed up."

"So, they may not have intended to kill him?"

"We have no way of determining that," Dr. Hidalgo said. "Whatever their intent they are culpable if they gave him Rohypnol and Scopolamine."

"Who would know how to do this?" Sanchez asked.

"Good question," Dr. Hidalgo answered. "Someone in the medical community, a psychiatrist or pharmacist, or someone who had conducted high-priority interviews for the intelligence community." She looked at Bruno and he nodded agreement.

"To recap: Eastwick let someone into his cabin, probably someone he knew. They drugged him and likely got the combination to his safe. At the end of the interrogation Eastwick died, so the assailant dragged him to the old conference center deck and then pushed him into the ocean."

"Yes," Dr. Hidalgo and Bruno said.

"What was Eastwick's build?"

"He weighed 191 pounds," Bruno said.

"So, it would have taken an effort to move him from his cabin to the deck?"

"Yes," Bruno said. "We believe they used a garbage cart to move the body."

"The kind of cart used to move big garbage cans?"

"Yes," Bruno said. "We think we located the cart used near the old conference center. We believe the assailant left Eastwick tied to the chair. They hoisted him up with the garbage cart and rolled it to the conference-center deck. Then, they untied Eastwick from the chair, pushed his body off the deck, rolled the cart back to where they found it, and replaced the chair in his residence." Bruno glanced at Dr. Hidalgo and then looked back at Laura Sanchez. "We found rope particles, that might have been used to tie him up, in Eastwick's room and on the conference-center deck. We also found cart tracks leading from Eastwick's cabin to the porch of the conference-center."

"So, Eastwick could have been murdered by a man or a woman?"

"That's right," Dr. Hidalgo answered. She turned to the detectives. "Did you have any suspicion that Eastwick might have been murdered?"

"We had a gut feeling that he had," O'Malley said. "Then this morning we learned the FBI has been to his San Francisco office."

"Why?"

"We're not certain," Sanchez said. "But we suspect that it has to do with irregularities in the Satori Institute accounts."

"What kind of irregularities?"

"There's a million dollars unaccounted for."

"Hmm. What does the FBI say?"

"Because there was no cell reception at Satori, we didn't follow on this until an hour ago," O'Malley said. "I contacted Lieutenant Perez and asked him to contact the San Francisco FBI office."

"So, you think the assailant was after the money?"

"Eastwick had a wall safe at his Satori cottage," Sanchez said. "Perhaps the assailant forced Eastwick to divulge the combination and removed the money."

"Did you examine the safe?"

"It was locked," Sanchez said. "We couldn't find the combination, but we did find Eastwick's laptop. Bruno has it."

Dr. Hidalgo turned to Bruno Oliver.

"Eastwick's Mac laptop is password protected," Bruno said. "I gave it to Julius, but he's been preoccupied with the trafficking website."

"Tell Julius to make Eastwick's laptop his number one priority," Hidalgo said. She folded her hands in front of her and turned to O'Malley and Sanchez. "I talked to Sheriff John, and he agreed that the two of us should handle the press. We'll have a briefing this afternoon. In the meantime, I probably don't have to say, don't talk to any reporters; you know that." O'Malley and Sanchez nodded. "Work through your chain of command and report new developments directly to me." Hidalgo frowned. "Do you believe the assailant left the Satori campus?"

"That would have made sense," O'Malley said. "But on Saturday and Sunday there wasn't much movement off the campus. So, he or she might still be there."

"We should warn them," Hidalgo said.

"We're in luck, in that regard," Sanchez said. "There's a US Marshal, Kate Swift, on the campus."

"What's a US Marshal doing there?"

"She's taking a psychological workshop," Sanchez said.

"And she knows about our investigation?"

"I informed her," Sanchez said. "Do you want me to keep her in the loop?"

"Yes. We're always shorthanded," Dr. Hidalgo said. "It will be good to have a continuous law enforcement presence on the Satori campus."

"I'll leave a message at the Institute front desk," Laura said. "I'll ask them to have Marshall Swift call me."

CHAPTER 19
(2PM): Tom

At 2pm the men returned to the Freud room.

"Any news about Greg?" I asked David.

"Nothing," David said. "He never officially checked out. I asked for housekeeping to check his room. They reported he'd removed his clothes; the only thing he forgot were some items in the medicine cabinet."

"Like what?"

"They mentioned his razor and a bottle of Valium."

"Strange." I shook my head.

"We'll continue going around the circle" David said. "Starting with Theo. Speak for as long as you want with, I hope, particular emphasis on what help you need."

Theo stood up. "I'm more relaxed. Feeling better." He turned to me and Otto. "It helps being able to talk to my new friends." He looked at David. "I've decided to leave oncology and become a GP; we need more people in family medicine and it's the easiest transition. I'm going to continue in therapy and strengthen my mediation practice." Theo looked around the group. "Like my friends, I had a dream I want to share."

"Go ahead," David said.

For the next half an hour, Theo explored his dream with the help of David and the other male participants. Not surprisingly, the dream had to do with Theo getting out from under his father's dominant spirit. David handed it expertly and at the end of the session, Theo was laughing.

When Theo was done, David asked, "What other help do you need?"

"Nothing for now. Thanks." Theo sat down.

David turned to Lucky. "How are you doing?"

Lucky jumped to his feet. "I'm like Theo. I'm doing better. The work I'm doing has helped me make new friends."

"Are you using?" David asked.

"No. There are drugs here, so I've thought about it. But I've been able to stop myself."

"Good. How can we help you?"

"I'm impressed by the risks everyone is taking," Lucky said. "I want to do a role play, where I talk to my father." Lucky looked around the group.

Otto and I looked at each other, as though one of us would volunteer; then Paul raised his hand. "I'll do it." Paul stood up and walked next to Lucky.

"Okay, Lucky," David said. "Tell us about your father."

Lucky took a deep breath. "His name is Paulo Moretti. He and my mom live on Long Island, near Stony Brook." He shook his body. "Since I came out, he's never accepted me. He says it's because he's a Catholic, but he's not observant. The only time he talks to me is when I call home to talk to my mother."

"What's the set up?" David asked.

"I call home to talk to him about Mom. She's been diagnosed with early-onset Alzheimer's. Dad's in denial, but mom has been having more 'episodes' and needs special care."

"Do you have siblings?" David asked.

"I have a younger brother, Leonardo. Leo. But he's an addict and we don't know where he is."

"Okay," David said. "Paul, have you got enough information?"

"I think so." Paul moved in front of Lucky.

Lucky made a motion like he was talking on the phone. "Dad, I'm glad you picked up. I want to talk to you about Mom."

"Just a second, I'll get her," Paul said, lowering his voice and affecting an Italian accent.

"No. Don't put the phone down," Lucky said. "We need to talk about her."

"You don't need to worry. I've got the situation under control. She'll be fine, she's just getting old."

"It's more than that, Dad. Donna said that when she arrived the other day, Mom was still in bed and didn't know who Donna was."

"Who is Donna?" Paul asked.

"She's the housekeeper. She used to come twice a week; now she comes every day."

"What do you want me to do?" Paul asked, as Lucky's father. "I'm doing the best I can."

"Mom needs to have a helper every day."

"I don't think I can afford that."

"Of course, you can, Dad. You have insurance and, besides that, you have lots of money." Lucky turned to David and the rest of the group. "My father owns a hardware store in Stony Brook."

"Well, I'm not sure," Paul said, deepening his voice.

"Go talk to the Gerontologist, Dr. Walker," Lucky said.

"I don't like her as much as the previous Gerontologist."

"Dr. Ricardo retired. You don't like Dr. Walker because she's a woman."

"Well, I don't know."

"I'll come over and go with you," Lucky said.

"You know I don't want you here," Paul said, as Lucky's father.

"I hear that, but we must put that aside for now. I need to help you with Mom."

"I'll never understand why you chose your lifestyle. You were such a popular boy in high school."

"Papa, we've been over that a hundred times," Lucky said. "I didn't choose to be who I am; it's my nature."

"I just don't understand. But you're right, we need to talk about this." Paul paused. "When do you want to come over?"

"I can come over tomorrow," Lucky spoke with a slight quiver. "Thank you, Papa."

Paul moved closer to Lucky and spoke in an even deeper Italian voice, "You know, Luciano. I've been talking to my friends at the club. One of them knows a therapist who can talk to you about your lifestyle. Maybe when you're here you could talk to this therapist; maybe you could explore converting."

Lucky's face got beet red, and he clenched his fists. He moved closer to Paul.

For a few seconds, Paul showed no expression. Then he cracked a smile, "Got you, didn't I?" he chortled.

"You tricked me," Lucky laughed. "Oh my God. Paul the priest tricked me."

All the men laughed.

"When's the last time you played a trick on someone?" Lucky asked Paul.

"Oh. Maybe ten years ago."

They hugged and exploded in laughter.

"Good work," David said with a smile. "Lucky, what more do you need from this group?"

"Nothing right now," Lucky shook his head and beamed at Paul.

"What about you, Paul?" David asked.

Paul remained standing. "Obviously, I've begun to have more fun. With my new friends." He nodded to Lucky, Theo, Otto, and me. "Over the last twenty-four hours I have had an epiphany of sorts. I realized that I can be spiritual without being part of the church. Jesus once said: 'Be in the world; not of it.' I realized that I could live a spiritual life outside of organized religion."

"What does that mean to you?" David asked.

"I'm not sure. It occurred to me that I could work here for a while, take some counseling courses, and help folks. That's all the further I've gotten."

"That's a good start," David said. "Do you want to take any questions?"

"Sure."

Lucky raised his hand. "This seems like a wise move, Paul. It would also be a wise move to be more social. You don't have to isolate yourself from the other members of the group.

"Thank you, Lucky."

I raised my hand, "I agree with Lucky. Several times I have seen you sitting by yourself in the dining area, Paul. I have wanted to invite you to eat with me and the other men, but I felt hesitant to do so. Now I want to formally invite you to join us."

"Thanks, Tom. I will join you." Paul sat down.

"Okay, then," David said. "We're done for today. Normally I would suggest that we reconvene with the women at 8, but from what Cheryl told me, I think the women are doing a process that will last until 10. So, I will see you tomorrow."

It was after 4PM. Lucky stood up, "Since we don't have to do anything tonight, why don't we all go out to dinner together."

I looked around and everyone nodded. "Sounds like a good idea," I said. "Where shall we go?"

"Why don't we go to the Big Sur Café," Theo said. "They have good food, and we shouldn't have to wait for a table."

We all agreed.

"Let me go tell Kate that I'm not going to have dinner with her," I said. I walked to the new conference room but stopped before I entered because I heard the women chanting inside. I wrote Kate a note and left it on the table near the main door.

As I walked by the dining room, I ran into David Sanders. "I've been thinking about Greg Tanaka," I said. "Could you have someone on the Satori staff check to see if his car is still around?"

"Good idea," David answered. "I'm worried about Greg, too."

CHAPTER 20
(3:30PM): Laura

The detectives were driving back to Monterey when Laura got a call from Kate on her cell. "The Institute office brought me a message that you needed to talk to me,"

"To give you a heads up," Laura said. "The autopsy indicates that Eastwick was murdered. The assailant probably filled him full of drugs until he divulged the combination to his wall safe. Once the perp got the money, they rolled Eastwick to the conference-center deck and threw him off."

"Cold. Sounds like a professional hit."

"That's what I thought. Someone who knew what they were doing." Laura paused. "One more thing, we consider it likely that the killer is still around. Unless they hiked in and out, the perp is still on campus."

"Wonderful. When are you guys coming back?"

"Probably not until Thursday. Tomorrow we're going to San Francisco to check Eastwick's other office and, hopefully, 'liaise' with the FBI."

"The masters of the liaison." Kate chuckled.

"Only following orders," Laura said.

"Okay. Thanks for the heads up. I'm going to go up to the Institute office and get my pistol out of their wall safe."

"Hopefully you won't have to use it," Laura said.

"Better to be prepared than sorry."

CHAPTER 21
(6PM): Tom

The outing at the Big Sur Café dinner was the first time we had operated as a six-person men's group.

The restaurant was housed in a non-descript one-story wood building a quarter of a mile south of the bridge over Pfeiffer canyon. I bought several bottles of a good chardonnay for our table, although I only had a sip because I was driving. The six of us dined in traditional Italian style: antipasto, minestrone soup, green salad, lasagna, chicken cacciatore, and gelato. The meal stretched out over more than two hours.

When we arrived at the cafe, I was worried about Paul and Rory fitting in, because they had been outliers, but the others easily accepted them. In fact, Lucky and Paul appeared to have a special affinity.

It was a classic men's gathering with lots of talk about what was wrong with the San Francisco Giants, even though Lucky was a Mets fan. For the first time, Paul seemed to relax, and I thought *we've become a cohesive group*. We lingered over the meal.

When we got ready to leave, Theo said, "Is it okay if I ride back with you, Otto, and Rory?" He smiled. "I want to give Lucky and Paul some privacy."

It was after nine, when the four of us arrived back at the Satori parking lot. Throughout dinner I had been worried about Greg. Instead of heading directly to the baths, I took a detour through the dining room and stopped at the bar to see if David Sanders was around. He was sitting at a small table, nursing a glass of white wine, and reading a paperback.

"Sit down Tom," David said. "How was your dinner?"

I pulled out a wooden chair and sat. "Fun. Good food." I waited a beat. "Did you find out anything more about Greg Tanaka?"

"Just enough to whet my curiosity. Greg's car isn't parked in the visitors' area, it's parked way up in the staff area, by the art cottage."

"That's strange." The art cottage was on the north end of the Satori campus, about half a mile from the dining room. "How did it end of there?"

"That's what I wondered," David said. "I asked staff to check the log at the north gate. They said that Greg's car, a Mercedes sedan, went through the keypad procedure at 2:38 AM last night."

"Anything of interest on the camera?"

"No. Whoever used the keypad knew about the camera and kept their face hidden beneath a hoodie."

"I don't like this," I said. "Tomorrow, when there's light, Kate and I will check out Greg's car."

"Good idea. His California license plate number is 6TR244."

ce

As I approached the baths, I could hear the women from our workshop laughing and singing Irish songs. Otto was waiting for me in an adjacent tub.

"I was too nervous to get in the women's tub on my own," he said with a smile.

With some trepidation, Otto and I approached the largest tub, which contained only the seven women from our workshop. "I'm not sure this is a good idea," Otto said. "They seem to be having a private party."

"We've come this far," I said. "Let's ask if they want us to join them."

Lois and Tammy were guarding the tub entrance. "Can we get in?" I asked.

Lois called to the others. "Tom and Otto are here. Do we want men to join us?"

The moon hadn't risen, and the night was dark enough that I couldn't see where Kate was. From the far end of the tub, I heard her say, "Only if the men are proven worthy. Only if Tom and Otto are willing to sing a song."

"The men can respond to this," Aoife led the seven women in "The Parting Glass**."

Of all the money that e'er I had
I spent it in good company
And all the harm I've ever done
Alas, it was to none but me

**A traditional Scottish song

Of all the comrades that e'er I had
They're sorry for my going away
And all the sweethearts that e'er I had
They'd wish me one more day to stay

But since it fell into my lot
That I should rise and you should not
I'll gently rise and softly call
Good night and joy be to you all

Fill to me the parting glass
And drink a health whate'er befalls
Then gently rise and softly call
Good night and joy be to you all.

When the women stooped singing, Otto and I stepped into the tub. "Stop there," Aoife said, "let's hear your song."

"I need your help," I said. "I'm not much of a singer."

"I have an idea," Otto said. "You should know this song." Otto launched into "The Hawaiian Wedding Song" and I followed with my thin baritone voices.

This is the moment
I've waited for...

The women applauded. "You have proven worthy," Aoife chuckled. "You may enter."

Otto and I waded across the tub to where most of the women had congregated. Kate was sitting against the far wall with Julie on one side and Lucy on the other. Lucy slid over so I could sit next to Kate.

"I did it," Kate said. "I'm in the hot tub and I'm naked."

"Congratulations. How are you feeling?"

"I was euphoric until you showed up. Now I'm embarrassed."

"I don't want you to be embarrassed," I said. "I'll go." I started to get up.

Kate clasped my hand. "Don't go yet." She sighed. "I want you here. I'm having fun."

"You're sending me a mixed message."

"I know," Kate sighed. "I worked on that in the group today. On the one hand I want you close and on the other hand I push you away. Cheryl helped me understand that's because I'm afraid to be vulnerable with you."

"That's understandable."

"You seem so reasonable, Tom. Are you feeling vulnerable?"

I thought for a second. "I am. But I'm blown away by the strong attraction I feel for you. Every time we get close, I feel this surge of energy between us."

Kate squeezed my hand. "I feel that, too."

"You guys are so cute," Julie said.

"When are you going to kiss?" Lucy asked.

"We're figuring out our relationship in front of an audience." I laughed.

"it's my fault," Kate said. "I talked about you in the women's group." She slid closer. "If it's any consolation, they like you."

"Except for Tammy," Lucy chortled.

"I understand," I said and lowered my voice. "So, we will move onward." Despite the hot water, I grew aroused.

"Yes." Kate moved her head so she could whisper in my ear. "We're going to..." she searched for the right phrase "...get together. But not tonight. I've had a great day with all the women but now I'm exhausted."

"Mama bear is tired," Julie said.

"Mama bear?"

"She adopted me and Lucy as her cubs," Julie said. "She's going to teach us Taekwondo and help us deal with Earle-world."

"So, I'm about to be surrounded by badasses?" I chuckled.

"As long as you treat Mama bear right, no harm will come to you," Lucy laughed.

"Uh huh." Kate was falling asleep. "I'm turning into a prune," she said. "I need to get out of the tub."

"I'll help you," I said.

Kate and I waded across the tub to the entrance. I helped Kate out of the tub and handed her a towel.

We walked to the showers. "Do me a favor and make sure no men are in the shower room," Kate said. "There were only women when we first got here."

I looked inside and saw only one young woman showering in the far corner. "The coast is clear," I said.

We entered the shower room, hung up our towels and turned on the hot water. The young woman exited.

In the subdued light in the shower room, water glistened on Kate's lithe body as she turned in the spray. My heart pounded.

"Why are you staring at me?" Kate asked.

"Two reasons. First, I'm admiring your beauty. And second, I'm making sure you don't have an 'Earle' tattoo."

Kate snorted. "You're awful." She sprayed me with hot water. "Okay, wise guy. Turn around so I can check you for Fiona tattoos."

"Not a one," I said, as I slowly turned around.

Kate reached out and pinched me on the left buttock.

"Something's very wrong with me," I laughed. "I like it when you do that."

Kate pulled me closer. Just then we heard a mixed group enter the dressing chamber. "Perhaps we should dry off," I said.

We moved to a corner of the dressing chamber, and I shielded Kate with my body while she dressed.

"I guess I'm more old-fashioned than I thought," Kate said. "I'm not used to all this nudity."

"If you want, I can close my eyes until you're finished dressing."

Kate chuckled. "That's a different problem." She sighed. "When you look at me, my heart gets tingly. It's disconcerting. I feel like I'm back in high school."

"I could promise not to look at you, but I would be lying. I like the way you look."

Kate tilted her head to one side, smiled, and finished dressing.

We began to walk up the hill toward the dining hall. Somewhere on the gravel path, we started holding hands.

"Do I remind you of Fiona?" Kate asked.

"You don't look alike, but there is something about your personality, your independence, that is similar."

"That's what Cheryl said."

"What else did she say?"

"She liked her. Cheryl said Fiona was very funny but not someone that suffered fools gladly. She said having seen you with Fiona helped her understand why you were attracted to me."

"Did this come up in the women's gathering?"

"A bit. As we went around, all the women talked about the men – or women in Lois' case – in their lives." Kate kept holding my hand. "When it came my turn, I said that you and I were beginning a relationship, but I was nervous because your wife had so recently died."

"I understand that, but I feel ready to start a new relationship." I tightened my grip on her hand. "I feel excited about getting to know you."

Kate stopped and tilted her head to one side. "You are tingling my heart again." She turned and led me further up the hill. "All the women in the group – except for Tammy – feel that it's a good idea for us to be together. Cheryl said she understood why I was nervous but that in her experience of you, she had found you to be an honorable man. She believed that you would be straight with me." She began to chuckle.

"What's funny?"

"Excuse me," Kate blushed. "I have a dirty mind. When I said that my mind went right into the gutter."

"I thought we were going to wait until tomorrow to get into the gutter."

Kate snorted. "We did. But I'm wavering."

We reached level ground and began to walk around the dining area. Kate stopped and changed the tone of her voice. "I need to tell you about the call I got from Laura Sanchez."

"What's happened?"

"The autopsy revealed that before his death, Malcolm Eastwick was pumped full of drugs."

"Wow. Did Laura explain what they think happened?"

"The deputies think Malcolm let someone into his cabin on Saturday. They had a drink and the assailant drugged him. While Malcolm was out, they tied him to a chair. Then they injected him with more drugs. When he woke up, he gave them the information they needed, probably the location of the missing money, and the combination of the wall safe."

"So, they think died in the chair?"

"Yes. And then the perp loaded him on a cart, rolled him to the conference-center deck, and tossed him down the cliff."

"In the middle of the night," I said.

"A very determined killer," Kate shuddered. "Laura and I think it might have been a professional hit."

I made a face.

"Laura warned me the killer may still be on campus."

"That's really creepy."

"I know, but she could be wrong," Kate said. "Whoever did this could be long gone; they probably got their money from Malcolm's safe and hit the road. That's what a professional would have done."

"What do you think?"

"I don't know. But I was concerned enough that I got my pistol out of the office safe."

"You're going to carry your gun around?"

"Yes." Kate tilted her head to one side and grinned. "Except in the baths and certain other situations."

"Good to know." I smiled. And stopped walking. "I have something interesting to tell you. Greg Tanaka has disappeared."

"Cheryl said he dropped out of the workshop."

"It's more complicated than that. He stopped coming to the workshop and didn't notify Cheryl or David. He checked out of his room but didn't inform the front office or housekeeping. And, the strangest thing of all, he didn't leave the Satori campus."

"How do you know that?"

"On Sunday, Greg drove into the campus in a Mercedes sedan and parked in the guest parking lot. In the middle of last night, Greg or someone else drove his Mercedes out of the guest parking lot and into the restricted staff parking lot half a mile up the road."

"There's a computer log?"

"Exactly. And a video record. Only it doesn't show much, just someone in a hoodie using the keypad." I frowned. "Greg's Mercedes is parked by the art studio. I thought tomorrow you and I could check it out before we go on our big date."

"Okay," Kate said. "But right now, I need to get into bed. I'm exhausted." We started walking again.

Five minutes later, we reached the door of her room.

Kate unlocked it, looked at me, and sighed. Then she kissed me on the cheek, turned around, and went inside, closing the door behind her.

WEDNESDAY

CHAPTER 22
(6:30AM): Tom

I woke at my usual time, made myself a cup of coffee, shaved, and headed for the hot tubs. The temperature was in the high fifties and a heavy fog covered the Satori grounds.

When I got to the tub area, the maintenance crew was still busy. They had drained my favorite tub and were busy cleaning the rock and concrete interior. I slipped into the adjacent large tub and floated on my back. I had the sensation that I was alone in the universe, encased in amniotic fluid.

The workshop is going well, I thought. David and Cheryl are doing a good job. And I like the men. When my mind regarded the workshop men, I thought of Greg Tanaka. *What happened to Greg? Why was his car moved?* I shuddered. *Something bad happened to him.*

As I floated the fog began to break up. My thoughts drifted to Malcolm Eastwick. *What went wrong with Malcolm? He was successful, but it was never enough.*

Malcolm and I had known each other a long time but had never been close. *One reason was Fiona; he was always making a play for Fiona. But she never took him seriously.* I asked her about that and she, famously, described him as the "eternal boy." But Fiona didn't trust Malcolm; she had learned early in her life to never be intimate with someone she "couldn't absolutely trust." And I realized that, like Fiona, I didn't trust Malcolm, either. *I can trust Kate. I can relax with her that I don't have to watch what I say or how I say it.*

Now I could faintly hear the maintenance crew filling the large tub. The surface of the pool area was covered with fog, but sun was breaking through directly overhead.

Malcolm was like Charlie Forest, I thought. Charlie had been a Stanford friend of mine. President of my fraternity when I was a sophomore. A guy who seemingly had everything going for him. He went to Stanford Law School, passed the bar, and got a job with a prestigious San Francisco firm. Ten years later he went to prison for stealing from his clients' trust accounts. Charlie had a gambling problem.

What was Malcolm's secret problem? I floated to the edge of the tub and looked down on the surf breaking over the rocks. *I bet it was avarice. Malcolm made a good living as a therapist and "guru," but he was around too many people who had a lot more money. I bet Malcolm was envious, he wanted more money and made a bad decision. He did something with the Satori accounts so he could get more money and his avarice came back to bite him. Malcolm skated out of a lot of problems during his life, but he couldn't get out of this one.*

When I got to the dining room, Kate wasn't there. I grabbed a cup of coffee and sat down next to Otto and Norma. It seemed like they were sitting closer together, but I thought it might have been my overactive imagination.

"Kate's running," Norma clarified.

I went through the food line and grabbed two plates in case Kate missed the serving window. I talked to Otto, Norma, Aoife, Julie, Lucy, Theo, Lucky, and Paul. We agreed we were enjoying the workshop.

Just after the food line closed, Kate hustled into the dining room and sat down next to me. Her hair was damp, and her face flushed. I was reminded of our brief interlude in the bath showers the previous night.

"Sometimes I really need to run," Kate said. "I have a lot on my mind."

CHAPTER 23
(7:30AM): Laura

"Why don't you drive?" Detective Sanchez said to Detective Sergeant O'Malley. "Obviously my driving bothers you. I'll pull over and you can drive." They were heading north from Monterey on the two and a half-hour drive to San Francisco. They had just passed Castroville.

"I don't like to drive on the Freeways," O'Malley said and turned back to studying his phone messages.

"Okay. Since you don't like freeways, when we get to Santa Cruz, we'll keep going on Highway One instead of taking Highway Seventeen over the hill. We'll go into San Francisco the back way."

"Fine with me as long as we get there in time for our ten o'clock appointment."

"Shouldn't be a problem," Sanchez said. "Are we going to work with the FBI? What did Lieutenant Perez find out?"

"Nothing, so far. I'm not sure what their problem is."

"I've heard they're difficult, but I've never worked with them before. Have you, Sarge?"

"One time, years ago. There was a high-profile kidnapping in Carmel, in the Pebble Beach area. We got started on the investigation and then the FBI got involved and shut us out."

"What happened?"

"Turned out that the kid was taken by a housekeeper and transported to Mexico. The FBI worked with the Mexican Federales and brought her back."

"Happy ending."

"Yeah. But the FBI guys were dicks."

"All guys?"

"Yeah."

"That explains it."

"Give me a break, Sanchez. Not all men are dicks."

"Nope. But a good number of male police officers are." She raised her eyebrows. "They haven't been through the sensitivity training that other Monterey officers have."

"What sensitivity training is that?"

"Don't tell me you missed it. I'm shocked, Sarge. I guess that I'm going to have to report you to HR."

"What?" O'Malley dropped his phone on the floor.

"In fact, I may have to do it the next time we stop." Sanchez struggled to maintain a straight face.

O'Malley scrutinized her. "You're putting me on, aren't you Sanchez?"

She exploded in laughter. "You're too easy, Sarge. Does Patty pull your leg, too?"

"No. She's very respectful. Not like you modern girls. Not like you, Sanchez. Not like Teresa." Teresa was O'Malley's youngest daughter.

"I bet Teresa pulls your leg. How is she doing? Still loving Cal?" Teresa was a junior.

"Too smart for own good," O'Malley said. "Now she wants to go to law school."

"Uh-oh. Watch out Sarge. Teresa will become a public defender."

O'Malley rolled his eyes. "That would be my luck."

∽∾

"Nice office," Sanchez said. They been shown into Malcolm Eastwick's San Francisco office on the second floor of a well-maintained four-story building on the corner of Lombard and Hyde Street. Eastwick's office manager, Penny Little, showed them into his office, where Sanchez and O'Malley sat on a comfortable couch and Penny settled into a modern leather chair.

"I don't know how long we can stay here," Penny said, as her eyes misted. "Everything's up in the air since Malcolm died."

"It must have come as a terrible shock to you," Sanchez said.

"It was," Penny said, as a tear rolled down her cheek. "Who would do such a thing? Malcolm was such a wonderful man."

Sanchez retrieved a box of tissues from Eastwick's desk for Penny, then sat back down.

"I just don't understand it," Penny sobbed. She rubbed her eyes then blew her nose.

"As far as you know, did Malcolm have any enemies?"

"No," Penny blubbered. "He was such a wonderful man. Everyone loved him." She cried into a cluster of tissues.

"By the way, Sarge," Sanchez said. "Did you remember to call Lieutenant Perez?"

"What?" O'Malley at first seemed shocked then he lumbered to his feet. "That's right, I need to call him. Excuse me, Miss Little. I'll go back to our car and call the Lieutenant." O'Malley left the office.

"I get the feeling that you and Malcolm were very close," Sanchez said.

"He said even though I was young, I understood him better than anyone," Penny sobbed.

"I can understand that. You're very accomplished." Sanchez studied the attractive blonde. "Sophisticated."

"Thank you. Malcolm appreciated me." The sobbing diminished and Penny dabbed her eyes.

"Since it's just the two of us, I'd like to ask you a personal question. You don't have to answer."

"Okay. I don't see what difference it makes now."

"Were you and Malcolm sleeping together?"

Penny blushed. "Why are you asking me that?"

Sanchez lowered her voice. "Because we think that Malcolm may have been murdered and we want to protect those who were closest to him."

"Murdered? Malcolm was murdered?" Penny raised her voice. "Who would do such a thing?"

"We're not sure but we came here to warn you and to see if we could gather information that would help us determine who might have done this."

Penny got up and got herself a bottle of Pellegrino from the small refrigerator behind Malcolm's desk. As she twisted off the top, she turned to Sanchez, "Would you like anything to drink Detective?"

"No thanks."

Penny sat down. "How can I help you with your investigation?"

Sanchez pulled out her notepad. "First of all, do you have any idea why the FBI talked to Malcolm?"

"None. He was as surprised as I was when they showed up."

"They didn't make an appointment?"

"No, they just showed up."

"When was this?"

"Roughly two weeks ago. I can look it up for you."

"Okay, we'll do that before I leave," Sanchez said. "Did the FBI agents leave their cards?"

"Yes. But Malcolm kept them."

"Do you happen to remember their names?"

"Yes. The man was Agent Anderson, and the woman was Agent Mulvaney."

"What did they talk about?"

"I don't know. Malcolm told me to take an early lunch and then he didn't want to talk about it."

"Was that unusual?"

"Yes." Penny hesitated. "We were intimate so he would usually talk to me about everything."

"But not this?"

"No. I could tell whatever it was bothered him. But he didn't say anything, and I knew better than to pry."

"Do you know if Malcolm had any financial problems?"

"Like what?"

"I'm not sure how to ask this question," Sanchez said. "I'm a detective not a businessperson. Satori had licensing agreements. Do you know if there are any problems with those agreements?"

"I don't know of any, but all the files are in Malcolm's safe."

"Where's the safe?"

"It's in the far wall, behind the Stanford poster."

"Do you know the combination?"

Penny blushed. "I guess it doesn't make any difference now. Malcolm never actually gave me the combination, but I watched him open the safe enough times that I learned it. Malcolm would mutter the numbers under his breath."

"You have a good memory."

"I do. It's one of things Malcolm liked about me."

"Excuse me, I'm going to text my partner." Sanchez pulled out her iPhone and texted O'Malley: "Found safe. Bring evidence kit."

૦૯૦

"The lieutenant wants us to wait for the FBI," O'Malley said. "Two agents, Anderson and Mulvaney, are on their way over."

"They're the ones who were here before," said Penny.

While we waited, Penny made some excellent coffee.

Sanchez asked Penny about her relationship with Malcolm Eastwick. They had met while she was an undergraduate at Stanford and attended a Satori fundraiser, in Atherton, hosted by her mother Jean. "We liked each other but didn't become lovers until I turned 21 and Malcom left his wife Bijou," Penny said.

Penny told them she not only worked as Eastwick's office manager, but also as his assistant at his occasional psychological seminars. Penny said she was preparing for her psychotherapist license by taking classes at the California Institute of Integral Studies in the Mission district.

Just after Penny left to get more coffee, Agents Anderson and Mulvaney showed up. Anderson was tall and ice-white blond. Mulvaney was Black and compact. A badass, Sanchez thought. Mulvaney was clearly the lead.

Sanchez explained the course of the interview that resulted in discovery of the safe and Penny's revelation of its code.

Penny returned with several pounds of Peet's French Roast and a dozen croissants. She made coffee while the agents devoured the pastries.

"Thanks for your hospitality, Penny," Sanchez said. "The agents believe we should begin right away."

Agent Mulvaney recorded Penny's assurance that she was opening the safe on her own volition and then filmed her as she twisted the dial back and forth four times and the safe clicked open. The agents and detectives all wore gloves.

Mulvaney reached into the safe, examined what she found, called out her observation, and then Sanchez recorded it and placed it on Eastwick's desk. First, they found a set of files, that appeared to contain financial records for Satori related products and projects. Next, they found Eastwick's passport and travel papers and a comparable set under an alternate identity, Wesley Boyd. Finally at the back of the safe, they found $527,000 in neatly packaged bundles of $100 bills.

CHAPTER 24
(9AM): Tom

Kate and I walked into the third full day of the Transitions workshop and took the same positions in the circle. At 9:05 Cheryl spoke: "Welcome to Wednesday." She looked at each person. "You're doing an extraordinary job. I'm not sure how the men's circle was, but the women's circle was a spectacular success. Do any of the women want to talk about it?"

Julie raised her hand. "I just want to thank my big sisters Kate, Norma, Aoife, and Lois for their love and support." She walked around the circle and gave each of these women a hug and a kiss on the cheek.

Lucy raised her hand. "Me, too." She followed suit, offering a hug and kiss, as well.

Kate raised her hand. "I want to thank you for encouraging me to let go of my inhibitions and get into the tubs. I love them. Thank you."

Norma raised her hand. "Me, too. Thanks."

DEATH IS POTENTIAL · BOB BURNETT

Aoife raised her hand. "I want you to know that I feel loved and supported here. I feel the safest I have in months, and I've finally been able to sleep through the night."

Tammy raised her hand. "This is the first group of this sort I have ever been in. It's not what I expected but I'm enjoying it. I'm learning a lot." She turned to Cheryl. "I've stopped thinking about shooting Ernie."

"Good," Cheryl said. She turned to David. "Nothing happened in the Men's circle?"

"Greg Tanaka left the group," David said, "but we soldiered on without him." He looked around at the men.

I raised my hand. "I enjoyed the men, but the highlight of the day was hearing the women singing in the tub."

Rory stood up. "I got Tom as my big brother. That meant a lot to me."

Lucy cackled, "Julie and I have Kate as our mama bear so watch out, Rory."

Everyone laughed.

David looked around at the men. "Anything else?"

Paul stood up. "Because of you, I've gained the courage to reexamine my life." He glanced at Lucky. "And to come out." He sat down.

Everyone applauded.

"Anything else?" Cheryl asked and waited a beat. "Okay. Today we're going to offer some of you a chance to come at your issues from a different perspective. We're going to create a series of family tableaus."

David looked around the room. "Who here has participated in a workshop where they used family tableaus?"

I put up my hand, as did Lois.

"Okay," David said. "This is going to take a little explanation. We're going to do a structured psychodrama involving role playing. Those of you who want to explore a particular family dynamic can ask members of the group to portray members of your family." David looked around the room and saw mostly blank faces. "Okay, I'm going to show you an example." He turned to Rory. "Rory, Cheryl and I did something like this when we worked with the residents on Saturday, do you remember?"

"Yes," Rory said. "I could use a family tableau to work on my issues with my mother and father."

"Perfect. Who here can play your mother and father?"

"I would like Tom to be my father."

I stood up.

"Okay," David said. "Who can play your mother?"

Rory scanned the women and I thought, for a second, he was going to choose Tammy and then he said, "Kate, I guess." Kate got up and took my hand and we moved to the center of the room.

"Okay," David said. "What's the setup that you want to explore?"

"I come home from SC and my mother and father are sitting in the family room. I say, 'Hi mom and dad. I'm home.'"

"What do they do?"

"My mother says, 'You look thin. I'll ask cook to make you a sandwich.' She gets up and goes into the kitchen."

"Okay, Kate," David said. "Can you do that?"

Kate went to Rory and said exactly those words. She walked past Rory and headed for the other side of the room. As she passed him, she gave his shoulder a squeeze.

"That's good," Rory said. "But my mom wouldn't touch me."

"Sorry," Kate frowned. "I forgot."

"What's does your father do?" David asked.

"Nothing. He keeps reading the paper or watching TV or whatever." Rory shrugged. "Unless SC is playing. Then he may say something like, 'What's wrong with Beckham?' Like I care."

"Okay. So, Tom does nothing."

"Yeah."

David looked around the group. "Has everyone got a good idea of Rory's family dynamics?" Most nodded. "Okay, now we're going to shake it up." David turned to Rory. "How would you like your mom and dad to respond when you come home?"

"I'd like to feel some warmth from them," Rory said. "I'd like to feel that they really care about me." His eyes misted.

"Okay. Let's go back to the beginning of the scene where you come home from SC and your parents are sitting in the family room. What would you like to happen?"

"I'd like my parent to be interested in me."

"Okay," David said. "Reenter the tableau. Kate and Tom, you respond as Rory requested."

Rory retreated to the edge of the circle and then turned around and walked to where Kate and I stood. "Hi Mom and Dad. I'm home."

Kate threw her arms around Rory. "Son. I'm so glad you are back. I've missed you." She hugged him tighter.

I hugged them both. "Rory. I'm glad to see you. Once you get settled let's grab a bite to eat and then hang out."

Rory began to cry.

"How does that feel?" David asked.

Rory clung to Kate and me. "Take your time," I whispered.

After a couple of minutes, Rory raised his head and looked at David. "This feels so good."

David watched us and then asked Rory, "Is there anything else you need?"

"I don't think so."

Rory indicated he was ready to take feedback. Several participants complimented Rory on his work. Two noted that their homes had been similar to Rory's.

"Good work, Rory," David said. "Good work, Kate, Tom, and Lucy. Let's take a ten-minute break."

When we finished the break, Cheryl addressed the room, "Who else would like to form a family tableau?" She looked around the circle.

Initially no one raised their hand, then Tammy spoke out, "If no one else is going to go, I could use this as an opportunity to talk to Ernie and our minister, John."

"That's fine," Cheryl said. Tammy walked into the center of the circle. "Who would like to be Ernie and John?"

Otto raised his hand, "I'll be Ernie."

Paul stood up. "And I can be the minister."

Cheryl moved closer to Tammy. "What's the set up?"

"We're in couples counseling. I'm complaining that Ernie has been catting around. The minister is advising us to read the Bible and pray together. I'm getting angry."

"Okay. Why don't you start by telling Ernie why you're angry?"

Tammy stood in front of Otto. "Ernie, you promised me that you are going to change your ways. But now you're banging Trixie. I'm sick and tired of this."

Otto, speaking as Ernie, responded, "Tammy you know that I love you but I'm a high energy guy with lots of needs. You can't satisfy all my needs, so I've got to have someone on the side. Someone like Trixie. You should be used to it now. It's been this way for twenty years and I always come back to you. Honey." Otto reached out for Tammy, but she batted his hand away.

Tammy began to cry.

Cheryl moved closer. "What does your minister, John, say?"

"John says wives need to be subordinate to their husbands. John says Ernie and I need to spend more time reading the Bible."

Some folks hissed.

Paul stepped close to Tammy and repeated John's lines.

Tears rolled down her cheeks.

"How are you feeling?" Cheryl asked.

"Sad. Tired. Frustrated."

"What do you want to do now?"

"I don't know."

"Would you like an ally?" Cheryl asked.

"What's that?"

"Someone to stand next to you and lend support."

"I guess. I'm not used to that."

Cheryl addressed the group. "Who would like to be Tammy's ally?"

Lois raised her hand and walked next to Tammy. "Ask Ernie how he would feel if your roles were reversed, and he was the one stuck at home and you were the one going out having a good time."

Tammy repeated what Lois said.

Otto speaking as Ernie said, "I wouldn't like it."

Paul in his role as the minister intervened. "That's not the way that it is, Tammy. You're the wife and you must reconcile yourself to loving Ernie no matter what he does."

Tammy cried. Lois whispered in her ear and Tammy shouted, "Fuck you, John."

Some of the participants clapped.

Lois whispered some more, and Tammy moved towards Otto. "I deserve to be happy, Ernie. I don't have to put up with your shit anymore. I'm leaving and I don't give a flying fuck what Pastor John says." Tammy burst into tears and Lois gave her a comforting hug.

The women began to whoop and clap.

Kate whispered in my ear, "Do you think Tammy realizes that Lois wants to fuck her?"

I shrugged. "Maybe you need to adopt her as one of your cubs."

Kate slugged me on the shoulder.

"Do you need anything more from the group?" Cheryl asked Tammy.

"No. Not right now. Thank you, Otto and Paul. And a special thank you to Lois." Tammy hugged Lois and they walked back to their seats.

"Good work everyone," Cheryl said. "This would be a good place to break for lunch. We'll reconvene at two."

"What did you think?" Kate asked.

"I'll tell you while we walk back to the dining room," I said. We gathered our things and walked out the conference room door.

On the table was a note: "Marshall Swift call Detective Sanchez."

CHAPTER 25

(noon): Laura

Detectives Sanchez and O'Malley were finishing the inventory of the contents of Malcolm Eastwick's safe when Sanchez' cellphone rang. "This is probably Marshal Kate Swift," Laura said. She picked up the phone. "Thanks for calling me back, Kate. I wanted to let you know what we found in Malcolm Eastwick's San Francisco office and ask you to do us a favor."

"It turned out that Eastwick has a safe here. Fortunately for us, his assistant Penny knows the combination. We opened the safe and found money and some potentially important papers."

"Is the FBI working with you?" Kate asked.

"Yes, and we're making good progress. The FBI took the files; they're making copies for us. When they're done with that, we're going to return to Monterey, lock the money in an evidence locker, and start studying the Satori licensing papers."

"How much money was in the safe?"

"Slightly more than half a million dollars."

"So, Eastwick got roughly a million dollars from the Satori 'licensing' scheme," Kate said. "Instead of turning it over to the

Satori accountant, he put half the money in his campus safe and the rest in his San Francisco office."

"That's what we're beginning to think, too," Laura said. "The FBI suspects Eastwick was involved in a money-laundering scheme, probably with the Russians."

"Folks who would not take kindly to the loss of $1 million."

"Exactly. Folks you do not want to mess around with." Laura changed her tone. "Listen, Kate, we want you to see if the combination for the San Francisco safe works for Eastwick's safe at Satori. Eastwick's assistant, Penny, is pretty sure it does."

"The same combination for both safes?"

"Penny says Eastwick didn't have a good memory and told her once that he was always forgetting the combination of his Satori safe. Therefore, he had the combination changed to match the one at San Francisco." Sanchez read off the combination.

Kate wrote it down and read it back.

"That's right. Our theory is that the assailant killed Eastwick after he got into the safe. There should be nothing in it."

"Where's Eastwick's cabin?"

"It's not far from where you are now. The Satori office knows the location. Take a look and call us back." Laura paused. "I don't have to remind you to be careful."

"That's why I have my trusty pistol," Kate said. "Hopefully the bad Russians are not around." She paused. "Before you hang up, I have something to tell you: one of our workshop men, Greg Tanaka, dropped out. His car is still here but no one has seen him."

"That's interesting. What do your instincts suggest?"

"Greg didn't fit in. And his story was strange. He looked like a body builder but said he was a CPA who got caught up in a money laundering scheme and was about to enter Federal Prison."

"Hmm," Laura Sanchez said. "Malcolm Eastwick might have been involved in a money laundering scheme and your Tanaka said he'd been involved in a money laundering scheme."

"And he didn't look like a CPA."

Laura paused. "Maybe Tanaka was a bag man for the Russians. Perhaps he came to Satori to collect the money from Eastwick and then something happened."

"Like what?"

"I have no idea." Sanchez paused. "Do me a favor, Kate, when you take a look at Eastwick's safe, also take a look at Tanaka's car and see if there's anything strange. By the way, do you have the car's license plate?"

Kate gave her the number. "California 6TR244."

"I'll call DMV and check it out."

CHAPTER 26

(12:15PM): Tom

"Did you catch that?" Kate asked after the call with Detective Sanchez.

"Most of it. They found another safe at Eastwick's office, got into it, and found a lot of money."

"They found almost half a million dollars and some paperwork related to the Satori licenses."

"Sanchez gave you a number that you wrote down."

"Yes. She thinks that the combination for the San Francisco safe will work for the safe here. She wants us to check it out and then take a look at Greg's car."

"Let's do it," I said.

"After lunch. I'm starving."

We got the key for Eastwick's cottage and walked north on the Satori grounds until we came to the semi-secluded location, about a hundred yards above the old conference center.

The modern wood building was built on a point overlooking the ocean.

Kate put down her backpack and put on gloves. Then she unlocked the door and swung it open. "Oh my god! Someone trashed this place."

The living room was in shambles; books were strewn on the floor and the furniture had been turned over and cut open.

"Stay back, Tom. This is a crime scene, and I don't want to contaminate it."

I backed off. "What are you going to do?"

"I didn't bring booties. I'm trying to get into the front room, and open the safe, in a way that doesn't contaminate the scene." Kate looked around and spotted a pile of old newspapers on the cottage porch. "This should work."

Kate laid down a path of newspapers between the front door and the location of the wall safe. She walked carefully on the newspapers, swung open the picture that hid the wall safe, and removed her note from a pocket. Kate turned the dial with her right gloved hand. There was an audible click and Kate swung open the steel door. "Empty."

Kate looked around the front room and turned to me, "Did you bring your iPhone with you?"

"Yes." I took it out of my pocked and handed it to her.

Kate snapped several pictures, backed out, and locked the front door. As she handed me back my iPhone, she said, "Someone had Eastwick's front room under surveillance. I spotted a spy camera between some books on his shelf."

"So, there would be a record of whoever broke in?"

"I think so," Kate said. "I'll tell Laura and she can ask her smart investigator, Bruno, to trace the camera."

⌾

Kate and I walked farther north until we came to Greg Tanaka's black Mercedes sedan, California license 6TR244.

"I'm going to treat this as a crime scene," Kate said. "I need you to stand back from Greg's car." She walked around the gravel area, where the car was parked. "There appear to be footprints by the trunk, so we need to not step on them." Kate reached into her backpack and took out a large flashlight. After turning it on, she peered through the Mercedes' windows. "Nothing in the front seat except for the car-rental agreement. His luggage is in the back seat. Now I will check the trunk."

Kate put the flashlight back into her backpack and removed a small crowbar. "One of my dad's tools," she said with a smile. "When I pop the trunk, I may trigger the car alarm so don't be startled."

She inserted the crowbar into the side of the trunk lid and forced it open. There was no sound.

Kate dropped the crowbar into her backpack, took out the flashlight and turned it on. "No body, but some physical evidence. There's a dark stain that is probably dried urine. And on the trunk lock there's a piece a fabric and possibly skin."

"So, you think Greg's body was in the trunk and then pulled out?" I asked.

"That's my working assumption." Kate lowered the trunk lid but did not lock it. She used some duct tape to secure the lid.

Kate scanned the area between the side of the Mercedes and the edge of a bluff about twenty-five yards distant. "Here's the track." She focused on a deep furrow the proceeded from the car towards the bluff edge. "The assailant probably loaded Greg's body into a wheelbarrow and wheeled it across this meadow to the cliff."

We followed the furrow across the sandy clay field until it reached the cliff edge. Kate illuminated the furrow termination. "Here's where the wheelbarrow was tipped up and Greg's body pitched out." Kate walked five yards north of the suspect area and looked down on the cliff face. "There's a plant dislodged, possibly by the impact of Greg's body. And there's another sliver of fabric." She shown the light all the way down to the waves surging into the cove. "If the water conditions were similar to what they are now, we'll never find Greg's body."

Kate stepped back from the edge. "We don't have the equipment needed to belay down the cliff and go into the sea cave and look for the body." She smiled. "Besides, I have to get ready for a hot date this evening."

"This is a job for Bruno and his guys," I said.

Kate took my hand. "We've done all we can do here. Let's walk back to the office and I'll call Laura Sanchez."

CHAPTER 27
(12:30PM): Laura

Detectives Sanchez and O'Malley were driving to the San Francisco FBI office when Sanchez' cellphone rang. "This is Marshall Swift," Laura said. "What did you find, Kate?"

"The good news is that the combination works. I was able to open the safe. The bad news is: there's nothing in it."

"So, the assailant got Eastwick to divulge the combination," Laura said. "They removed the money and killed Eastwick."

"Uh huh," Kate said. "There's more: someone reentered Eastwick's cabin and trashed it."

"So, the assailant went to a safe place, counted the money, realized that it wasn't all there and then – probably in the dead of night -- returned to Eastwick's place and trashed it looking for the rest of the money."

"That's one explanation," Kate said. "Whoever killed Eastwick was after money. After the deed was done, they had an opportunity to count the money and realized that it was about half of what they expected; they returned to the cottage and searched for another hiding place. But there's another explanation: Greg Tanaka was sent to Satori to collect money from Eastwick. When he learned he was dead, Greg Tanaka broke into Eastwick's bungalow and thoroughly searched it. By the way, when we were in Eastwick's front room, I spotted a spy camera. It could be that whoever killed Eastwick learned that Tanaka had burglarized Eastwick's cottage. Subsequently, they killed Greg. By the way, we searched his car."

"Let's come back to that," Laura said. "What you are saying is that the assailant knew about the Satori safe but not the one in San Francisco. That probably means they are on your campus and still searching for the money. They found out that Greg Tanaka was searching for the money and killed him. Is that what you think?"

"The physical evidence suggests that Greg was killed somewhere on campus, loaded into the trunk of his Mercedes, driven to the location by the art studio, removed from the trunk, placed into a wheelbarrow, moved to the edge of the bluff, and pitched into the ocean."

"Like Eastwick."

"Similar to the M.O. of the Eastwick murder but in this case the body was tossed over the cliff into a sea cave. It's likely we will never recover Tanaka's corpse."

"But there's physical evidence?" Laura asked.

"Yes," Kate answered. "We protected the physical evidence."

"Good work." Laura paused. "I don't like this situation. Is there any way to lock down the Satori campus?"

"Let me ask Tom." Kate had a mumbled conversation. "Tom says we won't be able to do that. There's a big fundraiser here tonight and some celebrities are driving in."

"This is not a good situation," Laura said. "There's no way O'Malley and I can get there until tomorrow morning." She sighed. "At least you're there, Kate. Call me if there's a development and I will send some deputies down to help you."

"Okay."

"Otherwise, I'll see you first thing in the morning."

CHAPTER 28
(2PM): Tom

Kate and I walked into the Wednesday afternoon session of the Transitions workshop. While we kept our same positions, the other participants changed their seats.

Cheryl stood up. "Are there any questions about what happened this morning?"

Tammy put her hand up. "I want to thank all of you for helping me this morning. Especially Lois." She sat down and clasped Lois' hand.

Cheryl looked around the group. "Does anyone else have a comment or question? Does anyone else wish to work with a family tableau?"

No one in the group responded.

"Okay. David and I thought this might happen. so I have a suggestion on what to do next. During the women's circle, there was an interesting discussion about how to feel safe with men. Not surprisingly, a lot of our women have had experiences where they did not feel safe with men. I thought it might be useful for the women to return to this topic and the men to listen. That is, the women would come to the center of the room and sit in a circle. The men would sit outside them and listen."

David said, "I want to reinforce what Cheryl said, men. We want you to listen only. This is necessary to establish a safe environment." He looked at the men. "Do you agree?"

The men nodded.

The women moved into a tight circle. We men moved into a looser circle around them. I sat behind Kate.

"Okay, women, who wants to begin?"

Julie inched forward. "This discussion began when I mentioned my experience working as a waitress at a bar in Missoula. I quit because I got tired of being groped. On Saturday night, especially after a big football game, all the guys would get drunk and then it was open season on the waitresses. They seemed to think it was a big joke to grab my ass or touch my breasts. I even had a couple of cowboys follow me into the ladies' room."

"And no one protected you?" Cheryl asked.

"No. The bartenders were too busy. The bouncers always had their hands full, and the boss didn't seem to give a shit. In fact, he hit on a couple of the younger waitresses."

"So, you quit?"

"I quit and, fortunately, got a job working at the hospital."

"Did you get hit on there?"

"Of course. But no one grabbed my tits or my ass." Julie sighed. "I've been hit on since I was fourteen. I'm sort of used to it."

"And you haven't given up on men?" Lois asked.

"No. Not yet," Julie laughed. "And meeting the men here has encouraged me, especially seeing Tom form a relationship with Kate."

"You told the women about your plans; perhaps share them with the men," Cheryl said.

"Okay." Julie stood up. "In the fall I'm going to reenter veterinary school, this time at UC Davis. With Kate's help, I'm going to find a Taekwondo dojo and begin training." She bumped fists with Kate.

"Taekwondo seemed to be a theme in the women's group," Cheryl said. "Aoife, Julie, and Lucy expressed an interest in learning Taekwondo with Kate."

"Me, too," Norma said, "If I end up moving to Northern California."

Julie sat down.

Cheryl turned to Kate. "Do you mind telling your story, Kate. The men might find it interesting."

"Sure." Kate slid forward on her pillow. "I grew up in Fresno. I went to Fresno schools and Fresno State University. My dad was a detective in the Fresno PD. We had a great relationship and I naturally gravitated to police work." She looked around at the men. "I was always athletic, a bit of a tomboy. When I was a teenager, my dad got me involved in martial arts. By the time I entered State I was working on a judo black belt. Then a Taekwondo dojo opened in Fresno, and I shifted my allegiance. During my senior year I played soccer and taught Taekwondo." Kate turned to look for her thermos. I handed it to her, and she winked at me.

Kate sipped water. "After I graduated from State, I applied to the Fresno PD and was accepted. There were women in the department, and I was Vern Swift's daughter; there wasn't a lot of sexism. Once in a while something would happen at a party, but nothing awful. After five years, I became a detective. Then I went to a regional peace officers meeting and learned that the San Francisco Marshal's office was looking for women. So, I applied and was accepted. I was thrilled." Kate shook her head. "I was so naïve. I showed up the first day and realized that there were no women in the office, other than a receptionist. They had recruited me as part of a settlement on discrimination in the Marshal's service. It wasn't just a sexist environment, it was hostile. I loved San Francisco and my apartment, but I hated my job. I had virtually no social life; when I had time off I either went home to Fresno or worked out at the Zanshin Dojo. The guys at the Marshal's office gave me every shit job they could, but I kept my head down and did the work. After a year, things got better."

Kate sipped water. "Then I made a mistake, I agreed to go out for drinks with the guys at their favorite bar in the Mission District. I only had one beer, but they got loaded and then the sex talk started." Kate flashed me a look with raised eyebrows that seemed to signify *Are you sure you want to hear this*. "One big guy, Elmer, went on and on about how I must be a lesbian because I never fucked any of them. I could have left but after a year I was so sick of that shit that I said, 'I'll make you a little bet, Elmer. You and I will have a wrestling match. If you go down first, then all this crap will stop. If I go down first, then

I'll blow you.' Of course, they lapped it up. I never did tell them I was a Taekwondo black belt – which was unethical. We went outside the bar, took off our Marshal's jackets and shirts. Elmer outweighed me by over 100 pounds. I think he figured he would grab my undershirt and fall on me. When he moved forward, I used *tool sul* and flipped him over my head. Elmer landed on his back on the pavement and was out cold. Unfortunately, it turned out that he dislocated his shoulder because of an old football injury."

Kate sighed. "What saved my ass was the female staff at the bar: the bartender and the waitress. They were willing to testify to what happened. So rather than fire me, the Marshal's Office gave me a promotion so long as I agreed not to press charges. Elmer was transferred to Huntsville, Alabama. A month later, two women joined as US Marshals. Once that happened, I called a meeting of my staff and said, 'We've had some sexism problems here. Today that's stopped. If I hear of any complaints, I'm not going through HR, I'm going to handle them personally. Does anyone have any questions?" Kate sipped water. "You know how it is with guys, they may be thinking, 'fuck you,' but they won't say anything. So, I called out each of the men and said, 'Joe, if you don't agree with this new policy, I can arrange for you to transfer. Do you agree?' They all backed down. And that was that."

"And your job is okay now?" Cheryl asked.

"Yes. Except for Earle but he's moving to Chicago." Kate lowered her voice. "And the dead bodies. But I don't want to talk about that now."

Kate sat down. Julie and Lucy hugged her.

"Before I let you off, Kate," Cheryl said. "Tell the men what you said to the women."

"I said, I haven't given up on men. My father was a good man, so I know there are good men. What I've learned is that if a woman is going to make her way in a man's world, she has to be able to take care of herself. That's what I'm teaching Julie, Lucy, and Aoife; and Norma if she wants."

"She scares me," Rory whispered.

"You'll be fine, as long as you follow my lead."

Cheryl called out. "Tom and Rory, I hear you talking. Do you want to share with the whole group what was said?"

"We're both scared to death."

Everyone laughed. Kate reached back and punched me on the leg. "I'd sue," I said, "but I'm too frightened."

⌒

The Transitions group broke up at four and many participants headed for the baths. Kate and I headed back to our rooms to prepare for our first "date."

At five, I knocked on her door. Kate was dressed in the same white linen jump-suit she'd worn the first night of the workshop, but it was highlighted by a red belt and a bright scarf. She wore gold hoop earrings and, for the first time, mascara that complimented her green eyes. "Wow," I said. "You look gorgeous."

Kate blushed. "You don't look so bad yourself."

"Perhaps, but no one is going to hit on me at the reception; I'm going to have to spend all evening beating away the wolves."

Kate kissed me on the cheek, locked the door, and took my hand. "We're off."

We walked down the stairs and headed north on the main Institute path. "I'm a little embarrassed about telling the whole group the Elmer story." Kate stopped and gripped my hand. "I don't want you to think badly of me; I don't want you to think I'm a slut."

"I would never think that of you. I think you are a courageous, honorable woman trying to make her way in a man's world."

"Thank you," Kate said. "You're sure you're not saying that because you want to get into my pants."

I laughed. "I do want to get into your pants." I squeezed her hand. "I'm saying that because I have a high opinion of you. I think you are smart and energetic and honorable."

"I think the same of you." Kate stopped. "Perhaps we can just skip the reception and go to your room and -- what was your expression? – ah yes, consummate our relationship."

I chuckled. "I can't wait to consummate with you, but I think it is a good idea for us to go to the reception." I held up three fingers. "First, I like the idea of us going on a real date before we fall into bed. Call me old-fashioned, call me romantic, call me whatever but I think it's the right thing to do."

"I like romantic. What are the other two reasons?"

"Two, it gives you a little insight into the world I move in." We started walking up the path. "I've been thinking about our relationship, trying to explain to myself what is happening and where it's going. I was reminded of a couple's book I read a long time ago that said all relationship are determined by the balance among money, sex, and power." Kate squeezed my hand. "The sex dimension is to be determined for us."

Kate kissed my hand.

"We are both powerful, in our own ways."

Kate shrugged.

"The last dimension is money. I've been fortunate and now, by most people's standards, I'm well off. I'm privileged. That could create problems for us. I don't know. But it occurred to me that going to the fundraiser would expose you to a slice of my world and you could see how you like it."

"Just so you know, I'm not indigent." Kate chuckled. "My grandfather owned a big ranch in the foothills east of Fresno. When he passed, it went to my father and his brother, Ben. My Uncle has been the working partner, but my father has stayed involved and they have a good relationship. When they die, God forbid, the ranch will be left to me and my cousin Sheila."

"What do you plan to do with your inheritance?"

"Sheila and I have talked this over and we plan to sell the ranch," Kate said.

"So, I was wrong. You're more familiar with the monied class than I expected."

"You've really thought about this haven't you?" Kate asked.

"Yes. I'm strongly attracted to you and have been asking myself, 'what is this all about?'"

"And did you get an answer to your question?"

"Yes."

"What was it?"

I blushed. "Now I'm embarrassed." I cleared my throat. "I told myself that I am in the process of falling in love with you."

"That's so sweet." Kate stopped walking. "You're so brave, Tom. So clear." Her eyes misted. "I'm not sure if what I feel for you is love or lust or longing or something else that begins with 'l', perhaps losing my mind. Whenever I see you, I have this overwhelming desire to touch you." She blushed. "To place my hand on your bare skin." She lowered her voice. "I feel like I'm fifteen years old."

"That is so nice to hear." I pulled her closer. "Maybe we should skip the reception."

Kate took a deep breath. "I think we should do the reception but not linger."

"Okay. We'll duck in and out."

Kate started walking. "What do you expect?"

"At the least, the fundraising staff is going to ask me to renew my donation to Satori. Probably, given the mess it's in, they're going to ask me to be on the board."

"Do you want to do that?"

"No."

"Then why are you going?"

"For one thing, I've gone to these events for years and the people are zany but fun. For another thing, Satori is a customer of our business. Finally, we might get a clue as to who killed Malcolm."

"You think somebody on the Satori staff killed Malcolm?"

"It could have been a mafia-style hit, someone sent here to off Malcom because he stole their money. But a lot of people on the staff didn't like Malcolm. It could be something simpler, like a jilted lover."

"Someone who got pissed off when Malcolm started sleeping with Penny?"

"Exactly."

We walked a little further, holding hands, until we came to a broad wooden bridge that forded Pfeiffer Creek. We walked across it, hearing the faint echo of our footsteps, and then turned west to the Old Conference Center.

We came to the steps of the old conference center, a rambling three-story wood building with a composition roof; a structure that looked as if it might have, at one time, been a hotel. "Here we are," I said. "Tonight, if anything seems strange to you, come and talk to me about it."

In the shadows at the corner of the building, I saw Cheryl Taylor smoking a cigarette. She was talking to two men in suits, who were also smoking. I remembered Fiona saying the only visible way Cheryl expressed anxiety was her cigarette addiction.

Kate and I walked onto the wood porch and were met by Marcia Ball. "Tom and Marshal Swift. So nice that you could join us. Most of the board is already in the main room." Marcia handed us each a name card and I was relieved that Kate's merely said "Kate Swift."

I helped Kate attach her name card and then took her hand as I walked into the spacious rectangular room.

Moments later, Cheryl greeted us. I almost didn't recognize her because she was dressed for the occasion. *Of course*, I thought, *now that Malcolm's gone, Cheryl must represent the Satori tradition.* In the workshop, Cheryl typically wore wire-rim glasses, no makeup, hair pulled back in a tight bun, and a loose, olive-brown pantsuit. Tonight, Cheryl had ditched her glasses; she wore glamorous makeup, diamond earrings, and a black strapless cocktail dress.

"You look wonderful," Kate said, at almost the same moment Cheryl told her she looked great. They both clasped hands and beamed.

"Watch out for the Hollywood guys, Kate," Cheryl whispered. "They can be very obnoxious."

"Tom promised to protect me." Kate said, tightening her grip on my arm.

Cheryl glanced at me and lifted her eyebrows, as if to say, *Kate doesn't need your protection, but it's the thought that counts.*

"I'm nervous," Kate said. "I'm not used to hobnobbing with the rich and famous."

"They're just like us," Cheryl said. "Only not as well adjusted."

The three of us laughed.

"Are you ready for your new role?" I asked Cheryl.

"As ready as I'll ever be." Cheryl glanced around the room. "I view it as an operational necessity."

We excused ourselves and walked further into the room. "Does Cheryl have a boyfriend?" Kate asked.

"I'm not sure. Fiona used to keep track of that. She tried to fix Cheryl up with people we know in the city, but with no success. A while back, Cheryl dated a military guy but I'm not sure what became of him."

Thirty people had already arrived at the reception. I recognized most of them, although I hadn't been to a Satori fundraiser for three years, since before Fiona suffered her final illness.

A waiter arrived with a tray containing flutes of champagne. I handed one to Kate, took another for myself, and touched the rim of her glass. "Here's to my beautiful friend."

Kate blushed. "Here's to our first date."

Over the next few minutes, we made our way among the participants, some staff, but mostly members of the board and donors. Several had not heard about Fiona, and were surprised to see me with a date, but it didn't feel awkward, as I explained what had happened and that Kate and I had just met at David and Cheryl's workshop.

Eventually we worked our way across the room, walked out of the room, and walked onto the deck overlooking a steep cliff. "So, this is where Malcolm died?" Kate said, looking down onto the waves crashing on the rocks below.

"Yes. Probably over there." I pointed to the corner of the deck that was the closest to the edge.

Kate walked to the corner, grabbed my hand, and looked down. "Malcolm might have fallen but it seems most probably that he was pushed."

I looked down at the rocks and then turned to look at the crowd in the main room. *I wonder if anyone here did it?*

Bruce James, the Institute executive director, walked up. "Tom and Marshal Swift, nice that you could join us. Even if this is a sad occasion." James briefly cast his eyes down. "Tom, has Jean Little talked to you, yet?"

"No. I haven't seen her."

"Well, when she does talk to you, don't mention I already talked to you. She wants to broach an idea we had."

I bet it's an idea involving my money, I thought.

A man whose name I did not remember walked up to us. He was a little younger than me with thinning bleached blonde hair arranged in an elaborate combover. His name tag read: Jerry Kermit. *The movie producer*, I realized. He was accompanied by a faintly attractive young woman with a weak chin and very large breasts. *Those have to be fake.* I glanced at Kate and she raised her eyebrows. The young woman's nametag read: Gwyneth Jones.

Jerry reached out with his hand, "Tom, I was very sorry to hear about Fiona's passing. She was quite a woman."

"Yes, she was." *And she was always trying to ward off your advances.*

"It must be tough living without her. She left big shoes to fill." Jerry glanced at Kate.

What a prick, I thought. "Fiona was unique. But so is my new partner, Kate Swift." I turned to Kate, and she stuck out her hand. *I need to develop a signal to tell Kate to flip guys like Jerry over her head.*

Jerry held Kate's hand a little too long. "Jerry Kermit. I'm a movie producer." He made no attempt to introduce his date.

I extended my hand to her. "Tom Scott."

"I'm Gwyneth. I'm an actress."

Of course, I thought.

"Are you in the entertainment business?" Gwyneth asked.

"I have an event-management company."

Bruce James broke away. "See you later, Tom. Marshal."

"Marshal?" Jerry said to Kate. "You're a US Marshal?"

"I am," Kate smiled and poked me in the ribs. "This is my assistant, Chester."

"Are you here to arrest anyone?" Jerry asked as his companion stood there with her mouth open.

"Possibly," Kate said with a straight face. "Would you mind if I search you for illegal substances?"

"With pleasure," Jerry smiled, as Gwyneth turned and walked inside.

I saw Marcia Ball waving to me. "I'm going to get the hand-cuffs," I said to Kate. "Remember to read Jerry his rights."

Kate thumped me on the shoulder. "Don't take too long, Chester."

I walked across the deck and onto the green carpet of the main room. Before I could reach Marcia, I was intercepted by a woman in a low-cut dress that appeared to have been attached to her tan body by super glue. *Oh, oh.* I thought. *Monique.*

She hugged me and tried to kiss me on the lips, but I turned my mouth away. "I'm so sorry to hear about Fiona," Monique said with her phony French accent. "When are you going to come visit me in Santa Monica?"

She never relents, I thought. Monique had been hitting on me for years. It had become a standing joke between Fiona and me. "My business is booming," I said. "I seldom get to Los Angeles."

Monique leaned forward so I had a clear view of her bosom. "You should visit. I could make it worth your while." *Monique is the Hollywood version of Tammy*, I thought.

Just then Marcia Ball interrupted us. "Jean Little wants to see you," she said. "She's over there with Dr. Badger." Marcia pointed across the room to the fireplace.

"Let me collect Kate," I said. "Then I'll talk to Marcia."

"Who is Kate?" Monique asked.

"My new partner," I replied and stuck out my hand. "Nice to see you, Monique."

She tried to pull me close, but I resisted, turned around and walked back to where Jerry was talking in an animated manner to Kate.

"Earle thinks I will be perfect for his new movie," Kate said. "He wants me to fly to Hollywood for a screen test."

"As your partner, I advise that you sign nothing until Jerry wires a signing bonus to our account."

Jerry's smile died.

"I'll let you work out the details, Chester. I'm going to find the ladies' room." Kate turned and walked off, giving her hips an enticing wiggle.

"Quite a woman," Jerry said.

"Yes. But dangerous."

"In what way?" The color drained out of his artificially tanned face.

"She's a Taekwondo expert. Her previous boyfriend got drunk and tried to force her into sex; she flipped him and broke his back."

Jerry's mouth dropped open.

"I'm very careful how I handle her."

"She has a gun?"

"Yes. And handcuffs." I leaned closer to Jerry. "I have an idea for you to consider. Make a remake of 'Dirty Harry,' call it 'Dirty Mary' and cast Kate as the lead."

"Good idea," Jerry stammered and backed up. "I should find Gwyneth." He walked back into the main room.

I waited on the deck until Kate came back. "Can we leave now? I think I've done my duty." She wrapped her left arm around me and bit me on the ear lobe.

"Yes. But on the way out, I promised Marcia Ball I would talk to Jean Little, who wants to ask for money."

"Okay. As long as it doesn't take too long." Kate ran her tongue over her lips. "I'm getting impatient."

"Believe me, I'm impatient, too."

"How did you get rid of my new best friend Jerry?"

I recounted what I'd shared.

"That explains Chester's limp," Kate chortled.

I wrapped my arm around her as we walked into the main room. "Did Jerry ever actually make a movie?" Kate asked.

"A couple, I think."

"Would I have seen one?"

"I doubt it. The most famous is titled, 'Space Pussy.'"

Kate laughed loudly, attracting the attention of several couples close to us. "You're making that up." She belted me on the shoulder.

"You can't make stuff like that up."

We found Jean Little. "Marcia said you wanted to talk to me. This is my partner, Kate Swift."

Kate stuck out her hand and Jean shook it.

"Is it okay if we talk about money in front of Ms. Swift?"

"We have no secrets."

Kate tilted her head to the side and raised her eyebrows.

"All right." Jean shuffled her feet and lowered her voice. "The unfortunate death of Malcolm leaves us at loose ends. The board and I were wondering if you would consider making a significant contribution?"

"What amount were you and the board thinking about?"

"At least one hundred thousand dollars," Jean said. "More if you can see your way clear."

Poor ask, I thought. "Fiona and I always treasured Satori," I said, pausing for emphasis. "Kate and I are in the process of reallocating our assets. I'm sure we can help in some fashion."

"Are you going to be in San Francisco, next week? Perhaps we could discuss this over lunch?"

"We won't be in the city next week. Kate and I are taking a little trip. I'll call you when we return." I reached out and shook her hand.

Kate followed my lead and shook Jean's hand.

We left the conference center and started the walk back to south campus.

When we were alone, Kate said, "You are a smooth talker, Chester." She punched me in the arm. "Am I your partner?"

"If you want to be. I wasn't sure what to call you. 'My guest' doesn't say enough. 'My girlfriend' sounds like high school. Technically you're not yet 'my lover,' and I would never call you that anyway. 'My significant other' sounds like a fucked-up contractual relationship. So, I settled on 'my partner.'"

Kate pulled me closer with her left arm. "I accept. I'll be your partner."

We continued walking. "My favorite line was 'Kate and I are in the process of reallocating our assets.'" Kate chortled.

"In about five minutes I plan to begin reallocating your assets," I laughed.

Kate snorted. "What am I going to do with you?"

"I have many ideas."

"I bet you do." She slugged me in the upper arm. "And what was that about our 'taking a little trip?'"

We reached the path intersection and turned right towards my cottage. "I'll tell you later."

"When I was in the line for the bathroom, I was looking at the historical Satori pictures on the wall. I found what I think was a picture of you, Fiona, Malcolm Eastwick, and Bruce Springsteen."

"Yeah. I'd forgotten about that picture. Bruce did a benefit for Satori, and we managed the event."

"Fiona and I don't look alike." Kate stopped walking. "I mean, I like the way she looked, she was very beautiful; but she and I have different colored hair and different body types."

"Does this surprise you?"

Kate sighed and clasped my hand. "I'm relieved. There's a part of me that is searching for proof that this won't work and, I guess, I had this voice telling me, 'Tom is trying to recreate Fiona.' And another voice saying, 'You'll never measure up to Fiona; she was Wonder Woman.'"

I pulled Kate closer. "Fiona was Fiona. You are Kate."

We reached the south campus. I could see my cottage across the lawn.

"I have a terrible confession to make," Kate said. "I haven't done anything about birth control. I stopped taking the pill and after Earle, I cut my diaphragm into shreds and flushed it down the toilet. I'm sorry."

"You don't have to be sorry. We don't need to worry; I've had a vasectomy."

Kate tilted her head and furrowed her brow. "Really, why?'

"After Fiona died, I did it as a symbolic act. Fiona had always wanted children and I told myself that I could never have a child without her." I sighed. "Fortunately, I planned ahead, the vasectomy can be reversed. And I made a 'deposit' in a sperm bank." I took both her hands. "So, if you are determined to have children, it's not out of the question."

"Wow," Kate said. "All the relationship stuff is coming at us fast and furious." She sighed. "I'd sort of given up the idea of having kids but..." she blushed, "last night I had a dream where we had kids." Kate pulled me closer. "However, to tell you the truth, I'm relieved. I want you all to myself and I don't want to worry about all the contraception crap." She laughed a throaty laugh. "Am I too awful? I just want you whenever I want you."

"No. That is not awful," I said. My heart was pounding so hard that I felt sure Kate could hear it.

We held hands and walked to my cottage, which was the northernmost of a set of three luxury suites. I unlocked the door and swung it open.

Kate moved close and I wrapped both arms around her. She tilted her head up and we kissed. I felt a surge of energy so strong that it almost knocked me off my feet. We staggered into the front room and collapsed on the floor. I kicked the door closed.

THURSDAY

CHAPTER 29
(2:10 AM): Tom

"You've turned me into a screamer," Kate rasped.

Our bare bodies were entwined, supported by several pillows, half sitting up in a queen-size bed. All the candles had burnt out except for one, which flickered on the redwood bureau at the far side of the room. The cotton window curtains were pulled to one side, exposing the west side of the room to the dark night. A few stars hovered over the moon-swept ocean. Surf pounded the granite cliff.

My body quivered with excitement. I was covered with a thin sheen of sweat. *I should be exhausted*, I thought. *But I'm too turned on.* "I want to please you," I said hoarsely. "When you screamed, I thought I was doing my job." I kissed her cheek.

"Oh my god, you are pleasing me." Kate purred. "it's just that I wasn't prepared for a climax like that." She pressed closer. "I'm not sure what I expected when we got together but not this. Not waves of orgasms." She sighed. "I thought you would be a more 'conventional' lover."

"What does that mean?"

"You're more attentive than I expected, more considerate. You talk to me. And you want to excite every part of my body. From the hair on my head to the soles of my feet, you've turned me into one big erogenous zone."

"As your lover, it's my job to please you."

"My wonderful lover." Kate kissed me.

I tightened both arms around her.

"I love the way you hold me," Kate said. "I crave physical contact with you. I'm insatiable." She tucked her head under my chin and curled on my chest.

"Me, too." My heart ached. "I hadn't realized how much I missed skin contact until I met you..."

"And I couldn't keep my hands off of you."

I kissed her hair. "I love it."

Kate inched higher until her mouth was next to my ear. "As I open to you, as I let myself be vulnerable," she whispered. "I realize how needy I am."

I pulled her closer. "You give me many gifts. When you open to me, I open to you." I turned my head and kissed her.

Kate pushed her tongue deep inside mine.

I grew aroused again.

"Tom, you are way more experienced than I am."

"Uh huh."

Kate whispered in my ear. "I have had a more sheltered sex life than you might have imagined. In high school and college, I was a cop's daughter, and my boyfriends were very careful with me." Her voice was barely audible. "Earle thought I was a prude because I wouldn't let him go down on me."

"Fuck Earle," I growled. "Earle was an idiot. You are a remarkable woman who requires special handling."

She snuggled closer. "Is that your secret skill? Special handling?"

"With you." I kissed her. "I handle you with care."

She ran her tongue around my lips and mouth. "You talk to me and reassure me when I am nervous."

My heart hammered. "I was never aware that you were nervous. I focused on appreciating every inch of your luscious body and listening to your feedback."

"My sighs and moans."

"Yes. I didn't have an agenda, but when I was kissing your stomach, you spread your legs, so I went lower."

"I wasn't thinking, I just did it."

"And you got very excited."

Kate panted and bit my lower lip. "You opened me."

"You gave me a special gift."

"And I screamed like I never have before." She bit my ear lobe. "I'm aroused again."

My erection throbbed. "So am I."

Kate chuckled and pushed against my erection. "Does it bother you that I am so loud?"

"No." I turned into her hips. "It turns me on. However, it might bother Tammy who rented the cottage two doors down."

"I don't give a flying fuck if I bother Tammy."

"It might bother the Benedictine monks who live in the monastery above Lucia."

"Their choice to be celibate," Kate laughed. "They don't know what they were missing." She ran the fingers of her left hand lightly down my chest and circled my belly button.

I inserted my tongue in her ear. "What turns you on, turns me on." I slid my left hand slowly down her stomach and reached her pubic hair.

Kate arched her back and then placed her hand on mine. She kissed me. "You know, Tom, you are so competent that it's tempting to let you take care of everything." She moved up so she was leaning on my chest looking into my eyes. "After you were finished 'appreciating' me, I lay there blissed out and thought, 'I'm going to stay here and have Tom make love to me forever.'" She furrowed her brow. "Then I thought, 'When does Tom go off duty? When does he get 'appreciated'?" She sat up. "So now you're going to take your turn. Just lay back and let me provide the special handling."

I started to tell Kate she didn't need to do anything for me, but she put her hand over my mouth. "Do what I tell you, Tom, or you will be punished." Kate chuckled. "Now lie flat and spread your legs."

Kate sat up. She reached into her purse, picked out a white headband, and slipped it over her head, pulling her hair back.

Kate kissed me for a long minute and then moved her lips everywhere on my head. She placed her left hand on my heart.

Her kisses moved to my neck. Kate lingered on the fleshy area of my clavicle and sucked hard. "While I'm at it, I'm putting my mark on you, so any woman, who sees you naked in the showers and admires your cute butt, will know you're taken."

My heart beat faster. I closed my eyes.

"Open your eyes, Tom. I want you fully awake for this." Kate's kisses moved to my chest. and she sucked on my right nipple. I moaned. "Good," Kate said. "Keep your eyes open and moan." She chuckled. "My new life objective is to make you moan every day." Her hand moved to my pubic hair. She sucked on my left nipple. "Your nipples have not been fully appreciated."

I moaned again and my penis quivered. Kate kissed my stomach and ran her tongue around my belly button. She paused to give me another hickey. "This is so much fun." She caressed my glans with her hair, as she gripped the base of my penis with her thumb and forefinger.

I moaned and arched my back.

"Just a little while longer, Tom." Kate moved her lips to the inside of my calves and gave me another love bite. She let her tongue trail all the way down my leg and then sucked two of my toes. "Umm."

Kate moved back up my legs, sliding her tongue over my skin, and then hovered over my erection.

We were both panting.

"Now I need to get us ready." Kate kissed the side of my penis as she placed several fingers inside her vagina. "I'm very wet. What do you think?" She placed her moist fingers on my lips.

I noisily sucked them.

Kate chuckled. "Now I need to get you ready for my Tantric fantasy." She licked my glans and then slid on top of me.

191

I moaned as I was embraced by her wet warmth. Sparks lit the backs of my eyes. All I could feel was Kate.

Her eyes widened. "Hold on, Tom. We're almost there." Kate's panting increased. "Keep your eyes open. And do exactly what I say, or you will be disciplined." She clenched her vagina.

"Brace your arms. I'm going to lean over you." I did what Kate said, and she was suspended over me. "Damn, I won't be able to kiss you." Kate shook her head, as she realized her lips would only come to my neck. "We'll work on that later. Now pull your legs together."

I did what she said. Kate moved her feet outside my legs until she was suspended over me.

"Good. We're almost there. Now take a deep breath."

We both inhaled and Kate lowered her body over mine until I could feel her erect nipples against my chest and her vagina enveloping my penis. I struggle to maintain control. We both moaned.

"Now exhale." Kate pushed up off me. "Oh god. I'm so close." Her eyes were intense. "Now inhale."

Again, Kate lowered her body over mine. I was so excited that I imagined my heart breaking through my chest.

"Now exhale." Kate pushed up off me. Her voice was a throaty whisper. "Almost there." Her body trembled. I focused on holding on. "Now inhale."

This time, when Kate lowered her body over mine, we both shook. "Now exhale."

As Kate pushed off, I could see her eyes were dilated and her pupils rolled up until the eyes surface was white. Her body convulsed. Kate collapsed on me and screamed.

I let go and joined her shouts.

CHAPTER 30
(6:10AM): Laura

"Sanchez here." Laura picked up her cellphone. "No, you didn't wake me up, Mr. James." Detective Laura Sanchez recognized the agitated voice of Bruce James, Satori Institute executive director.

"We have a problem," James said. "We found a dead body in the baths."

"That is a problem. Tell me what you found."

"The cleaning crew found the body in one of the private tubs – a one-person claw-foot tub. It was Bryn Moore, our accountant." James' voice broke. "They suspected foul play because Bryn was a straight arrow."

"Okay. Here's what you need to do: Close off the tubs and have everyone stay away from the area." Sanchez took a deep breath. "And close off all access to the Satori campus. Don't let anyone in or out."

"Okay. We can do that," James said. "When can you get here?"

"That's a problem. I'm up early because Sergeant O'Malley and I planned to drive down this morning. However, there's a fire at Garrapata State Park and the road is blocked. We can't drive down until that's under control."

"Can't you circle around, drive through San Luis Obispo County, and come up from San Simeon?"

"No. Believe it or not, there's a slide at Ragged Point and the road is blocked."

"So, you're not coming here today?"

"It's unlikely," Sanchez said. "Wake up Marshal Swift. Tell her what happened and that I want her to take charge until we arrive. She'll know what to do."

CHAPTER 31
(6:20 AM): Tom

Knocking woke me up. I was asleep on my back and Kate was lying on top of me. The knocking grew louder.

"What's that noise?" Kate asked.

"Someone at the door, sweetheart. I'll take care of it." I began to slide out from under her.

"Make them go away. I don't want us to be disturbed."

"I'll take care of it." I extricated myself and sat up.

"If it's Tammy, tell her to fuck off."

I struggled out of bed and found a path across the carpeted floor that was littered with our clothes. *I need to buy Kate a new linen outfit*, I thought, stepping over the remains of the white pantsuit she'd been wearing. I grabbed my dress shirt and wrapped it around my bare body. Peering through the wooden blinds, I saw Bruce James standing on the porch. I opened the door a few inches. "What's up?"

"Sorry to disturb you, Tom. I was wondering if I could speak to Marshal Swift."

"Why? What's happened?"

Before James could answer, Kate sat up on the bed. "Tell him that Tammy should get some ear plugs."

"I don't think this is about Tammy." I turned back to Bruce James. "What's happened?"

"There's a dead body in the tubs in what looks like suspicious circumstances. We talked to Detective Sanchez, and she wants Marshal Swift to take charge."

Kate walked behind me, stark naked. She leaned her head into the open-door space. "Block off all access to the baths. If any of your staff touched the body, have them stay in the bath area until I get there."

"Okay. What's the matter with your voice?"

"Hay-fever, I guess," Kate said. "Block off all access to the Satori campus. Probably the best way to do this is to move Satori vehicles into the driveway and lock them."

"Okay."

"How long before Sanchez and O'Malley get here?"

"Not today. Highway one is blocked by a fire at Garrapata and by a slide below Gorda."

"No shit? That's a mess."

"Yes," said James. "Anything else?"

"I need to take a quick shower. When I get to the baths, I'll need a box of rubber gloves, some large baggies, a magnifying glass, and a high-quality camera. I'll be there as soon as I can."

James turned around and I shut the door.

"Welcome to my world, partner." Kate kissed me. "Would you please fix me a cup of coffee while I shower? Do you have a razor?"

"There's one on the bathroom sink. How do you like your coffee?"

"Strong. Black. Put some in a thermos if you have it. What's the weather like outside?"

"Crisp. Probably high fifties."

"Okay. While I'm in the shower, honey, please go back to my room and have Norma find my jeans, my US Marshall sweatshirt, some underwear, and my tennis shoes."

I dropped my towel and bowed. "Your obedient servant." I remembered her commanding, *"Do what I say, or you will be disciplined."*

***

When we got to the baths, we found the maintenance crew sitting on a bench by the bathrooms. There were two young men and a woman. Work-study students, I guessed. They had blocked off access by moving portable tables across the path.

Kate asked their names. "I need one of you to go back to the tables and use masking tape to attach then to the wooden fence and each other; we don't have 'crime-scene' tape. The person that does this should make a big sign that says, 'Crime Scene: No Admittance.'"

"I'll do it," said the young woman.

"Let's go look at the dead guy," Kate said.

We walked into the upper part of the bath area, where there were smaller hot tubs. The cadaver was in an individual hot tub.

His skin color was gray, and his body slumped over against the porcelain edge.

"Who is this?" Kate asked.

"Bryn Moore," one of the men said.

"A drug user?"

"I don't think so, but I didn't know him very well. He worked here as a bookkeeper. He always struck me as kind of a nerd."

Kate looked around. "Okay, the first thing to do is to drop all the sun blinds so folks up at the dining room or in the conference rooms up above can't look down here, see the body, and take pictures. When that's done, we'll move a massage table next to the tub, lift Mr. Moore's body out of the tub, and place it on the table so I can examine it."

The two young men set about lowering the shades.

Kate turned to me. "My phone is locked in the safe with my badge. Can I borrow your iPhone, Tom? It probably has a better camera."

I unlocked my iPhone and handed it to Kate. She took multiple pictures of the victim.

"I don't think he was killed here," Kate said. "Let's go look in the massage rooms." We put on rubber gloves and walked down the hall. All the doors were locked. "One of the guys will have the keys."

We got the keys from Johnny, the youngest of the two men, and opened the doors. In the second room we saw men's clothes on a chair. "This was probably where it happened. We need to block off this door with tape and mark it as 'Crime Scene.'"

"Someone killed him here and then dragged him to the tub?" I asked.

"That would be my guess," Kate answered. "I need to take a closer look. For the time being, let's move a massage table out of a vacant room and place it next to the decedent."

The young men and I set up the sturdy table.

Kate studied the young people. "In a second, Tom and I are going to lift Moore's body out of the tub. We'll need assistance to do this. If you don't think you're capable of lifting the corpse, say something now."

One of the young men, Larry, blanched and stepped back. "I don't think I can do this."

"Okay, Larry. You're excused. You can leave the area but please don't tell anyone any details about what you've seen. If your friends ask you what happened, you can say, 'I saw a dead person in the tub; the cops are investigating.'"

Larry walked up the hill in the direction of the dining room.

Kate handed plastic gloves to the other two, Wendy and Johnny. "Wendy and I are going to lift the decedent's shoulders. Tom and Johnny have the tougher challenge, they're going to lift his thighs. We'll lift the body straight up and let the water drain off. Then we'll move the body across onto the table. Tom, that will mean you'll have to step around the end of the tub."

"That will be awkward, but I think I can do it," I said.

We positioned ourselves at the tubs, lowered our gloved hands into the water, and grabbed the corpse. "One, two, three, lift," Kate said.

We raised the body out of the tub and let the water drain off. The corpse was heavier than I expected.

"Now, one, two, three, shift," Kate said.

Because of my position I had to extend my arms to hold up the body as I skirted the edge of the tub. My arms shook as I lifted Bryn Moore. *Thank God I lift weights*, I thought.

I noticed a brown clump at the bottom of the vacated tub. "There's fecal matter in the tub," I said to Kate.

She grimaced. "We'll have to bag it. But we won't worry about that now."

Kate turned to Wendy. "Please run up to the kitchen and borrow something like a spatula that Tom can use to lift the fecal matter and place it in a bag." Wendy raced off.

Kate turned to Johnny. "I want more illumination over the corpse. Turn on all the lights and see if you can find something like a portable lamp that I can use." Johnny walked off.

"Now I'll use your iPhone for the examination," Kate said.

I unlocked my iPhone and handed it back to Kate.

"Here's something I forgot to say. I'm using your phone to take pictures and to record my observations of the corpse. There's a chance that your phone will be taken into evidence."

"That's okay. Everything is backed up. If they seize my phone, I'll buy a replacement."

"Thank you, Tom."

"You don't have to thank me, Kate. I'm your partner. We're a team."

"Oh." Kate tilted her head to sone side and smiled. "I'm still getting used to that." She moved to kiss me and then stopped and took a deep breath. "I need to focus." She took a step back and looked down at Moore. "I didn't ask you if you have a problem working with cadavers."

"I don't. My mother was a nurse and we used to talk about her work. She often took me into the hospital with her; a couple of times I saw dead people."

"My mother was a nurse, too. What about your dad?"

"He wasn't around. I'll tell you about it later."

"Okay," Kate said. "Let's get to work." She opened the victim's closed eyes and took pictures. "The pupils are dilated, which probably means there are drugs in his system." She used the light on the iPhone to illuminate her search area. When Kate saw something unusual, she used the magnifying glass. "There's bruising and slight traces of adhesive around his mouth; the victim was gagged with something, probably duct tape."

Kate worked her way down the chest. "Do me a favor, Tom. Lift his right arm."

I lifted Brynn's right arm until his hand was level with Kate's eyes. "There's bruising around his wrists. I don't think it was the result of a rope burn or a flex tie. Maybe a leather belt?"

"Or the restraints they use in hospitals," I suggested.

"That would do it. We'll have to examine the massage room for evidence of restraints."

Kate carefully examined the victim's forearm and upper arm. She leaned in and shone the iPhone light on his right armpit. "Here it is. Here's the puncture." Kate spread his armpit hair apart and invited me to study what she had found. An obvious puncture wound, surrounded by a ring of red.

"So, he was injected with something, and the perpetrator made an effort to hide it?"

"Exactly." Kate took several photos and then stepped back. "This is similar to what happened with Malcolm Eastwick, but in that instance, I don't believe the perp made any attempt to hide the puncture."

"Perhaps because they planned to throw Malcom in the ocean?"

"That would explain it," Kate said. "Or it could be they felt more emotion when they injected Malcolm."

Kate continued her investigation. We studied the left arm and found bruising around the left wrist.

Kate scanned the stomach and the pelvis area. "Do me a favor Tom and lift up his junk." I complied. Kate gingerly examined his left testicle. "There's a puncture mark back here. I'll take a picture."

"This is like Malcolm," Kate said. "The victim was drugged and probably questioned."

She scanned all the way to the feet. The ankles showed evidence of having been restrained. Kate found another puncture between the big toe and second toe on the left foot.

"I feel like there's something else," Kate said when she finished her examination.

"How did the assailant get the body here?"

"Malcolm's body was moved in a garbage cart. Maybe there's something like that around here."

We searched the entrance to baths and found a linen room with towels, and sheets for the massage tables. At the back was a cart used to transport fresh linen.

"This was probably what the perp used," Kate said. "Notice that most of the towels were strewn on the floor. The perp cleared off the cart and used it to transport the body from the room to the tub." She looked around. "This is evidence. We need to move it out of here into the massage room we blocked off."

We put on fresh gloves and I helped Kate maneuver the linen cart into the massage room. I stood in the door while Kate examined what she suspected was the scene of the crime. "There's a stain on the sheet; probably semen. Like you suggested, Tom, there are metal brackets on the table that could be used to hold leather restraints." She kneeled and examined the floor. "There are what appears to be leather shavings and perhaps a partial footprint here."

Kate joined me at the door, surveyed the scene of the crime, and ran her hand across her forehead.

"What are you thinking?" I asked.

"I suspect our perp believed that Malcom stashed more money somewhere on the Satori campus. The assailant figured that poor Bryn Moore would know where it was. They lured him into the massage room for a sexual liaison and then drugged him. When he came to, they interrogated him, but he didn't know anything, so they injected him with a lethal dose. Later, the killer moved Moore onto the line cart and rolled him to the tub."

"Why do you think they didn't pitch him into the ocean, like they did with Malcolm Eastwick?"

"Too many stone steps," Kate said. "It was a straight shot from the massage table to the solo tub, but ten or twelve steep steps to the edge of the cliff."

"Is there any possibility this was an S&M gig gone bad?" I asked.

"Nowadays they call it BDSM," Kate said. "I don't think so, but I don't know that much about BDSM. That could be the case, but the drug injections don't fit the pattern."

Kate locked the door and led me out of the bath area.

"What I want to do now is to talk to Sanchez and, hopefully, her coroner investigator," Kate said. "I want to see if there is any indication that Eastwick was restrained."

CHAPTER 32
(7:30 AM): Laura

"I'll put you on the speaker phone," Detective Sanchez said after she received Kate's phone call. "I've got Sergeant O'Malley here along with coroner's investigator Bruno Oliver. What happened to your voice?"

"I'm having troubles with seasonal allergies," Kate said.

"Trying gargling with salt water," O'Malley said. "What have you got for us?"

"Another killing occurred last night in the baths' area. The victim, Bryn Moore, a thirty-seven-year-old white non-Hispanic male was employed here as a bookkeeper. Last night he was lured into a massage room by an unknown individual, where they likely engaged in sexual activity. Subsequently, he was drugged, gagged, and probably tied to the massage table. The victim was probably questioned and then killed by means of a second drug overdose. After his death, he was likely placed on a cart and moved to an individual tub in the hot-tub area. Finally, his body seems to have been arranged in a manner to suggest that he had experienced an accidental drug overdose."

"A comprehensive report, Marshal Swift. Anything else?"

"The assailant could have been a woman. In the massage room we found semen stains on the sheets, suggesting there was sexual activity before the killing."

"The victim could have been with another man," O'Malley said.

"True. But that's not the impression I got from the crime scene."

"Tell me about your examination of the body." Oliver said.

Kate shared about the three hidden injections.

"So, you believe the assailant tried to hide the injections?"

"That was my impression."

"You think the victim was tied to the massage table?" Sanchez asked.

"Yes. The evidence indicates that Moore was restrained, probably by leather cuffs. There were bruises on his wrists and ankles consistent with the use of restraints."

"Did you find any physical evidence to support this?" Oliver asked.

"There wasn't any obvious evidence," Kate replied. "However, the massage table had metal brackets of the sort that could have been used with leather restraints. And I found shavings that might have come from such restraints; they were on the floor by the table. Along with a partial footprint."

"And you closed off the massage room?" O'Malley asked.

"Yes. I was very careful in my examination. That room is locked down, as is the tub where the victim was found."

"Good work," Sanchez said. "Did you take photos?"

"Yes. We didn't have access to a high-quality conventional camera, so we used my partner's big iPhone. We'll send those to you when the Internet is up."

"Good." Sanchez said. "Your partner is Tom Scott."

"That's right. He helped me with the photographs but otherwise stayed well back from the crime scenes," Kate said. "Investigator Oliver, did you find evidence that restraints were used during the interrogation of Malcolm Eastwick?"

"No. But I'm going to reexamine his clothing," Bruno said. "Eastwick was wearing clothes when we fished him out of the water. There weren't any obvious bruises on his wrists and ankles, but we might have missed something."

"So, Marshal Swift, are you suggesting that Eastwick was killed by a woman using the same M.O.?" Sanchez asked.

"Yes. My working hypothesis is that the perpetrator lured both victims into an assignation for the purpose of getting them into a vulnerable position. Then she drugged them in order to learn of the whereabout of a substantial amount of money." Kate paused and sipped tepid coffee. "This technique worked with Eastwick; he gave his assailant the combination for his safe. The technique didn't work with Moore because he didn't know anything."

"Why do you think that the perpetrator went after Moore?" O'Malley asked.

"I believe that the perpetrator realized that she had not obtained all the missing money when she opened Eastwick's safe, but she was not aware there was another safe in San Francisco.

She assumed that the remaining money was hidden on the Satori campus and that Moore, as the bookkeeper, knew where it was."

"But he didn't," Sanchez said. "Because Eastwick had taken the money to San Francisco." The detective looked at her associates. "Good work, Marshal. You're suggesting that the murderer is probably still on the Satori campus."

"Yes. Probably a board member or someone on the staff."

"I don't have to tell you to be careful."

"No, I understand the gravity of the situation. We've locked down the campus so no one can get in or out. When are you going to be able to get here?'

"Certainly not today," Sanchez said. "Maybe tomorrow if Cal Fire gets on top of the Garrapata blaze."

"Okay," Kate said. "In that case I want your help locking down communications. At the moment, the only working line is this landline in the main office. We can restrict that. As luck would have it, the internet connection has also been down; I'm not sure why. I want you to call the Satori Internet provider, Charter, and request that they disable the Satori router."

"I think that we can do that. Why?"

"Because I suspect that someone took a picture of Bryn Moore's body before we arrived, and I want to keep that from being broadcast on social media."

"Okay," O'Malley said. "But you understand that means the entire campus is cut off. Some of your board members may not like that."

"Tough," Kate said. "I have an investigation to do."

Sanchez chuckled. "Before you hang up, we should let you know what we found out about Greg Tanaka's automobile, a Mercedes Sedan with California plates 6TR244. This car was leased from Golden Gate Mercedes by Stephen Sato. Sato, real name Greg Yamamoto, is on the FBI watch list. He's a known bad guy wanted for a series of violent crimes."

"So, he was employed to come here, get the money from Eastwick, and take care of any problems," Kate said.

"Yes," Laura replied. "Except he ran into someone badder."

"Who's probably still here."

CHAPTER 33
(7:45AM): Tom

"So, we're on our own?" I said to Kate after the call.

"Yes. The Sheriff's Department will not be able to get here until tomorrow." Kate sighed. "I'm tired and hungry, let's get something to eat."

On our way out of the Satori main offices, Kate stopped at the main desk and asked Sequoyah to open the safe so she could retrieve her gun and handcuffs. "Best to be careful," Kate said, as she fastened the holster around her waist and slipped the cuffs into the front pocket of her US MARSHAL sweatshirt.

We stepped onto the path to the dining room. "How are you doing?" I asked.

Kate sighed and turned to me. "I'm frustrated. I was looking forward to spending the entire day in bed with you and now I can't."

"I'll make it up to you. In the future we can have many days in bed."

She kissed me and then stepped back. "That reminds me, you told Jean Little that we were going to take a little trip." She titled her head to one side and arched one eyebrow.

"Before we got together, last night, I was thinking about what we should do next, after we return to San Francisco. And it occurred to me that we should take a little trip and make sure we can stand each other every day. You know, there are couples who love each other, but maintain separate residences."

"I know that, but I don't understand it," Kate said. "My intent is to sleep with you every night. To be your partner."

"Me, too. But I suggest we take a little trip and make sure that everything works and, if so, then we can begin living together."

Kate's eyes misted. She took two deep breaths. "Okay. What were you thinking of?"

"Well, when I first had this idea, I imagined us backpacking in the Sierras. Then I remembered that I don't like sleeping on the ground."

"Or fucking on the ground."

I laughed. "That, too. So, I've been thinking about a nice resort or hotel."

"Not Las Vegas. That would be a showstopper."

"Not Las Vegas. I was thinking either Hawaii or Paris. Hawaii because it's warm and easy to get to. Paris because it's Paris."

"I would enjoy going to Hawaii with you but coming right after the workshop it's too much like Satori. I vote for Paris because we can stay in a comfortable bed, order room service, and go to art museums."

"You like art museums?"

"Duh. When I'm not working or at the Dojo, I paint."

"Did you tell me this? If you did, then I'm afraid I missed it."

"I thought I had, but maybe it was in the women's circle." Kate paused and looked over the Satori campus. "The only other time I have been to Satori was to do a painting workshop with Adam Wollstonecraft. My father was a painter; he thought it was a good way to dodge the stresses of cop-world. I love painting."

"So, you would be happy if we took a little trip to Paris?"

"Why are you asking me this, Tom? I would be crazy not to be happy. A vacation in Paris with my lover. What could be better?"

We went through the breakfast line and sat down with our workshop friends at the usual table by the west windows.

"Why are you wearing your US Marshal sweatshirt," Lucy asked Kate. "Did you have to deal with the dead body?"

When Kate started to answer, Julie interrupted. "What's wrong with your voice?"

"I think I caught Tom's cold," Kate said, pinching my leg under the table. She proceeded to tell them a sanitized version of our encounter with the cadaver.

"Sounds grim," Norma said.

"It was," Kate said. "But I learned an important thing this morning: Tom is not freaked out dealing with a dead body."

"What's going to happen now?" Julie asked.

"Well, after we finish eating breakfast," Kate said. "We have to move the decedent from the bath area to the cooler in the kitchen."

"I'll help," Julie said. "I've had a lot of experience moving around dead animals."

"I'm a doctor," Theo said.

"And I'll help," Norma said. "As a nurse I've seen more than my share of dead people."

Otto sighed. "I think I can do this. We'll be wearing gloves, right?"

"Of course," Kate said. "And you won't see the actual corpse. Tom and I and will go down first and wrap it in a sheet. Then we will wrap it a second time in canvas." She looked at the group. "Your gloved hands will only touch the canvas."

"In that case," Lucy said. "I think I can help, too. I'm kind of a wimp when it comes to dead people."

Just then David walked up to the table. "What's going on, Kate? I heard you and Tom got called out early to deal with the body in the bath area."

"Yes," Kate answered. "The situation is under control, but we need to move the cadaver out of the bath area into the kitchen refrigerator. I just recruited these guys to help so we're all going to be late to the workshop."

"It's a strange new team-building exercise," David said. "That's fine. Take your time. We'll start without you." He walked off.

Kate spoke to our friends. "Let's get this done and go on to the workshop."

We left the dining room and walked down the path to the point where Wendy and Johnny were still guarding the bath entrance. "We're going to move the body," Kate explained.

"We can help," Wendy said.

"I think we've got it handled. I'll let you know."

When we got to the dressing area, Kate and I went inside the utility closet and grabbed a king-size sheet and a gray tarpaulin. "Tom and I will go ahead and wrap the body," Kate told the group. "When it's done, we'll call you in."

We walked past the showers and came to the table where Moore's body lay. Kate and I put on gloves, wrapped the body in the king-size sheet, and called our friends to the table.

Kate handed out gloves. The group wrapped Moore's corpse in the tarpaulin, lifted it up, and proceeded out of the bath area. We went up the trail and stopped where Wendy and Johnny were guarding the path.

"You can remove this barrier," Kate said. "We can let everyone back into the bath area but cordon off the area around the tub where we found the body and the table where I examined it."

"Okay," Wendy said. "We know what to do."

Kate and I and the others carried Moore's corpse on up the trail. When we reached the top, we turned to the right to avoid the main entrance to the dining room, trying to attract as little attention as possible. Nonetheless, several people watched from the windows as we skirted the main area and entered the kitchen back door. One of the workers showed us where the big cooler was. We opened the door and laid down Moore's body onto a stainless-steel tray. *This is a very weird experience*, I thought, as the cooler door slammed shut.

⚬⚭⚬

After stopping at the restroom, Kate and I grabbed coffee and walked up hill to the workshop.

When we entered, and took our regular seats, David stopped talking and turned to Kate. "Marshal Swift, before we move on with our next exercise, perhaps you can explain to us what's been going on this morning."

Kate stood up. "Not all of you know that I am a US Marshal."

"What happened to your voice?" Lois asked.

"Too much singing in the hot tub," Kate started to say.

Lucy interrupted her. "Actually, too much screaming."

The group laughed.

Kate blushed and gave Lucy a soft punch in the arm. "Anyway. I've been here off duty, but this morning the Sheriff's Department asked me to help, because one of the cleaning crew found a dead body in the bath. The Sheriff couldn't get here because Highway One is blocked."

"How long will it be blocked?" Tammy asked.

"We think a day or two. They asked me to conduct the initial investigation to ensure an orderly inquiry, protect the corpse and crime scene, and to reopen most of the bath area."

"You regard this as a crime scene?" Theo asked.

"We regard this as a death in suspicious circumstances."

216

There was a low hum of conversation and then Cheryl spoke. "Do you think that this death is connected to the demise of Malcolm Eastwick?"

"I can't talk about that."

"Is this why access to the Satori campus is blocked?" Lucky asked.

"Yes. Because of the suspicious circumstances, we're treating this as a crime scene. We want everyone to stay on campus until we've had a chance to conduct a thorough investigation."

"Do you think we are in danger?" Tammy asked. "Is this like one of those movies where there is a party and then the lights go out and people start getting murdered?"

"I don't watch those movies," Kate said. "But no, I don't think any of you are in danger, but I will take every precaution to ensure you are safe."

There was a buzz of conversation.

"Does anyone else have questions for Marshal Swift?" David asked.

Rory raised his hand. "Do you know when the Internet will come back up?"

"I'm not sure. I think there's a problem with the router."

David looked around the room. "Okay, if there are no further questions, let's get back to work."

Bruce James entered the room. "Sorry to interrupt, David and Cheryl. Is it okay if I borrow Marshal Swift? The board wants to be briefed."

"Do you want me to go with you?" I asked Kate after she followed Bruce out of the conference room.

She stopped and looked at me. "Here's the problem, Tom. I know from experience that if I walk into that group with a man, particularly a handsome man who is taller than me, the crowd won't take me seriously. All the questions will be directed at you, even though you're not a peace officer."

I sighed. "That makes sense. But I don't want to be separated from you. And I do know this crowd." I took her hand. "How about if we walk down to the conference center together, then you go inside, while I sneak around to the deck entrance and watch?"

Kate clenched my hand. "Okay. I want to be with you, too. But you need to give me space to do my job."

"Are you going to tell them about the disappearance of Greg Tanaka?" I asked. "I noticed that you didn't mention it when you spoke to our workshop."

"No. I don't want people to freak out hearing that in the last four days, we believe that three people have been murdered here and we think the assailant is still on campus."

I took Kate's hand. "I'm not freaked out."

She smiled. "When you touch me, I freak out but that's a good thing."

We held hands and followed Bruce James north to the old conference center.

"Our guests are unhappy they can't leave," Bruce said.

"Uh huh," Kate said.

"Do you think this is connected to Malcolm's death?"

"Might be." Kate said. "My father was a homicide detective in Fresno. He always said his number one rule was to be careful and to do the investigation by the book. In this case, 'the book' means making sure that everyone is interviewed."

"Okay. You need to tell that to our guests."

We walked in silence to the old conference center. When Kate stepped onto the front porch, I went around to the back. The Satori board, and their guests, were in the great room, which was set with small tables. The crowed was drinking coffee and eating pastries.

Bruce James stopped at the great-room door and announced, "Ladies and gentlemen, I know that you have questions about what's going on. I've brought you the person in charge, US Marshal Kate Swift." He stepped back.

Kate stepped forward. "I met some of you last night when I was at your fundraiser. I'm here on vacation, attending a workshop. However, I am an active-duty US Marshal. The Monterey County Sheriff's Department knew that and asked me, this morning, to take charge of the investigation until they arrive."

There was a murmur of voices.

Kate spoke louder. "This morning, shortly after 6AM, the Sheriff's Department contacted me because the bathhouse cleaning crew found a dead body in a tub. The Sheriff's Detectives couldn't get here because Highway One is blocked."

Again, a buzz of voices.

"I investigated and found a male dead in a tub. Further analysis indicated there were suspicious circumstances. As a consequence, the Sheriff's Department asked that the campus be locked down."

Murmurs of disapproval. Someone shouted, "This is an outrage."

I slipped into the back of the room.

Bruce James stepped forward. "Marshall Swift, how long do you believe the campus will be shut down?"

"I'm not sure. Highway one is blocked in both directions. I can't imagine it will stay closed more than a day or two."

"My client has an important engagement in Los Angeles," a well-dressed woman said. *Roddy Gallagher's agent*, I thought. "Can we arrange for a helicopter to land here, so he can keep his appointment?"

"I'm sorry but I cannot permit that," Kate said. "My instructions are to keep everyone here until they can be interviewed by the Sheriff's Department."

Gwyneth Jones, Jerry Kermit's date raised her hand. "Marshall Swift, do you believe that the latest death is connected to the death of Malcolm Eastwick?"

"It could be. Both deaths occurred under suspicious circumstances."

"I thought Malcolm's death was an accident?" Gwyneth asked.

"The Monterey medical examiner has yet to make a determination," Kate said.

"So," Monique said, "There is a possibility that Malcolm and the man found in the baths were both murdered?"

"That's a possibility, but it's up to the Monterey County Sheriff's Department to make that determination."

"So, we could be at risk?"

"My job is to ensure that you are safe," Kate said. "The institute staff and I will work to ensure that."

There were hostile mutterings. Roddy Gallagher nodded at a large man lounging against the back wall. The man walked through the crowd and approached Kate. "I hear what you say, Marshall Swift, but my client will be safer with me than with you."

I moved forward in the room, but Kate motioned me back. "Who are you and who is your client?"

"My name is Ivan, and I am chief of security for Roddy Gallagher."

"Nice to meet you, Ivan. Now sit down."

"I'm removing my client from this location."

"That's not happening."

"What are you going to do, honey? Shoot me?"

"I won't have to shoot you, Ivan." Kate raised her voice. "It's a federal crime to interfere with a US Marshal in the performance of her duty. In addition, you should know that I have a Taekwondo black belt."

"Sure you do, honey." Ivan stepped forward and raised two giant hands as if to throw Kate out of the way.

Kate moved so fast that her hands were almost a blur. Her right fist hit Ivan in the solar plexus and left chopped down on his neck. Ivan fell forward like a stone statue, so hard that the floor shook. *Oh my god, he's dead*, I thought before I heard Ivan moan.

"Tom," Kate said. "Pull his arms behind him." I ran forward and did what she said and Kate cuffed Ivan behind his back.

"Now search his legs for weapons." I patted his left leg and found a sheath knife; I patted his right leg and found a small handgun in a holster attached to a Velcro band. I pulled both off.

Roddy Gallagher got up from his chair and stepped forward. "Tom, this is all a big misunderstanding, I'm sure that you and I can come to an accommodation."

I picked up the handgun, still in the holster. "Sit the fuck down, Roddy. Your bodyguard just threatened my partner. Very bad mistake." My voice was shaking.

"Tom, put down the gun," Kate said in a calm, raspy voice.

I put the gun in my right pocket. I put Ivan's knife in my other pocket. I took a deep breath and stood up.

Kate removed another gun from Ivan. She shoved it in the center pocket of her US Marshall's sweatshirt then turned to Bruce James. "Bruce, I want you and your staff to write down the names and contact information for everyone in this room." She turned to face the audience. "You all have been witnesses to an attempted assault on a US Marshal. You all may be contacted by a US Attorney." She took a deep breath. "In the meantime, Ivan will be removed from these premises and housed in..." she looked at Bruce James.

"I guess the infirmary."

"Ivan will be housed in the infirmary. You all will remain here. The institute staff and I will provide for your security. Get up Ivan."

Ivan staggered to his feet. His nose was purple.

"Go out the door and head up the hill," Kate ordered. Ivan left the room and we followed.

There was a smattering of applause.

"Tom, find out where the infirmary is."

Marcia Ball was on the porch. "I can show you."

She walked ahead of Bruno as we trudged back towards the main building.

"How are you?" I asked Kate.

"Ask me in a few minutes." She said with a slight quiver.

It turned out that the infirmary was a sterile set of rooms next to the executive offices. One of the rooms had a hospital bed and a toilet.

"This is perfect," Kate said. "It has a door that can be locked from the outside and no window."

We walked into the room and Kate instructed Ivan, who was glaring at her, to sit on the chair.

"Marcia, you should wait outside." Kate said and waited until Marcia left the infirmary space. "Ivan, here's what's going to happen. Tom is going to remove your shoes, belt and pants. We're also going to take your wallet and your phone. We're going to put all of these in a safe."

Ivan nodded.

I took Ivan's clothes and dumped them in the hall.

"You're going to be kept in here until the Sheriff's Department shows up and then they will determine the next steps."

"I want to talk to an attorney."

"When there's phone service, we will arrange for you to talk to an attorney. In the meantime, I want you to promise to behave yourself. If you do, I will remove your cuffs and you will be served regular Satori food. If you don't, I will cuff you to this bed and you will be served oatmeal and water."

"I will behave."

Kate handed me the handcuff key. "I will stand here and Tom will remove your cuffs. If you touch Tom or try to escape, I will kneecap you."

Ivan nodded.

I removed the handcuffs and Ivan didn't move. Kate and I backed out of the room and I picked up Ivan's clothes.

When we exited the infirmary, Marcia was waiting. She locked the door and handed Kate the key.

"Now we need to put Ivan's clothes in the safe.'

We followed Marcia back to the executive suite. No one was around. "I know the combination," Marcia said. She pulled back the Satori picture, dialed the combination, and opened the safe. Kate rolled Ivan's clothes into a compact bundle and shoved them to the back of the steel chamber.

"Thanks," Kate said to Marcia. "Tom and I are going to go into the vacant office and make a call."

"Okay. Let me know if you need anything." Marcia left the executive suite.

Kate and I went into the vacant office. I closed the door.

Kate wrapped her arms around me. Her body was shaking all over. "Oh God, I hate this shit."

I kissed her hair.

"Thank God you are here, Tom. I want you to hold me forever."

"I thought you were remarkable, Kate. You were so cool."

"I didn't feel cool. I thought, 'These people expect me to protect them, and I don't know what's going on.'"

"And then Ivan."

"That fucking Ivan. What an asshole. He made me so angry and then, for a moment, I thought I might have killed him."

"You didn't though."

"What's his story? Who is Roddy Gallagher?"

I laughed. "You don't know who Roddy Gallagher is? He's a big action-movie star."

"Really? Do you and Roddy have a history?"

"Roddy and Fiona had a history. He was always trying to hit on her and she was always telling him to fuck off. One time he had the balls to tell me that if she slept with him, he would give her a million-dollar movie contract."

"No shit."

"God's truth."

"But you wouldn't shoot him, would you?"

I laughed. "I don't even know how to operate a gun. I just pointed the thing in his direction because I was pissed off that he had his goon go after you."

"And you stepped forward to protect me."

"Yes, even though I didn't know what the fuck I was doing."

"Were you scared? Did it upset you when I used my martial-arts skills?"

"No. I was impressed and turned on." I smiled. "The only time I've been scared with you was last night when we were making love. I got so excited that I thought I might have a heart attack."

DEATH IS POTENTIAL • BOB BURNETT

Kate laughed loudly. "I thought of that, too. In the middle of the night, I thought, 'It would be ironic if I have a heart attack after I have my first complete orgasm.'" She tipped her head back and kissed me.

"We need to keep each other healthy."

Kate held me close. "You've been a good boy, Tom. You deserve a reward."

I got an erection.

Kate chuckled. "Your body wants to be rewarded."

I tightened my clasp. "That's because you've turned me into a horny seventeen-year-old. On the exterior I may look like forty-year-old business executive. On the inside I'm a pool of molten testosterone."

"Sounds hot." Kate ground against me.

I leaned to the left and locked the office door.

Kate dropped to her knees and unzipped my jeans. She pulled my erect penis out of my shorts. "You've turned me into a naughty girl." She licked my glans and then slid her mouth over me and began sucking noisily.

I moaned.

"Not so loud," Kate said. "they'll hear us." She resumed sucking.

I bit down on my sweatshirt sleeve.

When I thought I couldn't hold out any longer, I pulled Kate's head back. "We can do this another time, but right now I want you to join me in my 'improvement' over last night's sexual gymnastics."

Kate stood up and smiled. "Tom's fantasy."

"First we both remove our clothes." Kate and I stripped naked.

"Now I make sure that you're ready." I dropped to my knees and licked her vagina and clitoris.

"Next I sit on the edge of this table." I moved back and sat on the redwood table with my feet tapping the floor.

"Now, you, athletic Kate, climb on the table."

Kate bounded up.

"Finally, you very carefully sit on my penis and wrap your arms and legs around me."

Kate slid onto my erection. We both moaned. She was looking almost directly at me.

"As I hoped, we can now kiss as we enjoy each other."

I gripped her firm butt with my both my hands and pulled her up as Kate's mouth closed over mine. She wrapped her strong arms around my chest, and we rocked back and forth.

I grabbed Kate's US MARSHALL sweatshirt and pulled it over one shoulder. "When we let go, we can bite down on this."

Kate murmured. "This is so good. I keep thinking it can't get any better and it does." Her *oohs* turned into growls. "Oh, so good. I'm losing it." Kate's body shook and then she screamed into the sweatshirt.

I kissed her face. Licked the tears from her eye lids.

She tightened her grip on me. "Oh my God."

My chest was constricted but I kept kissing her.

"Do me a favor, Tom. Never let go of me." Kate gasped for breath. She loosened her arms and pulled her head back. "You didn't come."

"I got so absorbed in pleasing you that I didn't."

"That's not fair."

"It's okay. It'll all balance out."

She shook her head. "I've been down this road before." Kate affected a whiney voice, "I'm sorry, girl. I'll take care of you next time." She ran her tongue over my lips. "Do what I say, or you will be disciplined."

My penis snapped to attention.

"Look into my eyes." Kate began to move up and down on my penis. "Good. I can feel you expanding." She chortled. "Like a balloon that is getting larger and larger."

My heart was pounding.

"Bite down on the sweatshirt, Tom."

I moaned.

"You're getting bigger and bigger. Now is the time to explode, to fill me up."

I let go and screamed into the sweatshirt.

We heard knocking on the office door.

CHAPTER 34
(11:30 AM): Laura

"What's up?" Kate Swift rasped.

"Your voice sounds terrible," Laura said. "Are you sure you only have allergies? You sound like you might have bronchitis."

Laura heard muffled laughing in the background.

"Or maybe you are having too much fun?" Laura heard Kate chuckle.

"Sergeant O'Malley is here. I'm going to put you on speakerphone. We want to tell you what we learned from the FBI."

"They're cooperating?"

"I know, big surprise. But, for whatever reason, they are cooperating."

"What did they say?"

"The San Francisco office has been investigating Malcolm Eastwick for involvement in money laundering."

"I thought it was something like that," Kate said. "Where's the money come from?"

"They think Eastwick was getting money from the Russian Mafia and washing it through Satori subsidiaries."

DEATH IS POTENTIAL · BOB BURNETT

They heard a muffled conversation.

Laura spoke. "Tom says that Satori has been holding workshops with Russian 'intellectuals.' That's probably the basis for the contact with the Mafia."

"That makes sense," Sanchez said. "Anyway, the FBI thinks that the cash in the safe wasn't being skimmed by Eastwick; it was merely the latest installment in a long-standing relationship."

"So, Eastwick was getting paid as part of the 'investment stream' from the Satori licenses?"

"That's what the FBI thinks."

"How did the FBI find out about this?" Kate asked.

"That's why we called you. They got an anonymous phone tip."

"How does that help?"

"The caller was a woman, and the call was made from a cell-phone in your area."

"There's no cell tower here," Kate said.

"We know," Sanchez said. "The FBI used their technology to trace the call to a router on the Satori campus."

"So, the informant was a woman calling from here," Kate said.

"Exactly. Another reason for you to be very careful."

CHAPTER 35
(11:40am): Tom

Kate and I got dressed. "Should we go to lunch?" I asked.

Kate chuckled. "I've decided I'm going to alternate between my two identities: responsible adult and naughty teenager. My responsible adult is going to get a quick shower. Then I'll meet you at the dining room."

"In that case I will force my horny teenager to take a bath and join you for lunch." I paused. "Before you leave, I have something to ask you."

"Okay."

"You said you were 'inexperienced' sexually but then you taught me a wonderful tantric sex ritual. Where did that come from?"

Kate giggled. "From my 'Introduction to Tantric Sex' DVD."

"Did you try that with Earle?"

"No way," Kate said. "I bought it as a kind of present for myself, hoping someday I would find the right partner to join me in the exercises." She kissed me. "And here you are."

❦

Kate and I met at the lunch line, loaded our plates, and sat down our workshop friends.

"Is it true you coldcocked Roddy Gallagher's bodyguard?" Lucy asked Kate.

The others pressed close to hear her response.

"Mr. Gallagher's associate would not obey the lawful order of a US Marshal," Kate said. "He initiated an assault and I responded with reasonable force."

"He went down like a giant redwood," I added.

"How big was he?" Otto asked.

"About the same size as Shaq," I said.

"Who's that?" Kate asked.

"Shaquille O'Neal, a former basketball player." I turned to Otto. "Ivan is a very big Russian."

"I bet Roddy Gallagher peed his pants," Lucy chortled.

"Tom threatened to shoot him," Kate said.

"No way." Lucy and the others leaned forward.

"For just a moment, I lost my cool," I said.

"Apparently, Tom and Roddy have a history," Kate said.

"Tell us about it," Lucy said.

"I don't like Roddy's attitude and I was particularly incensed that he sent his goon after Kate, so I pointed a gun at him."

"Technically, Tom pointed a holster at him," Kate said. "The gun was in a holster and Tom doesn't know much about guns."

Everybody laughed.

"Where is the bodyguard now?" Aoife asked.

"There's no regular detention facility here," Kate said. "So, we locked him a room in the infirmary."

"He won't be a problem," I said. "We took his shoes and pants."

The group laughed and began to ask Kate questions.

"That reminds me," I said to Kate. "We should take some food to Ivan."

"You go through the line again and then I'll go with you to his room."

When we got to the infirmary room, Kate shouted through the door, "We're here with lunch, Ivan. Stand back from the door."

Kate unlocked the door and peered inside. Ivan was sitting in a chair reading an old copy of National Geographic.

I set the tray on the floor. Kate relocked the door.

Bruce James met us as we left the infirmary. "Do you have time to talk to Roddy? I think he wants to apologize."

"I have no interest in talking to him," Kate said. "Why don't you handle this, partner." She walked off in the direction of the dining room.

I followed James into his office where Roddy Gallagher was sitting in a chair. He was wearing an unusual tan leather coat.

"Nice jacket, Roddy."

"I'm glad you like it. One of a kind. From the skin of an albino Mongolian yak."

Bruce James cleared his throat. "Roddy, you had something to say to Tom and the Marshal."

"That's right. I apologize for our little kerfuffle. I want to set things right with us."

"It was more than a 'kerfuffle.' Ivan attacked my partner."

"And she taught him a valuable lesson. I'm sure Ivan is as embarrassed as I am."

Bruce James rubbed his hands together. "Mr. Gallagher is thinking of making a donation to the Institute if charges are dropped."

What a surprise, I thought. "How much?" I asked Roddy.

"Fifty grand and we'll throw some business your way."

"We already do business with you, Roddy. We're providing protection when you perform at Coachella." I stroked my forehead. "Of course, I have to discuss this with my partner, but I believe she would be willing to drop all charges for a $250,000 donation." *And then she wouldn't have to spend days filling out all the Federal paperwork.*

"That's a lot of money," Roddy said.

"But better to spend that money than see a headline in *The Reporter* that reads, 'Roddy Gallagher involved in drunken battle at celebrity benefit.'"

Roddy sat back in his chair and studied me. "You're probably right."

"Let me talk to Kate."

"She's quite a woman," Roddy said. "I don't suppose she would be interested in being in my next picture?"

"I thought Sheena was your costar?"

"Sadly, she has developed a substance abuse problem."

"I'll ask Kate, but I suspect her answer will be no. She's expressed interest in a new business development."

"What's that?" Bruce asked.

"I'm afraid it's too early to talk about in public." *And I haven't figured out what it is.*

I stood up and stuck out my hand. Roddy shook it. "Or you could give me your coat," I said.

"Sorry, Tom. I'm very fond of this coat."

I walked back to the dining room where Kate was talking to Aoife, Lucy, and Julie. "What did Roddy have to say?"

"He apologizes for the little 'kerfuffle.'"

"Kerfuffle?"

"His word. He requested that we overlook what happened in return for a substantial donation to the Institute."

"How much?"

"Two hundred and fifty grand."

The women gasped. "This is why I let Tom handle our business affairs," Kate chuckled.

"Of course, I said that you would make the decision."

Kate tilted her head to one side. "Yes. That way I don't have to fill out any of the fucking paperwork."

"What about Ivan?"

"We'll leave him there until Roddy gives Bruce James a check. Then we'll let him go but keep his gun." Kate kissed me. "Good job, partner."

"Oh. One more thing. Roddy asked if you would be interested in being in his next picture."

"You should do it," Lucy blurted.

"In twenty-four hours, I've had two movie offers," Kate laughed.

"What was the other one?" Julie asked.

"At last night's fundraiser, some bozo producer asked me if I'd be in his latest epic. I don't know the name."

"The sequel to 'Space Pussy.'"

All the women squealed.

"And now Roddy Gallagher wants me to be in the latest episode of 'Mission Improbable.'"

"Why don't you want to do it?" Lucy asked.

"Because Tom and I are in the process of..." Kate paused, tilted her head to one side, and smiled, "Reallocating our assets."

"What does that mean?" Aoife chuckled.

"It means that we are considering a joint business venture," I said. "This is confidential but Kate and I thinking about starting a home for wayward girls and women."

Everyone laughed.

"I want to be in it," Lucy said.

"You will be our anchor tenant."

"I'll be in veterinary school, but can I come on the weekends?" Julie asked.

"I have an eleven-year-old daughter, Siobhan, who would be perfect," Aoife said.

"It's settled then," Kate said, wrapping her left arm around my waist. "Instead of becoming a Hollywood movie star, I'm going into business with Tom."

At 2PM, Kate and I went back to the Transitions workshop and took our accustomed seats in the group. "Welcome back Kate and Tom," Cheryl said. "We hope that your afternoon will be calmer than the morning." Everyone laughed.

"This week there's been a lot of talk and concern about death. David and I decided to build on this and do a classic Gestalt death exercise. Please choose a partner."

"Will you be my partner?" Kate asked, tilting her head to one side, with her characteristic smile.

"My pleasure." I slid my pillow out and sat across from her.

"Once you have a partner, meditate on this situation: You've just been told that you're going to die in thirty days. You're sitting with your partner, and you tell them what you'd like to do in your final days. This can be simple or complex but should come from the heart. Take a few minutes and then decide which of you will begin; that person will talk for ten minutes. We'll call the time. Then the roles will switch, and the previous speaker will become the listener and vice-versa. Any questions?" There were none. "Okay, let's begin."

"I want to go first," Kate said, "because there is something that I have been meaning to tell you: I really appreciated the support you have given me this morning."

"You're welcome," I said, "but I'm your partner."

"I know but consider what you've done this morning. You didn't have to go with me to the baths, but you did. You didn't have to help me deal with the corpse, but you did. You didn't have to go with me to talk to the donors, but you did. You didn't have to help me deal with Ivan, but you did."

I interrupted. "I didn't really do anything."

"But you were willing to confront Ivan, who is a beast. Most men would have backed off, but you stepped up. You helped me deal with Ivan and with Roddy. You negotiated a reasonable settlement." Kate paused to take a breath. "You are supporting me."

"Of course." I took her hand.

Kate teared up. "Being a female US Marshal is lonely. Since my father died, I haven't had strong support. Bad shit happens, I deal with it, and then I go home and brood, because I have no one to talk to." She clasped my hand. "Now I have you." She pounded her free hand on her heart.

"I am your partner."

"You are and I can't tell you how much it means to me." Kate paused and looked off into space. She looked back at me and then frowned.

"What is it?"

"Nothing." She shook her head. "It's my ambivalence showing up. I'm worried there is something about you that I don't know about, something I would hate."

"Like what?"

"Like maybe you have one of those yappy little dogs."

"So," I laughed. "If I owned a Chihuahua, that would be a showstopper?"

"I'm afraid so," Kate chortled.

"Fortunately, I don't own any pets." I reached out for her hand. "You're not a Republican, are you?"

"God no. Do I act like a Republican?"

"No." I pulled her closer. "You seem like a tidy person. Am I right?"

"OCD some would say. Are you the kind of guy who drops their dirty clothes on the floor and never picks them up?"

"No. Also, OCD." I kissed her hand. "Here's the big one: what do you think about taking out the garbage?"

Kate laughed. "I live alone. I take out my own garbage." She sighed. "I took out Earle."

"And Elmer," I chuckled. "It sounds like we are perfectly compatible, but I recommend a shake-down cruise."

"I'm ready."

I leaned closer and lowered my voice. "My penis wants to know if you'd be interested in a play date."

"Before we do that – before I quit being responsible adult and become naughty teenager -- there's something else I need to tell you," Kate said. "I am seriously thinking about leaving the Marshal's service. I know that it's a bad idea to change your vocation at the same time you are entering a new relationship, but there it is."

"Okay. You don't have to decide right away. You can think about this while we are taking our 'shake-down cruise.'"

Kate laughed. "I know. But I wanted to be honest with you, there's a part of me that wants to nestle in your arms and be your..." she searched for a word, "concubine."

"That sounds good to me, but I bet it would get boring for you after a while."

"Time," Cheryl said. "The talker becomes the listener and vice-versa."

"What did Fiona want to do in her final days?" Kate asked.

"She was tired, so she didn't want to do something like take a big trip." I ran my hand across my forehead. "She tried to work as long as she could because she enjoyed that. And then she hung out with me and Stella, her sister. And her friends."

"Did Fiona have a hobby?"

"When I first met her, she danced. She'd studied ballet and she was in a small independent dance company in the city. Then we got involved and our business grew, and she didn't have the time to dance." I paused. "She kept in shape, but she wasn't as athletic as you and she didn't have a hobby like painting."

"Do you have a hobby?"

"Not like you. I work out, at the Olympic Club. At night, I listen to jazz and read."

"I like jazz; my father listened to jazz."

"Who did he like?"

"Dave Brubeck. Miles Davis. Django something."

"Django Reinhardt. When we go to Paris, if you want, we can go to a jazz club."

"I'd like that." Kate leaned forward. "What do you read?"

"Fiction. I'm always looking for a really good book." I took her hand. "When I was at Stanford, I was an unusual techy in the sense that I liked literature classes. Sometimes I read poetry and plays."

"Like Shakespeare?"

"I like Shakespeare, but I haven't read any recently. Occasionally, I see a Shakespeare play."

"Can I ask you something?"

"Of course."

"When we are together, in the city, could we read Shakespeare together? My mother and father used to do that."

"We could read plays in the nude."

Kate laughed. "Not 'King Lear.'"

"What about 'As You Like It?'"

Kate grinned and shook her head, as if to say *You're incorrigible*. "Tell me what you would want to do if you only had thirty days to live?"

"Pretty much what you and I plan to do: hang out and go to Paris. Oh, and go to New Orleans. For some reason, I've never visited New Orleans. I'd like to go there and listen to jazz and blues."

"That sounds like another trip we should take."

We paused and studied each other.

"Is there anything bad about you that I should know?" Kate said with a smile, tilting her head to one side.

"Nothing that I think you don't already know. I'm impulsive. Like when I started to get between you and Ivan; even though he probably would have kicked my ass."

"Impulsive but brave."

I felt vaguely embarrassed. "And, if I don't watch myself, these days I will work way too much."

"Join the club."

"Fiona and I acted as checks on each other. One of us would say: 'time for fun.' And we'd go do something fun."

"Like?"

"Go dancing. Or go to Yosemite for the weekend."

"I'm ready," Kate said.

"Time," Cheryl called out.

CHAPTER 36
(5:15PM): Laura

"Thanks for calling, Marshall Swift," Laura Sanchez said. "Sergeant O'Malley is here. I'm going to put you on the speakerphone."

"What's up?"

"Nothing on our investigation, here. We want you to help us out some more. It turns out that the Garrapata fire is bigger than they thought. We're not going to be able to get to Satori tomorrow. For that reason, we need you to interview some of the folks that we would have talked to, the people that worked with Bryn Moore, particularly the administrative staff."

"Fine. I would be glad to do that."

Sergeant O'Malley spoke up. "We want you to tape these. You don't have to read the interviewees their rights, but we don't want anyone else present."

"You don't want my boyfriend, Tom, to be present." *How stupid does he think I am?* "Of course."

"Let us know what you find out, Kate."

243

"That was fast, Kate," Laura said, when Kate called back two hours later.

"What did you learn, Marshal?" O'Malley asked.

"I'll let you be the judge." Kate cleared her throat. "I began by interviewing Bruce James. He had no idea who would harm Mr. Moore. He claimed that he was an exemplary employee, who pretty much kept to himself." Kate paused. "I felt something was off, so I pushed him on the nature of 'Bryn Moore's relationship with Malcolm Eastwick. Bruce James hemmed and hawed and then said, 'This is all hearsay, but I think they had (ahem) an unusual relationship.'"

"Meaning what?" O'Malley asked.

"Meaning that Bruce James believed that Malcolm Eastwick and Bryn Moore had a sexual relationship."

"Sounds like Eastwick was boinking everyone," O'Malley said. Sanchez laughed.

"Next, I interviewed Carl Oliver, the HR guy. He knew nothing. He'd met Bryn Moore, because they worked in the administrative offices, but he claimed he didn't know him socially. Oliver has only been on the job for two months."

"No complaints about Moore?" Sanchez asked.

"I asked and Oliver said Moore's personnel jacket was clean."

"Who else did you talk to?" O'Malley asked.

"Next, I talked to Marcia Ball, the Satori development director. She claimed to have a cordial relationship with Moore and had no idea why anyone would kill him. I could tell she was lying, but at the time I had no idea how to get her to open up."

"Why did you believe she was lying?" Laura asked.

"She had two tells: whenever she got ready to lie, she would look up into the corner of the room, and she would wring her hands."

"Good catch," Laura said.

"Thanks. Next, I interviewed Sequoyah the administrative assistant, real name Simone Wertheimer. She's getting ready to leave Satori, feeling that she is not working in the 'psychologically mature' organization she was led to believe it was. She admitted that, to use your words Sergeant, everyone was 'boinking' everyone. Sequoyah said that she slept with Malcolm Eastwick to get her job; she said that after that one night, he treated her 'like dirt.' She said that Bryn Moore and Malcolm Eastwick had an ongoing sexual relationship; she felt it meant more to Moore than to Eastwick, whom she described as 'an amoral dickhead.' Sequoyah indicated that Marcia Ball had had a sexual relationship with Eastwick but that it was over; next Marcia Ball had a relationship with Bruce James, but it also had ended. She indicated that James now has a long-term relationship with a Carmel psychotherapist named Mary. Sequoyah believed that Marcia Ball and Bryn Moore had a sexual relationship of 'convenience.'"

"What does that mean?" Laura asked.

"Sequoyah indicated that Moore sold favors. And that Marcia Ball periodically paid him to service her."

"He was a male escort?" O'Malley asked.

"However you want to describe it, Brynn Scott apparently turned tricks for money or drugs."

"Lord have mercy," O'Malley said.

"Do you want to ask questions, or shall I continue?" Kate asked.

"Continue, please," Laura said.

"There's a founders' office in the administrative section. Apparently, Malcolm used it intermittently. Since his demise, it's been occupied by Cheryl Taylor, the last remaining founder. She signs certain documents, such as Bruce James' paycheck."

"You interviewed her?" Laura asked.

"Cheryl showed up as I was ending my interview with Sequoyah, so I interviewed her."

"And?" O'Malley asked.

"You're aware that Cheryl is one of the leaders of the workshop that I'm in?"

"Yes."

"Given that I have somewhat of a personal relationship, I was circumspect with her. I asked her about Bryn Moore, and she said she didn't know him well; she indicated he was one of Malcolm's clients."

"Malcolm was Moore's therapist?" Laura asked.

"That's what Cheryl said."

"He was 'boinking' his client," O'Malley said.

"That seems to be the case," Kate said. "I asked Cheryl about Marcia Ball, but she wouldn't talk about her as Marcia is one of her clients."

"What else?" Laura asked.

"I asked Cheryl if she knew about the money said to be missing from the Satori accounts, she indicated that Bruce James had informed her of the situation. Cheryl said that when her husband, Richard Staybrook died, she and Malcolm agreed that he would become the Satori managing partner."

"What does that mean?" O'Malley asked.

"They agreed that Malcolm would handle the business side of Satori."

"Anything else?"

"I told Cheryl that I had heard rumors that Malcolm had 'inappropriate' relationships with his therapy clients. Cheryl laughed and indicated that had been a long-term problem. She said that because of client complaints Malcolm had been placed on probation by the California agency that credentials psychotherapists. Apparently, he had cut back on his practice and, therefore, had some money problems."

"Did you ask Cheryl who she thought killed Bryn Moore?" O'Malley asked.

"No. Given the context, I didn't think that would be a useful line of questioning."

"Thank you, Kate," Laura said. "I'm very impressed by the results of your interviews."

"Amen," O'Malley said.

"One more thing," Kate said. "Can I examine Bryn Moore's cottage?"

"Good idea," O'Malley said.

"Can I have my partner, Tom, accompany me?"

"Yes," Laura said. "Just don't use the bed."

Both women laughed.

CHAPTER 37
(7:15PM): Tom

After the afternoon workshop session, Kate and I took a break. She returned to the room she shared with Norma to wash her hair. I returned to my cottage, straightened up, and then took a brief but satisfying nap. I woke up at six-thirty and hit the dining-room dinner line just before it closed. I didn't see Kate, so I grabbed enough food that she would have something if she was running late. That turned out to be propitious; when I sat down at our usual table, Norma handed me Kate's note that explained she was tied up doing interviews for the Sheriff's Department.

At 7:45Pm Kate ran in and sat down next to me. "Thanks for saving me food, I was running errands for Laura and O'Malley."

"How'd it go?"

"I'll tell you later."

❦

At a little bit after eight, Kate and I went to the last evening session of the Transitions workshop and sat in our accustomed seats. I noticed that Lois and Tammy were sitting close together.

"I think Lois and Tammy hooked up," Lucy whispered.

"Welcome to what normally would be the last session of the Transitions workshop," David said. "Usually, we have a talent show tonight, but considering the circumstances, we decided against it."

Cheryl shifted forward, "We thought that we would open up the group so that any of you who haven't had a chance to fully express yourselves could."

Across the room, I saw Lois nudge Tammy, who slowly got to her feet. I noticed that instead of dressing like she was about to play golf at the country club, Tammy was wearing more casual clothes and a grey-brown shawl around her shoulders. She'd let her hair down into a long braid. "I don't know what I expected when I came here. I was stuck in loveless relationship and couldn't see a way out. And then Lois befriended me."

"I bet she 'befriended' her," Kate whispered.

I bit my tongue.

"Mama bear," Lucy whispered. "Can you teach me about befriending?"

Kate, Julie, and I struggled not to crack up.

David shot us a "get it together" look.

Fortunately, Tammy didn't hear us.

Tammy took a long time to tell us that Lois had helped her understand that "love has many faces" and, in the process, Tammy had experienced a level of sexual pleasure she hadn't known before. I was happy for Tammy, but I couldn't fully appreciate what she had to share because I kept dozing off. Several times, Kate woke me by whispering, "Tom, you're snoring."

"Who wants to go next?" Cheryl asked.

Rory raised his hand. He explained that he had met a new girl in the work-study group, but instead of asking her to go to the baths he was "going slow." Rory got accolades for this, but I wondered how long his restraint would last. *Rory needs a real father*, I said to myself and wondered if I had the time to take him on as "project."

Aoife raised her hand. She'd received a phone call from her husband, who was home caring for their daughters. The Berkeley police had arrested her stalker, Ray, for setting a fire in a homeless encampment; he was in jail and likely to stay there for a considerable period.

"Anyone else?" Cheryl asked and looked slowly around the room. "Okay. That's it for tonight. We'll see you tomorrow at 9AM for what probably is our wrap-up session."

⌇

"I'm not ready to go to the baths," Kate said.

"I'm not sure if I'm going to be ready to go anytime soon," I said. "I have your bite marks all over my body."

"What a baby," Kate said, giving me a punch on the arm. "Just wait until it gets darker."

"I guess."

"Anyway, I want to check Bryn Moore's cottage before it gets too dark. Want to go with me?"

"Of course."

We walked north through the campus and Kate briefed me on her interviews. "Talk about incestuous," I said.

"I know. Eastwick didn't have any boundaries and it rubbed off on his staff."

"Speaking of boundaries," I said. "I'm monogamous. I'm not sharing you with anyone in the universe."

"Good. Since I'm not sharing you, either." She stopped and gave me a warm kiss.

"I'm in responsible adult mode. That will end when we get into the baths."

Bryn Moore lived in a one-bedroom cottage slightly to the north of Malcom Eastwick's home. We put on gloves and then Kate fished Moore's key out of her pocket and opened the door.

I stayed in the doorway.

Once again, the residence had been trashed.

Kate slipped on booties before she stepped inside and turned on the light. "Similar to what we saw at Eastwick's." The mattress had been slit open and the books pulled off the bookshelves. The side table had been pulled over. Kate straightened it and opened the drawer. "Various kinds of drugs." There was a plastic bowl on the floor. "Drug pipes and sex toys." Kate went into the bathroom and opened the medicine cabinet. "More drugs. I bet there are some hidden. Tom, put on gloves and booties and help me with the search."

We found the trapdoor when we moved Moore's couch and rug. Kate carefully pulled open the door, revealing a sizable concrete basement. "I saw a setup like this when I was with Fresno

P.D." She shone a flashlight into the secret room. "Tom, hand me a big throw pillow."

I pulled a pillow off Moore's couch and handed it to Kate.

She centered it over the opening and dropped it. A gun went off and the pillow exploded. I smelled something like fireworks.

"Can't be too safe," Kate said. "Look around and see if you can find a long-handled broom."

I found what she wanted in a closet off the kitchen. Kate lowered the broom into the secret room and twirled it around. Then she swept it over the steel-rung ladder. "Looks safe. I'm going down."

I thought about telling Kate to be careful but decided against it.

"This isn't a drug lab," Kate said. "More like a place where Moore stored drugs and occasionally cut big portions into smaller units. Tom, please hand me your phone."

I leaned into the drug room and handed Kate my iPhone.

She turned the flashlight on and scanned the walls. "There's one wall for cannabis products and another for drugs," Kate said. "There's a third wall with a mixing board. There's a bottle of white powder, maybe Levamisole. On the last wall there's a safe."

"Any chance we can open it?"

"None unless you have some sketchy talents I'm not aware of."

"Sorry. I'm terminally straight."

Kate chortled. "I like that about you. Let me look closer at the drug shelf." She began taking photos. "Bags of cocaine. A box of blue pills that may be Fentanyl. Tabs of what could be LSD or some other psychedelic."

"See if there are any roofies."

"Rohypnol. Good idea." Kate shone the flashlight around the shelf. "Here's a plastic container with olive-green pills. They could be roofies."

"What about the other drug they found in Malcolm? The one that was injected."

"I forgot the name," Kate said. "I don't see any syringes here or vials of injectable drugs." She took more photos. "Tom, look into my kit bag and removed the spool of police masking tape."

I found what she wanted and tossed it to Kate. She covered the safe with yellow police tape. She similarly demarcated the cannabis and loose drug shelves. When Kate was done, she tossed me the tape and climbed up the steel ladder. We closed the trap door and covered it with yellow police tape.

"Anything else," she asked.

I pointed to a spy camera perched on a living room shelf atop a stack of CDs. Kate took a photo of it and then led me out of Moore's cabin.

We stood on the porch and pulled off our gloves and booties. "Let's go call Laura."

CHAPTER 38

(9:45PM): Laura

"Find another body?" Laura Sanchez asked in a raspy tone.

"What happened to your voice?" Kate asked.

"Sleep happened," Laura laughed. "You remember sleep, don't you Kate? It's what you used to do at night before you met your boyfriend."

"Oh yes. Someday I will sleep again." Kate chuckled. "But right now, I'm busy doing your job for you. Tom and I just checked out Bryn Moore's cottage."

"Did you try out the bed?"

"We were going to, but the cottage had been tossed."

"Like Eastwick's?"

"Similar but that's not why I called you. There were a lot of drugs around and I had the suspicion that Moore might have been a dealer. Tom and I moved the couch and living-room rug. There was a trap door in the wooden floor."

"Wow."

"I was worried that it might be booby-trapped so I threw a heavy pillow down the stairs. A hidden gun blew it apart."

"Wow. Sounds like a serious drug cache."

"From the looks of it, I'd say that Bryn Moore was the major dealer for the Satori area."

"What kind of drugs did you find?" Laura asked.

"On one wall was a pile of cannabis products. On another wall were a variety of drugs: cocaine, fentanyl, and other pills. One set might be roofies. The third wall was a mixing bench. The fourth wall was a safe."

"No chance the safe was open?"

"No. I took photos and plastered everything with police tape."

Tom whispered in Kate's ear.

"By the way, we spotted another spy camera in Moore's bookshelf."

"Hmm. What do you think?" Laura asked.

"Clearly Bryn Moore was a bad guy, but my gut tells me that he didn't kill Eastwick or Tanaka."

"Why?"

"I could be wrong, and if I am, we'll know it when you open Moore's safe, but I don't think Moore had anything to do with Eastwick's money-laundering adventures. I think he was killed by the main assailant because he might have been aware of what Eastwick was up to."

"And the spy camera?"

"I think the spy camera was planted by whoever killed Moore. Now they know we've been in his cabin."

"Just like they know you've been in Eastwick's cabin." Laura paused. "I don't like the direction this case is moving in, Kate. You have to be very careful."

"Believe me, I understand that."

CHAPTER 39
(10PM): Tom

Kate led me out the door of the administration offices and we headed to the baths.

When we got to the dressing room, none of the members of our group were there or in the showers. Kate and I hurriedly stripped, showered, and wrapped towels around our bodies. We walked to the largest tub and found members of our group singing songs, led by Aoife.

We got in the tub and paddled to a vacant location against the rock wall overlooking the ocean.

We sang "The Parting Glass" and "Carrickfergus." When the group finished, we applauded Aoife. She thanked everyone and turned to Kate, "You have a lovely alto, Kate. Are you singing in a group?"

"No. not since high school." Kate leaned into me, and I wrapped my right arm around her.

"Nice hickey," Julie smirked, observing the blue bruise on my shoulder.

"I've marked Tom as mine," Kate said and then growled.

Everyone laughed.

"Relics of our 'befriending' ceremony," I said with a straight face.

Everyone laughed and moved closer.

"Show us other marks," Lucy chuckled.

I sunk down in the hot water until only my head showed.

"You can see them when Tom takes a shower," Kate said, tilting her head to one side. "But you will have to pay."

"Will you accept checks?" Aoife laughed.

"Cash, check, or credit card."

"I'm staying here until you all leave," I said.

"I know how to empty the tub," Otto said.

"I'll get my camera," Julie chortled.

We both started laughing and everyone joined us.

Within a few minutes, the group was singing again.

Thick fog descended on the tub. Kate and I felt it was time to leave our happy group. We showered and dressed in silence and walked together up the path to the dining room. I led Kate back to my suite.

⌒⌒⌒

Unlike the previous night, we slowly undressed each other, embraced and sat on the king-size bed. "What would you like to do?" We said at the same time.

"Let's go slow," I said.

"Slow is good."

⌒⌒⌒

Forty-five minutes later we were lying side by side, panting, drenched in sweat. Kate ran her left hand up my chest and stopped at my chin. "I have a confession to make. Everything has been so good, I'm afraid something awful will happened and spoil it."

"Me, too. I'm still scarred from Fiona's death."

Kate pulled me close. "I'm sorry."

"You don't have to be sorry. It's not you or me, it's existential. I'm aware of the fragility of life. I'm aware of how precious each day is." I kissed Kate. "How precious you are."

FRIDAY

CHAPTER 40
(1:50AM): Tom

We were awoken by pounding on the door. A man's voice asked, "Tom and Kate, are you there?"

Kate groaned. I stumbled to the door and turned on the porchlight. I recognized Otto and Norma. "What's happened?"

"I was walking Norma back to her room and we saw a strange person coming out the door. We were worried about Kate, so we rushed over here."

Kate, stark naked, pressed against my back. "I'm okay but I want to check out our room. Give me a second to get dressed."

"We'll be out in a second," I said, closing the door.

"I'm not going to have time to do more than brush my teeth," Kate said as she walked to the bathroom.

After dressing, Kate strapped on her pistol. I finished dressing and we stepped outside to join Norma and Otto.

"What happened?" Kate asked, as we walked to the room she shared with Norma.

"Otto and I stayed up late talking," Norma said. "He walked me back to my room and when we were two doors down, we saw someone slip out the front door and disappear around the corner of the building. I knew right away it wasn't you."

"What did this person look like?" Kate asked.

"They were about your size but dressed in a black sweatshirt with a hood."

"Man or woman?" I asked.

"We couldn't tell," Otto answered.

When we got to the room, Kate had us stand back. She unlocked the door, flung it open and straddled the opening with her gun in a shooting stance. "No one is here."

We followed Kate into the room. She turned on the overhead light. "Does anything look different?" She asked Norma.

"No."

Kate threw open the bathroom door and flipped on the light. "Clear." She turned to Norma. "Does this look the same?"

Norma stuck her head in and looked around. "Yes."

Kate and Norma moved to the center of the bedroom. "Look around," Kate said. "Is there anything out of place?"

The four of us scanned the room. "There's something strange on the top row of the bookshelf," Norma said.

I climbed onto a chair to check out the rectangular object crammed between two books. "It's another camera," I said.

"What's a camera doing there?" Otto asked.

"Let's talk about this outside," Kate said.

We trooped out of the cabin and stood in the middle of a parking space. "Someone is stashing spy cameras around the campus," Kate said. "I assume that it has something to do with the deaths of Eastwick and Moore."

"So, they want to spy on you?" Norma asked.

"Yes. Probably because I'm running the investigation until the Monterey Sheriff's Department can get back here."

"Do you think I'm safe in our room?" Norma asked.

"I'd prefer it if you stayed somewhere else," Kate said. "You could stay with us or perhaps with Otto."

"I'll stay with Otto," Norma said, taking his hand.

"Good idea," Otto said with a grin.

"Wait here while I get my things," Norma said.

We all waited while Norma collected what she needed. Then we walked south to the end of the parking lot. We said good night and Norma and Otto headed for his room and Kate and I walked back to our suite.

"Do you think we're in danger?" I asked Kate.

"Only in the sense that we're being stalked." She frowned. "I don't think we know enough to threaten the assailant; they're watching us to make sure we don't learn anything that would jeopardize them."

⌒⌒⌒

Kate and I returned to our suite, stripped, and got into bed. "I notice that even though there's a serial killer loose and we're being stalked, it hasn't diminished my sex drive," I said.

"I've noticed that too." Kate said. She was lying naked next to me, slowly caressing the left side of my body with her right hand.

I cupped her soft butt with my left hand and moved her into my erection.

"When you touch me, I lose control." She slid me inside of her and began a rhythmic movement.

CHAPTER 41

(7:30AM): Laura

"Sanchez here."

"Things are stable, but I believe our perpetrator is getting nervous," Kate said. "They've planted spy cameras around the campus. Last night we found a camera in the room that I've been sharing with another workshop member."

"Did they get footage of you and Tom? I bet that would be a big hit on You Tube."

Kate laughed. "Not to my knowledge." The tone of her voice changed. "I think they're getting nervous. When are you guys going to be able to get here?"

"O'Malley just talked to Cal Fire, and they think the blaze will be under control by midday. So, maybe later this afternoon."

"The sooner the better. The natives are getting restless."

CHAPTER 42

(8:30 AM): Tom

We barely got to the dining-room before the breakfast line closed. We filled our trays and headed for the familiar table, where our friends had gathered.

"You two look happy," Julie chuckled.

Kate and I grinned. A few minutes later, Norma and Otto joined us.

"How's it going?" Kate asked Norma.

"I think everything is going to be just fine," Norma said with a blush.

Everyone had questions about the status of the fire and when Highway One would reopen.

"Sounds like the northern part of highway one may open before nightfall," I said. "We'll probably see the Sheriff's deputies tonight or tomorrow."

○ℓ○

At nine we walked to the Carl Rogers conference room for what we expected to be the last workshop. Kate and I took

264

our usual seats. David and Cheryl waited five minutes before starting.

Cheryl said. "Now let's go around the room to say good-bye. Everyone can speak for as long as they want. We'll start with Tom."

I stood up. "I'll always remember this workshop as the moment when Kate and I became a couple. The moment we formed a powerful bond." I looked at Kate and she broke into a big smile. "Of course, lots of other things have been happening this week: the death of Malcolm Eastwick and the death of Bryn Moore."

"Don't forget Kate clobbering Ivan," Lucy yelled.

Everyone laughed.

"Yes. I won't forget seeing Kate using her formidable Taekwondo skills to floor Ivan the giant." I smiled. "A lot's happened this week, but at the center has been this group. There was deep sharing. I made a lot of new friends. Thanks to all of you and thanks to Cheryl and David for being such effective leaders." I sat down.

Kate bounded up. "I came here to get over being a US Marshall and I ended up back in my law-enforcement role. And that was okay."

"We appreciate all that you did," David said. The group applauded.

"It helped that I found a partner in Tom. It meant a lot to me that I had him to cover my back." Kate's voice caught as she said this and when she looked at me her eyes were wet. "I came here with two heavy burdens: I didn't like my job and I felt that I was a total failure at relationships. I still don't like my job and, when I get back to San Francisco, I need to figure out what to do about that. However, I'm beginning to believe that maybe I can be my ornery self and still have a great relationship. So, I'm hopeful." Kate smiled at me. "Thanks to all of you for being so open, so supportive. Thanks to Cheryl and David for being skilled workshop leaders. And thanks to Tom." She walked back and kissed me and slid into my lap.

Everyone applauded.

When the applause died down, Rory scooted forward. "This workshop has meant a lot to me; I've learned a lot. Thanks to Cheryl and David. Thanks to all of you. Thanks to Tom, who has become my surrogate dad. I look forward to visiting you in San Francisco."

Rory and I had made plans to go to a Giants' game.

Rory scooted back and Lucy scooted forward. "I've been taking better care of myself. I've made some new friends." She turned and looked at Kate. "I plan to spend some time with Kate and Tom. Thank you, all."

Julie went next. "Thank you, Cheryl, and David. This has been a good workshop for me. I haven't found true love, like some others, but I have gotten clearer about who I am and what I want. In the fall, I'm going to enter the veterinary school at UC Davis. In the meantime, I'm going to hang out in San Francisco a lot; spend time with Kate and Tom and my other new friends. Thank you all."

Aoife spoke, "This has been a good workshop for me. I've had a break from my stressful home life, and I've made new friends. As I mentioned, my stalker has been incarcerated; that's a great relief; I'll be able to return to teaching."

Norma went next. "Thank you, Cheryl, and David. Thank you all." She took a deep breath. "I've made some good friends here and that's important to me." She looked around the circle at each of us. "I've been reminded that life is precious and to have happiness sometimes you must take risks. Otto is starting a new life and he has invited me to be part of it."

The participants applauded.

Norma blushed. "So, for those of you in the bay area, you'll be seeing more of me. And Otto." She reached out for Otto's hand.

Otto spoke. "This has been a memorable workshop. It has had excellent leadership from Cheryl and David. Thank you." Otto nodded at Cheryl and David and lead a round of applause. "As someone who is launching a career as a psychotherapist, your leadership has been inspirational." He looked around the group. "And all of you have been brave and warm workshop members. It's rare to find a workshop like this, where all the participants fully participate." He took Norma's hand. "I'm starting a new adventure and I'm proud that Norma is joining me."

Theo scooted forward on his pillow. "I echo the sentiments expressed by the others. Although I haven't said much, this has been a good workshop for me. I've resolved to move out of oncology into family medicine; I've resolved to take better care of my mental health. And I've resolved to spend more time with friends." Theo nodded to me. "One of the things I realized in the group is that I enjoy hanging out with 'the guys.' When I get back to Palo Alto, I plan to spend more time with my friends."

Tammy spoke. "I'm leaving Ernie. I'm going back to Fresno and filing for divorce." She clasped Lois' hand. "Then I'm going to come back here and see what happens. Thank you, everyone."

Lois stood up. "I enjoyed this workshop." She smiled at Tammy. "I'd given up on love and then I was surprised." Lois sighed. "I enjoyed the women's gathering. Even though most of the women are straight, I felt respected and included. I'm hopeful."

Lucky scooted forward. "By nature, I am a positive person, but I was depressed coming into this workshop. Now I'm not." He squeezed Paul's hand. "This was a warm supportive group and some of us found love. What could be better?"

Paul spoke. "I've closed one door and opened another." He looked at Lucky. "The other night, in the baths, I realized that for years I've felt completely isolated. Now I don't. There's a refrain from a blues song, 'this is a mean old world to have to live in by yourself.' It helps having a friend, a partner."

Kate squeezed my hand.

"Thanks to all of you for your hard work," David said. "This has been an amazing group, particularly considering the unusual circumstances. I've been running this workshop for more than twenty years and this group rates among the very best I've been part of." David ran his hand over his forehead. "There are several reasons: you have several folks who have experienced intensive workshops and, as a group, you are willing to take risks. The other thing I noticed is that you're very supportive of one another, particularly the women." He turned to Cheryl.

"I would agree with what David said: this has been an unusually strong group. I can't remember when I've been part of a stronger group of women. It may not seem like it, but Satori has often been a bastion of the patriarchy. That hasn't been the way this group operated and for that, I'm thankful." Cheryl sat down.

David remained standing. "I thought for an ending, Aoife could lead us in a song."

Aoife stood up and we all followed her lead and clasped hands. "Here's a song you all know."

*Amazing grace***
How sweet the sound
That saved a wretch like me
I once was lost, but now I'm found
Was blind, but now I see

'Twas grace that taught my heart to fear
And grace my fears relieved
How precious did that grace appear
The hour I first received.

We hugged and then we all left the Carl Rogers room and trooped down the hill to the dining room.

⁓

Kate and I and our workshop friends were sitting on the deck, enjoying the sunny day, when Detective Laura Sanchez and Detective Sergeant Dan O'Malley walked up.

"Looks like it's time to go to work," Kate said. She kissed me and went off with the detectives.

---

* Public Domain

CHAPTER 43

(3PM): Laura

O'Malley and Sanchez walked with Kate to the executive conference room. "Where should we start?" Laura asked.

"Let's start with Greg Tanaka," Kate said. "I'll walk you to his car and then you guys can take over.

The trio left the conference room and were joined by coroner's investigator Bruno Oliver as they walked up the gravel path. "By the way," Laura said. "We have six police officers interviewing all the Satori guests who were in the old conference room. And another crew took Bryn Moore's body out of the freezer and is transporting it back to Salinas for an autopsy.

"Sounds good," Kate said. "Here's Tanaka's car. I popped the trunk because I thought there was a possibility his body was inside. Otherwise, I stayed away from the car."

Bruno used a tool to open the car doors. "There's nothing here except for a carryall. Let's look in the trunk." Bruno carefully moved to the side of the trunk and lifted the lid that Kate had taped down. "A stain and several segments of clothing." He studied the soft ground directly beneath the trunk. "Probably a footprint." Bruno turned towards the ocean. "Here's the track Kate talked about, probably a wheelbarrow." He led them to the edge of the bluff. "This looks like where the assailant pitched Tanaka into the surf." He turned to Laura. "My crew brought some climbing gear. We'll belay down the cliff and see if we can find anything."

The group headed back to Tanaka's Mercedes. Bruno turned to Kate. "Do you have any idea where the wheelbarrow ended up?"

"Just east of here there's a maintenance shed," Kate answered. "I got close but didn't open the doors because, once again, the ground was soft, and I worried I might inadvertently destroy some evidence."

"Let's take a look," Bruno said and led the group up a small hill. When they got near the shed, Bruno laid two boards down and used them to protect the ground while he opened the shed door. "Just like you thought, there's a wheelbarrow here." He used a flashlight to illuminate the inside of the shed. "There may be clothing particles attached." Bruno shut the shed door and marked it with yellow police tape.

"How far is Bryn Moore's cottage?" Laura asked.

"Just south of here," Kate answered and led them to Moore's one-bedroom dwelling. Kate put on gloves and booties before opening the door. "We were careful and didn't tough anything except the trap door." The group walked across the floor until they came to the trap door marked with masking tape.

"Looks sinister," Laura said.

"It reminded me of a drug den we found when I was in the Fresno P.D.," Kate said. "Wait until you see."

Bruno swung the door open and shined his flashlight inside.

"Whoa," Laura said. "Serious drugs."

"And a safe," Kate said. "Could be the location of the missing Satori money but I suspect it's not."

Bruno climbed down the steel ladder and examined the safe. "I'm pretty sure I can open this with a device I have in our van."

"That would be awesome," Laura said.

Bruno peeled off to get his specialized device.

"While we are here," Kate said, "I want to point out the spy camera in the bookcase." She pointed to the northeast corner of Moore's living room.

"I see it," Laura said. "You saw a similar camera in Eastwick's cabin?"

"Yes. And we found one in the room I was sharing with my workshop friend Norma."

"Let's take a look," Laura said.

Kate, Laura, and O'Malley trekked south across the Satori campus and reached Kate's room. She unlocked the door and pointed out where the spy camera was positioned.

"I see it," Laura said. "Let's go outside and talk about this."

"I'm going to go up to the old conference center and see how the interviews are going," O'Malley said. He walked away, leaving Kate and Laura alone.

"What do you think is going on with the cameras?" Laura asked.

"I think the assailant planted the cameras," Kate replied. "After they killed Eastwick, they posted a camera to see who came nosing around. The camera likely picked up Greg Tanaka looking for Eastwick's money. The assailant decided that Tanaka was probably the mob's bag man and, therefore, they killed him and disposed of his body. Once the assailant counted the money, they realized some was missing. They reasoned that Bryn Moore was likely to have collaborated with Eastwick. They planted a camera in Moore's cabin and discovered he had a trapdoor leading to a secret room. The assailant waylaid Moore, pumped him full of drugs, and interrogated him. When they realized Moore wasn't in cahoots with Eastwick, they killed him with a drug overdose. This time, they couldn't dump him in the ocean, so they tried to make his death look like an accident."

"I buy all that," Laura said. "Why do you think that they placed a camera in the cabin you shared with Norma?"

"Because they wanted to watch me?"

"If that's true, then there should be another spy camera in Tom's room," Laura said.

"You're right. We should take a look."

Kate led Laura to Tom's suite.

"Very nice," Laura said. "Do you mind if I stay here for a couple of days?"

"That wouldn't work out." Kate laughed. "The unit next door is vacant. You can rent that."

"I'll consider it." Laura chuckled. "But I hear the neighbors are very noisy." She walked around the suite. "I don't see a camera in your bookshelves." She pointed to loft area. "Take a look up there."

Kate climbed up the wooden ladder and found a spy camera lodged between the top rung and the wall. "Here it is."

After Kate climbed down, Laura suggested they walk outside to talk. "I don't want to take a chance that someone will over-hear us."

They walked down a gravel path and found two weathered Adirondack chairs looking out over the ocean.

"What do you think?" Kate asked.

"One possibility is that someone viewed your active sex life as a business opportunity. They captured it on video, and they plan to sell it via pay-per-view."

Kate chortled. "Exciting new internet portal: the 'bang-of-the-month club.'"

Laura laughed so hard she started coughing. "For a US Marshall, you have a twisted sense of humor."

When the laughter abated, Kate asked, "Seriously, why do you think the assailant planted the cameras?"

"I think they are after you."

"Why?" Kate asked. "Why come after me?"

"I don't think you're the target; I think they're planning to kill Tom."

"Oh my god," Kate exclaimed. "That never occurred to me. Why are they after Tom?"

"My guess is that the assailant believes that Tom knows some-thing that will reveal their identity."

Kate thought for a moment. "The assailant must know that Tom and I are in a relationship. This didn't make any difference to them until Thursday morning when the fire shut down Highway One and I had to temporarily take over the murder investigation. Then the assailant had an 'oh shit' moment when they realized Tom knows something important. So, then they decided to go after us."

"They decided to break into your suite and kill Tom, and you, too, if you happened to be there."

"Only my security was too good so they couldn't get in," Kate said.

"What security?" Laura asked. "Your suite looked pretty insecure to me."

Kate got up from her Adirondack. "Let's go back to the suite and I'll show you."

When they entered, Kate pointed out a black door guard on the floor. "Every access is protected by locks. I'm a little paranoid about being assaulted during the night, so whenever I travel, I always bring door and window guards with me."

Laura raised her eyebrows.

"When I was with the Fresno P.D., I worked on a horrific rape case. A woman was asleep in bed when an intruder came through the patio sliding glass door; he tied her up, raped her, and cut her."

"Did she survive?"

"Barely. She was severely damaged." Kate growled. "Fortunately, we caught the guy and sent him away."

"I can see why you're so careful. Do you mind if I look at the doors and windows in this unit."

"Be my guest."

Laura walked around the suite and checked the five windows and the sliding glass door leading to the deck. "Pretty impressive security. Do you mind if I remove the sliding-door guard?"

"Go ahead."

Laura removed the door guard, slid open the door, and checked the area near the exterior handle. "There are pry marks here. Someone tried to get in but failed to open the door. They were stymied by the steel door guard."

"Fuck," Kate exclaimed as she bent over to examine the area where the wood was fractured. "Sometimes it's good to be paranoid."

"For sure." They went back inside the suite and closed the door.

Kate repositioned the door guard. She growled and banged her right fist into her open left hand.

CHAPTER 44

(4:30PM): Tom

Our workshop friends went back and forth between the dining-room deck and the baths. I sat in a painted Adirondack chair and waited for Kate. Periodically, I saw her walking around campus with Detective Laura Sanchez.

I was about to get a glass of wine when Gwyneth Jones approached me, wearing a low-cut, flower-strewn summer dress. She had dark circles under her eyes and furrows on her forehead. "Is Marshall Kate here?" Gwyneth asked.

"She's out helping the Monterey Police. I'm waiting for her. If you want, you can wait with me." She nodded. "I was about to get a glass of white wine. Would you like a glass?"

"That would be nice," she said. "Thank you."

Gwyneth sat down in my chair. I walked to the bar, bought two glasses of wine, walked back, pulled up another chair, and sat down next to Gwyneth.

"Are you okay?" I asked.

"Not really. I'm having problems with Jerry, and I witnessed something that I need to tell Marshal Kate about." She sipped her wine and leaned closer. "I'm going to leave Jerry." She sipped more. "I should have done this months ago. Now I realize that he's a fake. And a flake." For the first time she smiled. "I've been living with a flakey fake and wasting my life." She gulped her wine.

I handed her my glass, which I hadn't touched.

"Thanks." She took a sip. "After we go back to LA, I'm going to pack my stuff and drive back to Winnetka. Then I'm going to reenroll at Northwestern and get my degree in interior design." She sipped more wine, and her words began to slur. "I'm going to do what my mother keeps telling me to do: exercise common sense."

"So, you are abandoning your plan to be an actress?"

Gwyneth laughed. "I was deluding myself. Jerry, and other Hollywood guys, aren't interested in any of my talents beyond these." She lifted up her breasts.

Kate walked up with Laura Sanchez. "What's going on?" She asked, tilting her head to one side with a bemused expression.

"Gwyneth wants to talk to you. She's leaving Jerry Kermit because he doesn't appreciate her."

Gwyneth nodded. "I need to tell you something important.'

"Why don't I go back to the executive conference room?" Laura said. "When you guys finish talking to Gwyneth, come join me." She walked off.

"Sit down in my chair, Kate," I said. "I'll get some more wine."

I walked back to the bar and got three glasses of white wine. When I returned, I pulled up a redwood Adirondack and listened to the animated conversation. Gwyneth was telling Kate about Jerry's inadequacies. Kate was nodding sympathetically. I handed out the wine.

"What did you want to tell me, Gwyneth?" Kate asked.

"First, I want to apologize. I should have come to you on Tuesday morning, but Jerry talked me out of it. He said, 'we shouldn't get involved.'"

"What happened?"

"It wasn't until after I realized that I was in an abusive relationship that I saw that Jerry had asked me to do something illegal. I'm sorry."

"Okay," Kate said, "I get it. What happened?"

Gwyneth talked faster. "On Wednesday, when I met you at the Satori function, I could have taken you aside and talked to you. But you intimidated me."

"I didn't mean to be intimidating," Kate said.

"I know." Gwyneth laughed. "You just are."

We all laughed.

"Then on Thursday, when you beat up that awful Ivan, I knew that I had to talk to you." Gwyneth took a deep breath. "But they wouldn't let us out of the old conference building. Until now. After I was interviewed."

Kate patted her hand. "I'm glad you decided to talk to me. What happened?"

"I saw a murder," Gwyneth said in a choked voice. "Or at least part of one."

"Is it okay if I record this?" Kate asked. She put out her right hand and I handed her my iPhone. "Thanks." She turned on record. "This is Kate Swift recording Gwyneth James. Gwyneth tell me what you saw."

"I arrived on Monday afternoon. Jerry promised me that we would be taking a romantic vacation. He said that it would be an opportunity for us to 'rekindle our relationship.'" Gwyneth's eyes filled with tears. "But once we got here it was the same old story: Jerry trying to be a big man. There was an open bar and, as usual, he drank too much. When we got back to the room, he wanted sex, but he couldn't get it up and he blamed me." Tears rolled down her cheeks.

"What did you do?" Kate asked.

"At first, I tried to go to sleep, but Jerry was snoring. So, I got up, made myself some herbal tea and sat in our dark room. That's when I decided to leave him. Once I made up my mind, I realized I couldn't go back to sleep, so I changed into my work-out outfit, put on a sweatshirt, left our room and the old conference building, and started walking north on the campus road."

"What time was this?'

"It was almost 3AM, Tuesday morning. I remember looking at my watch and thinking, 'It's almost 5 o'clock in Winnetka. The milk trucks will start their rounds.'"

"You walked north on the Satori campus road?"

"I walked north and just after I passed the art studio, I saw a car coming. So, I left the road and hid behind some bushes."

"And then what happened?"

"The car was a Mercedes. It pulled over by an open area and the driver turned off the engine. The driver got out and walked to the rear of the car and opened the trunk. They hesitated for a moment and then they walked south on the road to where there was a maintenance shed. They opened the door of the shed and then came back rolling a wheelbarrow."

"During this period could you determine if the person you were watching was a man or a woman?"

"I couldn't tell. They were wearing loose pants and an oversize hoodie sweatshirt."

"What happened next?" Kate asked.

"The person in the sweatshirt pushed the wheelbarrow next to the rear of the Mercedes and then they pulled a body out of the trunk."

"You're sure you saw a body?"

"Positive. They pulled the legs out first and then the torso. When they pulled out the upper body, the head flopped in my direction, and I could tell it was a man."

"Why could you tell that?"

"Because his hair was short, and his face was sharp and masculine."

"Could it possibly have been a woman?"

"I don't think so. The body was too heavily muscled."

"Okay," Kate said. "What happened next?"

"Once the person in the sweatshirt loaded the body into the wheelbarrow, they started pushing it across the open field."

"What direction was this?"

"West, towards the ocean."

"What happened next?"

"The person in the sweatshirt had a hard time pushing the wheelbarrow across the field. They had to stop several times;

I guess because the body was heavy. Eventually they reached the edge of the bluff. The sweatshirt person tipped the wheelbarrow over and the body fell out and disappeared; I assume it rolled down the cliff into the water." Gwyneth shivered. "It was terrifying."

"Sounds like it. What happened next?"

"Sweatshirt person pushed the wheelbarrow back across the field to the shed. They returned the wheelbarrow to wherever it had been in the shed and closed the wooden door."

"And then?"

"Then the person in the sweatshirt walked onto the campus road and headed south. And I followed them."

"You followed them. Why?"

"I know in retrospect it seems crazy, but I wanted to see where they went. I thought if they went into the old conference center, I wasn't going to go in. I was worried they might kill someone else, maybe me."

"What happened?"

"They turned onto the little bridge that leads to the old conference center. And then they stopped."

"Why did they stop?"

"They stopped in the middle of the bridge, threw back their hoodie, and lit a cigarette."

"Amazing," Kate said.

"When they got out their lighter, I could see who it was."

"And."

"It was the woman who helped found Satori. Cheryl Taylor."

"Wow." Kate paused and looked at me.

I raised my eyebrows and inhaled.

"You're sure that it was Cheryl?" Kate asked.

"Certain. I'd met her that evening. She came over to the bar in the old conference center to say hello to everyone. Jerry introduced us."

"Wow. This is important information, Gwyneth. One more thing: when Cheryl walked down the path, where did she go?"

"She went to a little cottage across the lawn from the old conference center. I watched her walk to her cottage, unlock the door, enter, and turn on the light."

Kate turned to me. "I'm asking a question of Tom Scott who has witnessed this interview. Tom, what is the location of Cheryl Taylor's residence on the Satori campus?'

"It's across the lawn from the old conference center."

CHAPTER 45
(5PM): Laura

Detectives O'Malley and Sanchez were sitting at the long table in the Satori executive conference room when they were joined by Bruno Oliver, Kate Swift, and Tom Scott.

"Is it okay if Tom joins us?" Kate asked. "We have something important to report and Tom has a vital role."

O'Malley opened his mouth to object, but Laura spoke first, "Sure. Tom can stay." She turned to O'Malley, "Trust me Sarge, this is the right thing to do."

"Why don't you go first, Bruno?" Laura said to the coroner's investigator.

As Bruno delivered his report, he only looked at Sanchez. "I was able to get Bryn Moore's safe open. It contained $22,500 in cash, a Ruger GP100 pistol, and two bags filled with what I believe are high-quality heroin and cocaine."

"So, nowhere near the $500,000 that our assailant was looking for?" Laura said.

"That's right. The cash was in the range one would expect to find in the lair of a drug dealer."

"Any indication the safe had been tampered with?"

"No," Bruno answered. "We dusted for prints, and it appears that only Bryn Moore touched the safe."

Laura turned to the others. "So, our working theory is that the assailant observed Bryn Moore on the spy camera. When they saw him open the trap door to his cellar, they marked him as someone who could have been collaborating with Malcom Eastwick. The assailant waylaid Moore in the baths and interrogated him using drugs. When they realized that Moore had nothing to do with Eastwick, they administered an overdose."

"Moore's death was a byproduct of the assailant's search for the missing money," Kate added. "They had no idea that Eastwick had moved the money to San Francisco."

"That's right," Laura said.

The five sat in silence.

Laura turned to Kate. "Tell us what you've found out."

Kate recapped her conversation with Gwyneth Jones. "She says the hooded figure she saw was Cheryl Taylor."

"Whoa," Laura said. "Our first eyewitness." She looked at Kate and Tom. "Do you believe her?"

"Yes,' Kate said. "She'd met Cheryl and there's no reason for Gwyneth to lie."

"Still, it was dark," O'Malley said. "And Gwyneth Jones waited several days before coming forward as a witness."

"We need some collaboration," Laura said.

The five sat in silence. After several minutes, Bruno turned to Laura. "Can I say something?"

"Sure."

"I think we need to reframe our perspective. The eyewitness is important, but she won't be enough to convict Dr. Taylor."

"Because?" Laura asked.

"Because the perpetrator has to be someone who knows about using drugs as tools for interrogation."

"What's this about interrogation drugs?" Tom asked.

Bruno responded but kept his eyes on Laura. "Malcolm Eastwick was interrogated using a sophisticated drug named Scopolamine."

"Who uses Scopolamine?" Tom asked.

"As far as we know, only the spooks," Bruno said.

Tom slapped his hand against his forehead. "I forgot something important. Cheryl worked with the spooks." He got up from his chair. "I want to show you an interesting picture, but it will require all of us to take a little walk."

Behind Tom, Kate winked at Laura as if to say, *you were right - Tom did know something that would reveal the identity of the assailant.*

⤸⤺

Tom led the group of five out of the Satori office, north onto the main campus path, across the wooden footbridge, and west to the old conference center. They walked into the main room, and Tom began to examine the historic Satori photographs.

"What are you looking for?" Kate asked.

"There's someone in the Satori past who was a professional interrogator. I'm hoping there is a picture of him with Cheryl."

Tom started to work through the chronological sequence. "I think the photo I'm looking was taken around the time of the Gulf War."

Laura called out, "Here's a picture of Bruce Springsteen with Tom and a gorgeous woman."

Kate rushed over. "That's Tom's deceased wife, Fiona."

Laura stepped back. "You don't look like her." She shouted across the room. "How lucky are you, Tom, to have two smart gorgeous women in your life."

Tom looked at them. "Believe me, I know that. I was blessed to be with Fiona and now I'm blessed to be with Kate."

Tom kept scanning the photos. "I don't think we're looking for a group shot, this is a photo of a couple."

Bruno called out. "I may have found it."

The others rushed to look at the photo.

"That's Cheryl Taylor, all dolled up," Kate said. "Who's the good-looking guy?"

"Hal Chesterton, Tom said. "He was a former Navy SEAL who ended up teaching at the Navy's Monterey Postgraduate school. Among other things, he taught a course in interrogation."

"How did Cheryl get involved with him?" Kate asked.

"After her first husband, Richard, died, Cheryl bought a house in Monterey and started a therapy practice there. She met Hal and they developed a relationship. Hal was working on rapid interrogation methods. He was interested in possibly using psycho-active drugs as an accelerant."

"How do you know this?" Kate asked.

"At one point, Cheryl and Fiona were very close. After Richard's death, Cheryl was at loose ends. During this period, she stayed with Fiona and Stella in San Francisco. Fiona and Cheryl drove up the coast and ended up at Hollyhock in BC."

"So, they became friends?"

"Yes. When Fiona met me, she asked Cheryl to check me out. When Cheryl met Hal, she asked Fiona to check him out."

"Did you meet Hal Chesterton?" Laura asked.

"We had dinner once."

"What was your impression of him?" Bruno asked.

"Smart guy. Tough – he had the same 'don't mess with me' vibe that Kate has."

"Except with you." Kate slipped her arm around my waist.

"Except with me." Tom continued. "He was secretive. I've never been around many spooks, but he fits the narrative I've heard about them: polite, well-spoken, and guarded."

"What happened to Chesterton?" Laura asked.

"Around 1993, maybe later, he disappeared. Cheryl knew that he was going on a 'special mission,' probably Iraq. He never returned. Months later, she got a call from his sister saying the Navy had formally notified her that Hal was MIA."

Laura said, "So, do you think that Cheryl was involved in Chesterton's interrogation research? You believe that she knows how to use Scopolamine?"

"Yes. Cheryl knows how to use a lot of drugs. At one time, she taught a Satori course on Shamanism. Recently, she had a grant to study using Psilocybin in the treatment of PTSD."

"We should talk to her," Kate said.

The five of us walked outside the old conference center and stood in the shade of a redwood tree. "I don't think it's a good idea to let Marshal Kate and her boyfriend interview our primary suspect," O'Malley said.

"It's not by the book," Laura responded. "But Tom has known Cheryl a long time and if anyone can put her at ease, he can. And Kate just came out of a workshop with Cheryl, and we all know that Kate is a skilled interrogator." O'Malley frowned but didn't say anything. "What do you think, Bruno?"

"It's not by the book," Bruno said. "But I agree that it would be the most effective interview strategy."

CHAPTER 46
(5:30PM): Tom

The five of us trekked in silence back to the Satori offices. I asked Sequoyah if Cheryl was there. She buzzed her and told us, "Cheryl will see you now."

Kate and I entered Cheryl's office. She was sitting behind her desk, drinking what I took to be tea. Behind her the drapes were open and we could see the south lawn running down to the cliff edge, and the ocean beyond. It was a beautiful day with only a slight breeze.

"We want to talk to you about Malcom Eastwick's murder," Kate said. "We have some questions."

"I'm all ears," Cheryl said, moving her hands off the table and into her lap.

Kate took out my iPhone and turned it on. Kate began speaking for the recorder. "This is Marshal Kate Swift. I'm interviewing Cheryl Taylor in her Satori Institute office. In the room with me is a civilian, Tom Scott, who has known Cheryl for many years."

"Yes," Cheryl said. "Tom has known me for many years. He probably knows my secrets."

Cheryl smiled but her eyes were cold. I shivered.

"Cheryl," Kate said. "We have a witness who can link you to the death of Greg Tanaka."

"A witness," Cheryl said without emotion. "That's interesting. Who is this witness?"

"Someone who was out walking by the art studio, early Tuesday morning. They saw you park Tanaka's car, open the trunk, take out his body, place it in a wheelbarrow, roll it to the edge of the cliff, and pitch it into the Pacific."

"Interesting. They saw me in the dark?" Cheryl's voice remained flat, but her right eyelid began to twitch.

"Contact with that witness prompted us to reexamine your relationship to the Eastwick case. Tom remembered your relationship with Hal Chesterton. He recalled that you knew about advanced interrogation techniques. We deduced that you knew how to use Scopolamine."

"I was afraid Tom would recall my relationship with Hal," Cheryl said. She withdrew her right hand from below the table-top and reached for her cigarettes, which were on the right side of her desk. Then she reconsidered and withdrew her hand.

"You were afraid Tom would recall your relationship with Hal and, therefore, you tried to kill him."

I opened my mouth to speak but Kate waved her hand for me to stay quiet.

"You can't prove that," Cheryl said.

"Once we have your phone, we can link it to the spy cameras."

Cheryl's iPhone sat on the left of the desk. She eyed it and squirmed in her chair.

"I'm now going to read you your rights," Kate said. She read them out while Cheryl stared at us.

"Why did you kill Malcolm Eastwick?"

Cheryl remained silent for more than a minute and then took a deep breath. "Malcolm and I had a long and difficult relationship. I met him and my deceased husband, Richard, at the same Stanford fraternity party. They both tried to date me. I chose Richard." Cheryl briefly closed her eyes. "They'd been friends for years. We used to call them 'the gold-dust twins.' Both handsome and talented. Richard was more spiritual, Malcom more adventurous. And lucky. Malcolm liked to experiment with drugs, and he would drag Richard along. Malcolm discovered Ayahuasca and talked Richard into taking it; they went for a hike behind the Satori campus and Richard fell off a cliff." Cheryl sighed.

"Malcolm got into trouble," Kate said.

"Malcolm got into trouble and usually skated away from it. In recent years, Malcolm's womanizing caught up with him. Satori had to pay off women that Malcolm had..." Cheryl searched for a word "...befriended. Malcom had inappropriate relationships with clients and was suspended by CPA."

"Malcolm needed money," Kate said. "How did you find out about that?"

"Marcia Ball is my client," Cheryl said. "Poor Marcia. Ten years ago, she slept with Malcolm a couple of times and never got over it." Cheryl shook her head. "She should have left Satori years ago, but kept hanging on, hoping that Malcolm would come back to her. Unrequited love. So sad."

"Marcia knew that Malcolm had taken the license money?"

"It's more complicated. Marcia started a sexual relationship with Bryn Moore, and he told her."

"They seem an unlikely pair," Kate said.

Cheryl raised her eyebrows. "Not all love is romantic, Marshal. Marcia was desperate and Bryn was a predator. She came to me with horrifying tales of their sexual encounters. I urged her to break off the relationship, but she wasn't strong enough." Cheryl looked at me. "And drugs were involved."

Cheryl continued "Finally, Marcia came to me and said that she was leaving Satori. She'd talked to some hotshot LA attorney who'd convinced her that she could file a sexual abuse complaint against Satori."

"How did you respond?"

"I tried to be measured. I said that I understood her grievance, but I did not understand why she didn't simply sue Malcolm. Marcia answered that it wouldn't do any good to sue Malcom because he didn't have any money. She told me, 'Malcolm is so broke, he's been embezzling from Satori.'"

"That's when you understood what Malcolm was doing with the license money," Kate said it.

"I know that makes me look like an idiot, but it never occurred to me that Malcolm would steal from Satori." Cheryl sighed. "After Richard died, Malcolm did his best to comfort me. We came to an agreement. Malcolm would become the managing partner and I would be, in effect, the silent partner. I withdrew from day-to-day Satori operations and concentrated on being a therapist." She shrugged. "I put my head in the sand and refused to look up. Until it was too late."

"So, you arranged to talk to Malcolm, when he came to Satori for the board meeting," Kate said.

"Yes. By that time, I realized he had been lying to me for years, so I anticipated a 'hostile negotiation.' I brought a nice Cabernet with me and when I was filling his glass, I slipped Rohypnol into it. While Malcolm was unconscious, I tied him up and injected him with Scopolamine. It all went according to plan. When Malcolm woke up, he told me where the money was and gave me the combination of his safe. Unfortunately, I got the Scopolamine dosage wrong, and Malcolm's heart stopped."

"That was probably because he hadn't eaten that day and he had a weak heart," Kate said.

Cheryl shook her head and her voice faltered. "I didn't intend to kill Malcolm, but I did." She reached for her cigarette package, withdrew a Marlboro, lit it, inhaled, and blew the smoke in our direction. "After that, things went downhill."

Kate kept up her questioning. "You disposed of Malcolm's body and then discovered that you hadn't collected all the money. That's when you installed the spy camera."

"Yes. That's how I caught Greg Tanaka breaking into Malcolm's cottage."

"And you snuck into Tanaka's room, knocked him out, and interrogated him."

"But he didn't know anything," Cheryl said. "He was just the mob's bag man."

"So, you killed him."

Cheryl nodded.

"Cheryl Taylor nodded yes," Kate said for the recording. "Why did you kill him?"

Cheryl smoked her cigarette. "I have no defense. I panicked. First, I killed Malcolm and then this mob guy starts snooping around." She snuffed out her Marlboro in an ashtray. "I killed Tanaka and then disposed of his body the same way I had dealt with Malcolm."

"You dragged his body into his car, drove it to the area by the art studio, dragged Tanaka out, and pitched him into the ocean."

"At least this time you never found the body." Cheryl flashed a grim smile.

"Why did you kill Bryn Moore?" Kate asked.

"For two reasons," Cheryl said. "I thought that he might know where Malcolm had stashed the rest of the money – this was before Jean Little told me the money was in Malcolm's safe in San Francisco. And I didn't like Bryn. He was a predator." Cheryl raised her chin and looked at Kate. "I'm tired of predators."

"So, you put a spy camera in his cabin. You saw that he had a trapdoor leading to his drug stash. You assumed he hid Malcolm's money there?"

"It was a logical assumption. Wednesday night, Bryn and Marcia had a regular assignation in one of the bath massage rooms. I waited until they were finished, Marcia had left, and Bryn was asleep. Then I filled him full of Scopolamine. But to no avail, Bryn didn't know anything."

"So, you killed him?"

Cheryl didn't say anything.

"At this point you had killed three people, but you weren't content to stop there. You planted spy cameras in our rooms with the intent of killing Tom and possibly me as collateral damage."

"It wasn't personal. I realized Tom could link me to chemical interrogation and I thought it would be best to eliminate him."

Kate growled. "Of course, it was personal, Cheryl. Tom thought he was your friend. For the record, he suggested that after he and I had established our new San Francisco residence, we might invite you up for the weekend."

Cheryl looked down.

I don't know Cheryl anymore, I thought. *She's not the person that Fiona and I once knew. Maybe she never was.*

Cheryl brought her hands onto the table and pointed a gun at me.

Kate shot from her lap.

I heard a snap, a boom, and then Cheryl fell over backwards, hitting her head on a small teak bookshelf. A framed picture fell.

"This is Marshal Kate Swift concluding the interview with Cheryl Taylor." Kate turned off the recorder. She turned to me, "For the record, you're my man. No one messes with you."

My heart was booming. "I'm so glad you're my partner." I took her hand.

"Don't move," Kate said. "I'm going to check Cheryl."

Laura Sanchez, Dan O'Malley, and Bruno Oliver opened the office door. "What the fuck happened?" Laura asked.

"The good news is that Cheryl confessed, and I got it on tape. The bad news is that she pulled a gun on us, and I shot her in the head." Kate looked down at what I presumed was

Cheryl's corpse. "Aimed for the forehead, got her in the bridge of the nose."

"Don't touch anything," O'Malley growled.

I stifled my impulse to slug him and remained seated.

Kate walked back around the table and sat down next to me. She clasped my hand and kissed it.

Laura looked up from Cheryl's body. "An amazing shot, Kate. You shot through the desk and hit her in the head."

For the first time, I saw the bullet hole in the desktop in front of Kate.

Bruno put on gloves and picked up Cheryl's gun. "A Sig Sauer P365." He turned to Laura. "I'll take care of the body," Bruno said.

"Thanks, Bruno," Laura said. She motioned to Kate and me. "Let's go into the executive conference room. I want to hear your tape."

CHAPTER 47
(6PM): Laura

As we left Cheryl Taylor's office, Sequoyah was standing by the door. "What happened?" She asked.

"There was a shooting," Laura said. "Do me a favor and don't let anyone in."

Laura led Tom, Kate, and Sergeant O'Malley into the conference room.

"Please play your taped interview with Cheryl Taylor."

Kate put the iPhone on the table and turned on the recording. When I reheard the gun shot, I flinched.

"Excellent interview, Marshal Swift," O'Malley said. "And you were convinced that you had no other choice other than to shoot Cheryl Taylor?"

"She pointed her gun at Tom. I thought she was going to shoot, so I shot first."

Laura studied Kate's face and smiled. "You were angry."

"Yes, I was. Cheryl had admitted her intent to kill Tom, and me as collateral damage, and now she was pointing a gun at Tom." Kate growled.

"Remind me never to get on your bad side," Laura said.

We all sat in silence. Finally, Laura said, "This is how it how it all ends, with a bang and a shitload of paperwork."

"Paraphrasing T.S. Eliot," Kate said with a smile.

"My favorite poet," Laura answered.

O'Malley shook his head.

Laura got up and summoned Sequoyah. "We're going to be here for a while. Would you have the kitchen bring us some food and coffee? Thanks." She closed the door.

O'Malley and Sanchez interviewed Tom while Kate, a peace officer, wrote a narrative of the shooting on an official Monterey County Sheriff's Department form.

"Were you surprised to find that Cheryl Taylor was the perpetrator?" O'Malley asked.

"Surprised isn't a strong enough word," Tom said. "I'd known her a long time. When Fiona was alive, we'd been friends." Tom shook his head. "The Cheryl we talked to this evening was someone I'd never encountered before."

"What do you think happened to her?" Laura asked.

Tom rubbed his hand on his forehead. "Obviously, Cheryl was really pissed off at Malcolm for stealing money from Sartori. Maybe after she accidentally killed him, something snapped, and it became easier for her to kill again."

"She tried to kill you," Laura said.

"Yes. But Kate never told me that. I guess the two of you knew." Tom wiped his hand over his forehead. "On the one hand, it made sense, because I was the only one around here who could link her to Hal Chesterton and his drug research. On the other hand, we were friends. It was very cold."

"To say the least."

"So, you believe that Kate Swift was justified in shooting Cheryl Taylor," O'Malley asked.

"Absolutely. When Cheryl brought out her gun, I believed she was going to shoot both of us."

○<0

O'Malley and Sanchez had Tom leave the room and then Kate entered. Kate read the narrative she had written and then signed it. Sanchez and O'Malley signed as witnesses. "We'll need you to come to Salinas tomorrow for more interviews," Laura said.

"That's what I expected," Kate replied.

Laura put her iPhone on the table and hit record. "This is Detective Laura Sanchez interviewing US Marshal Kate Swift. Also present is Detective Sergeant Dan O'Malley. We have read her statement regarding the shooting. A few additional questions: Marshal Swift, did you consider warning Cheryl Taylor?"

"No. She surprised us with a handgun. I believed I was dealing with a perpetrator who had already killed three persons. I thought there was a high probability that she was going to shoot Tom Scott. Considering this, I felt I had no choice but to shoot her."

"Marshal Swift, have you ever shot anyone before?"

"No."

"Marshal Swift, have you ever used your gun in the line of duty?"

"Not as a US Marshal. As a Fresno police officer, I fired my weapon twice. Once during a large gang fight, I fired my weapon in the air to distract the combatants. Once during a car chase, I fired at the vehicle being driven by a perpetrator who had abducted a young woman."

"In the second instance, did you hit anything?"

"In that instance, I hit the car tire and the car spun out of control into a field."

"You're a good shot."

"In my father's terms, I am an above average shot, but not a marksman."

"In this instance, you were holding a gun in your lap when Cheryl Taylor threatened you. Why was that?" Laura asked.

"I knew that I was dealing with an assailant who had tried to kill me and Tom Scott. I prepared myself for the worst by holding my Glock 22 in my hand, out of her sight."

"Beneath the table surface?"

"Beneath the surface so Cheryl would not see it."

"When she pulled out her weapon, you shot through the table and hit her in the forehead."

"Yes."

"That sounds like expert shooting."

"I suppose. I didn't think, I reacted."

"To repeat," Laura said. "You shot Cheryl Taylor because you believed that you had no choice?"

"That's correct. I felt that to protect the life of Tom Scott I was justified using deadly force."

Laura looked at Dan O'Malley. "Any further questions?"

O'Malley leaned forward. "Have you informed the US Marshal's office of this event?"

"I will after we finish this interview."

"What do you expect their actions to be?"

"I will be placed on further administrative leave. I will arrange for this interview to be forwarded to the San Francisco office. When I return to San Francisco, I will go into the Marshal's office and be interviewed. Then I will fill out many, many forms."

O'Malley grunted and leaned back.

Laura waited a moment. "I am concluding the interview with Marshal Kate Swift." Laura noted the date and time and turned off the recorder. "Thanks, Kate. You can go now. We'll see you tomorrow."

CHAPTER 48
(7PM): Tom

I waited in the Satori administration lobby while Kate was being interviewed by Sanchez and O'Malley. When Kate finally emerged from the executive conference room, I stood up and hugged her. "How are you?"

Kate collapsed into my arms. "Tired and stirred up emotionally. I feel relieved that we figured out who killed Malcolm and the others, and depressed that it was Cheryl. I feel angry."

"Did you know you growled after you shot her?"

"No. But I'm not surprised. I was really pissed off when I learned she had tried to break into our room to kill you."

"Is that why you had your gun out under the table?"

"Maybe. It was an unusual situation: we were confronting a dangerous suspect and we couldn't see her hands. I got my pistol out so I would be ready if she did something crazy."

"And she did."

Kate pulled back from my embrace and looked up at me. "At the end, Cheryl got really crazy."

"I know. When you were interviewing her, I kept asking myself, '*What happened to Cheryl? She doesn't seem anything like the Cheryl that Fiona and I knew.*'"

Kate shook her head. "So sad." She stepped back. "Is it okay with you if we don't stay here tonight? I don't think I can sleep in our suite. It will be restimulating."

"I thought you might feel like that, so I made a reservation at a nice hotel in Monterey. I reserved the honeymoon suite."

Kate kissed me. "You are such a romantic, Tom. Thank you. By the way, I have to go into Salinas tomorrow for another round of interviews and more paperwork."

"That's okay. I'll find something to do. Maybe hang out with Bruno."

Kate snorted. "You can help him with an autopsy."

"Whatever." I paused. "Do you want to drive back with me? That would be most convenient."

"Yes." Kate kissed me again. "I have a confession: I want you to take care of me for a couple of days."

"That's my job as your partner." I pulled her close. "How's your car going to get back to San Francisco?"

"I had already talked to Julie about driving back with me. I think she would agree to drive my Honda back and even stay at my place for a few days." Kate stepped back. "Before we pack up and leave, I want to say goodbye to our friends."

⤜⤝

As we left the Satori Administration area, we ran into David Sanders who was sitting on a bench. "What happened? I heard there was a shooting in the executive offices. Sequoyah wouldn't let me in."

I sat down next to David. "There is no simple way to tell you this, David. It turned out that Cheryl killed Malcolm and the two others. When Kate and I interviewed her, she initially was cooperative, then she pulled a gun on us. Kate shot her. Cheryl is dead."

"Oh no!" David's shoulders slumped and tears filled his eyes. His body shook with emotion. "It's hard to take this in. For the last couple of weeks, I knew Cheryl wasn't right, but..."

"It all came as a big shock to me," I said. "I believe Cheryl killed Malcolm because she discovered he had been embezzling money from Satori."

"Malcolm was so fucked up." David shook his head. A tear rolled down his cheek. "Recently, Cheryl told me she felt she was a hypocrite. She'd been advising her clients to set firm limits with their child or partner or whomever, but she had never been able to set limits with Malcolm."

"If it's any consolation, I don't believe Cheryl intended to kill Malcolm. She injected him with a kind of 'truth serum,' but got the dosage wrong and he succumbed."

"Then she killed Bryn?"

"Yes. And Greg Tanaka."

"Greg, too? I thought he dropped out and left the campus."

"It turns out that Greg enrolled in your workshop under false pretenses. He wasn't a fallen CPA on his way to prison, he was a bagman sent by the mob to collect money from Malcolm."

"Wow." David ran his hand over his face. "I thought something about Greg was off, but I never suspected..." his voice trailed off. "Wow."

"At the end, Cheryl got crazy. After Malcolm's death, she killed Greg and Bryn. Then she stalked me and Kate but didn't succeed breaking into our room. Then when Kate confronted her, Cheryl pulled a gun, and Kate shot her."

David covered his face with his hands.

I placed my hand on his shoulder and felt his body quiver.

For several minutes, we stayed like that. Then David spoke softly. "Cheryl was good to me. We loved each other."

"I never suspected that."

David turned his head towards me. "We weren't lovers because of my strange history. But in most circumstances, we would have been."

I didn't ask David about his "strange history."

"Cheryl was lonely. She'd lost her husband and then Hal. She spent all her time being a therapist. Taking in the pain of others." David's eyes were wet. "I suspect that when she found out about Malcolm's..." he searched for a word "...treachery, something snapped." He looked down at the floor.

I kept my hand on his shoulder.

After a few more minutes, David looked up at Kate who was standing next to where we were seated. "How are you doing, Kate? This must have been very hard on you."

Kate's voice shook. "I feel overwhelmed." She placed her hand on my shoulder. "On the one hand, I feel betrayed by Cheryl. On the other hand, I feel terrible about shooting her." She tightened her grip on my shoulder. "I'm very glad I have Tom to take care of me."

"I bet," David said. "What about you, Tom?"

"You know me. I've switched into problem-solving mode. I'll probably be hit by a tidal wave of emotions tomorrow."

David shook his head. "It's a lot to take in." He sighed.

"Are you going to be all right?" I asked.

"I don't know. I'm going to take a few days off and stay in my place in Carmel. See if I can work out things with June." June was David's girlfriend, a sometimes Satori massage therapist.

"We're going to say goodbye to our workshop friends, pack up, and go to Monterey tonight. Tomorrow, Kate has to check in with the Sheriff's Department in Salinas."

David straightened up. "Lots of paperwork, I bet."

"Too much," Kate said.

"When are you guys going back to San Francisco?"

"In a couple of days," Kate replied. "Why don't you and June come visit us some time?"

"Maybe we'll do that," David said. He stood up. "I think I'll head back to my place, pack some stuff, and head to Carmel." He hugged me and then he hugged Kate.

We watched David shuffle off.

"So sad," Kate said.

CHAPTER 49
(7:30 PM) Tom

Kate and I walked to the dining room and found most of our workshop friends sitting at our usual table. Tammy and Lois had already driven back to Lois' Carmel house. Aoife and Theo had left to be with their families.

"What happened?" Lucy asked. "We heard there was a shooting."

I looked at Julie, Lucy, Norma, Otto, Lucky, and Paul. "Kate and I have something heavy to tell you, but we don't want to do it here. Why don't we walk up to the Carl Rogers' workshop room?"

The eight of us trekked back up the familiar path to the room where we'd been in the transitions workshop. Kate turned on the light. We got out pillows and sat in a tight circle. At Paul's suggestion, we held hands.

I looked at Kate and realized she was in no condition to tell the others what had happened. "I have bad news, I said.

I gave our friends the same abbreviated version I had given to David Sanders. Kate sat beside me and clutched my hand.

Lucy began to cry. "Cheryl was my therapist." She sobbed on Kate's shoulder. Julie and Norma helped comfort her.

We sat in silence, holding hands.

Finally, Otto asked me, "You've known Cheryl a long time. What do you think happened to her?"

I told them what David had said.

"Sounds like Cheryl burnt out and had no one to turn to," Paul said. "I know something about that." He put his arm around Lucky. "Then Malcolm betrayed her and that was the final straw."

"I felt like killing my stepfather," Lucy said in a choked voice. "But then he saved me the trouble by dying in a car crash." Kate hugged her tight.

"In her closing remarks to the group," Julie said. "Cheryl talked about Satori being a patriarchy."

"Like most of the world," Norma said.

We sat in silence for a few more minutes.

"At the risk of being prosaic," Paul said. "I think we should try to remember Cheryl for the good she did rather than the bad."

"I agree," I said. "I'm attempting to think of her as Fiona's friend and not as the sick person she became."

"That's right," Otto said. "Satori wore Cheryl down and then she succumbed to mental illness."

There was a murmur of agreement.

Kate closed her eyes and didn't say anything. I thought *Kate will have a hard time forgiving Cheryl for trying to kill us.*

"Are you guys, okay?" Otto asked Kate and me.

"We're shaken," I said. Kate closed her eyes and leaned her head against my shoulder.

"I bet you are," Norma said.

"We're not going to stay here tonight." Kate opened her eyes. "Tom got us a room in a Monterey hotel." She squeezed my hand.

"You shot Cheryl through her desk?" Lucy asked. "That's fucking amazing."

"My primitive instincts kicked in," Kate said, as a tear rolled down her cheek.

We sat on the floor for a few more minutes. Then got up, still holding hands, and walked back to the Satori dining room.

⤸⤹

"Before you leave, can we do a group photo?" Lucy asked.

The eight of us dutifully assembled on the stairs outside the dining room.

Marcia Ball agreed to be our photographer. Kate and I were in the front row with Julie, and Lucy. The second row had Norma, Otto, Lucky, and Paul.

"Say cheese," Marcia called out as she took several shots.

Sergeant O'Malley, Laura Sanchez, and Bruno Oliver walked across the lawn. "Why don't you join us?" Kate called out.

O'Malley demurred. "I'm not photogenic. I'll sit this one out."

Kate had Laura stand on one side of her and Bruno on the other side, next to Lucy.

After Stacey snapped the photo, Lucy turned to Bruno. "I'm Lucy. Are you one of the Sheriff's detectives?"

"I'm an investigator for the coroner," Bruno said.

"What's that mean?"

"It means that I specialize in dealing with suspicious deaths."

"Hmm. What do you do for fun?" Lucy asked.

"I study poisons and I walk my dog, Mendeleev."

"I like dogs."

"Lucy is shy, Bruno." Kate said. "I think she likes you."

"That's good to hear. She is very attractive."

∾

Kate and I packed our bags and walked to my car. "Did Julie agree to drive your car back to San Francisco?" I asked.

"Yes. I'm driving with you in your...?"

"BMW SUV."

When we got to the parking lot, I clicked the remote control and the back of my SUV opened. We loaded our luggage. Kate put out her hand for the remote. "I'm driving."

"It's a big car. Goes fast."

"I'm a big girl. Trained to drive police pursuit cars by my father; and a graduate of Bondurant Driving School at Laguna Seca." Kate punched me on the shoulder. "You're in safe hands, stud."

Once we got into the car and Kate adjusted the driver's side seat, steering wheel, and rear-vision mirrors, she took out her iPhone. "Show me how to pair this with your BMW."

"Why?"

"Duh. You don't have a phone. Laura, or someone else, may try to contact us." She gave me a critical look. "This is another part of 'reallocating our assets.'"

I paired the phone. Kate started the SUV, backed out of the parking space, and headed up the driveway.

Her finger was poised over the radio power-on button. "Here comes a critical point in our relationship. I'm going to turn on the radio. If I don't like what I hear, I may have to let you out." She smiled. "Hopefully it's not Fox News, or sports talk – God forbid, or 'greatest hits of Kid Rock.'" She hit the button.

A jazz channel came on. "I know that song, but I don't re-member the pianist," Kate said.

"'Round Midnight' by Thelonious Monk." I smiled. "Did I pass the test?"

"For now. Don't get overconfident."

We drove north and soon passed by the famous Nepenthe restaurant. The phone rang. Kate put it on speaker.

Laura Sanchez said, "I want to thank you again for your help."

"You're welcome, Laura. I meant to tell you this, but I nev-er got a chance to talk to you in private. When you're in San Francisco, give me a call and we can hang out. Maybe the four of us can go out to dinner. Tom will pay for everything." Kate squeezed my hand.

"I'd like that," Laura said. "But I'll probably see you tomorrow at the Salinas office. By the way, the press just got wind of this case; Sheriff John had a news conference. Good luck." Sanchez hung up.

"Fuck," Kate said. "I'd forgotten about the press."

"Don't worry," I said. "I talked to my partner about it. When we get back to San Francisco, you're doing an in-depth interview with Laura Davis who is our friend at the Chronicle. And then you are doing a TV interview with Wendy Kim at KPIX."

Kate looked at me out of the corner of her eye. "You are so competent. It would be easy to just lay back and let you manage my life. Be your courtesan."

"But you won't do that."

"No. I won't do that because it would mean the death of our relationship. We both need to do our thing." She smiled. "Besides, I have the feeling that we bring out the best in each other. I look forward to the challenge."

We drove through Big Sur village and past Molera beach. When we got to Garrapata State Park, we saw fire trucks and road-repair equipment where the road had been closed.

Kate pulled over at China Lookout. "Indulge me." She got out of the car and pulled out her phone. "Come here Tom. I'm going to take a picture of you and me and the view." She held out the phone, capturing us with a backdrop of the California coastline. "Kate and Tom and infinite horizons."